NO REST
for the
Wicked

Wolfe Cotto

VAMPIRES *of* LONDON
BOOK ONE

BLACK CROW
PUBLISHING LIMITED, LONDON

Paperback ISBN - 978-0-9931576-0-8
Mobi ISBN - 978-0-9931576-1-5
ePub ISBN - 978-0-9931576-2-2

Published by Black Crow Publishing Limited, London.
Print and e-edition published worldwide 2014

Cover design and illustration by Andrew McColm

Contents

DEDICATION

This book is for Batman, Peanut and Monkey

ABOUT THE BOOK

Dear Reader

This book is a work of fiction.
It is the first instalment of the Vampires of London series.
Many of the historical facts are true, many aren't. I have used quotes from a number of sources, including: Tori Amos, Emily Dickinson, G. Eliot, F. S. Fitzgerald, among others. If a quote is unattributed it is most likely Shakespeare.
This is a love story, and the object of affection is London. She is a city of contradictions, freedom, dirt and magic.
If you believe vampires exist, be sure they nestle in her greasy bosom.
In the words of Samuel Johnson
'Sir, when a man is tired of London, he is tired of life; for there is in London all that life can afford.'

If you come across a word or a phrase you don't understand, it is probably either Cockney Rhyming Slang or Hungarian. Refer to the Glossary for the translation.

Yours
Wolfe

CHAPTER ONE

Eddy

I wake from a bad dream, except I know it wasn't just a dream. My head hurts, my hands shake and my ripping teeth are distended.

Jackie is gone, probably for good.

I push the heavy granite slab aside and crawl out of my crypt. The basement is silent and cold, crowded with junk, crates and my favourite things. Nothing unusual here, except a ratcheting up of the ever present atmosphere of waiting that emanates from the basement well. Tonight, the miasma of patient malevolence presses down on me and feels like a harbinger of impending doom. Some years before, I inadvertently introduced an entity to my well and my uninvited guest has provided uneasy, but thankfully predictable, company ever since – until tonight. Something has rattled its cage and the dread mood has intensified along with the patch of bone-chilling cold. It is the last straw. A sound starts from low in my gut, rises to a keening scream before ripening to a throat-shredding roar.

I run full tilt, headlong at the far, red brick, foundation wall. I smash my head into it a couple more times for good measure until I see stars and taste thick oily blood.

In three bounds, I leap up the three sets of stairs that give access to the subterranean levels of my home and emerge on the ground floor with another almighty roar. To hell with the neighbours.

Two-inch fingernails dig into my palms as my hands form fists that I drive into the opposite wall. The plaster cracks all the way to the ceiling coving and a patch falls away, exposing more red London brick.

I stretch my mouth open as wide as I can and believe me that's wide. Think 'flip top head' wide, exposing my rows of sharp teeth crowned by vicious canines, dripping with my own blood and serum. I've been gnashing in my sleep, my jaws ache, the stress has brought on a nasty bout of bruxism. 'Cheese and rice' all I need is for that bollocks to start again.

Copious reddish brown saliva drips down my chin and plops onto the parquet floor. Like human tears, the chemical composition of my saliva, serum, or venom produced by my parotid salivary glands, changes with my state of mind. Most of the time the synthesised serum sits in large alveoli behind my eyes, waiting to be injected into my prey via ducts that transit straight through my hollow fangs. The Zootoxins deliver a powerful dose of anticoagulant while taking care of any unwanted nervous or muscular impulse to resist or flee and effectively immobilise my victim. A cocktail of enzymes help me efficiently digest blood and flesh. Tonight I know my saliva will be full of virulent bacteria and septic pathogens that would cause any creature I bite or even scrape with my teeth, to contract sepsis. It wouldn't do you much good if I spit in your eye either. I am literally toxic.

I flex and twist my neck until the veins and muscles bulge and tendrils of knotted tendon run up across my cheeks to my forehead.

It has been days since I last fed and my naked body appears translucent blue, white, bony, reptilian.

I catch my reflection in the hall mirror. The sight sobers me up and snaps me out of it.

'Mop and bucket!'. Someone got out of the wrong side of the crypt this evening.

CHAPTER TWO

Getting Acquainted

My name is Herronimus Raphael Edward Basarab-DeVere. It's a bit of a mouthful so I've shortened it in recent times to Edward DeVere, but nevertheless it is my legal name and has been for some years now.

My home is London, the perfect place for me and the monsters she breeds. A city built on death – centuries of it. Thomas Carlyle called it 'the Great Maw' and he was right.

When human builders began the ground works for the foundations of St Paul's, they realised it was to be built over at least eighteen feet of stacked graves, one on top of the other, Saxon on British on Roman on Britons. The humans are always shocked, perhaps humbled, when they stumble upon the evidence of their own mortality preserved in the earth beneath their very own busy feet. Below this vibrant city throbbing with life, death is ever present.

I, on the other hand come alive under ground and revel in the dark places deep beneath the city, there I rub shoulders with human remains, still at last, freed from their relentless fidgeting. Even above ground, during the comfort of night, I can find peace as I move through any one of London's 'Great Gardens of Sleep'. The city's cemeteries, created to honour her citizens' final and well earned rest, soothe my ever hungry heart. I no longer feel alone or afraid of my own distant, yet inevitable death. I no longer give way to guilty thoughts and fears of punishment in some afterlife dreamed up by the wishful.

The humans need hope, the hope that they can somehow beat death, it helps them step out into the dangerous world they've helped create. Every one of them willing to gamble on that long shot. They will survive; a world without them, unthinkable. There must be a chance. A chance that this one time, in their case, things will be different, that they will live forever. Hope: now that is a powerful force. It is hope that keeps their warm hearts beating through their meagre span, helped by copious quantities of java. They all taste like latte these days. I watch them flower and wither, while my cold organ of circulation beats relentlessly on, driven by the insatiable hunger and increasingly, a simmering rage.

But I too hope. Here is my secret. I hope for love. Don't laugh.

Some nights I stroll through Highgate's neo-Gothic Valhalla and read the inscriptions of love; of loss; of longing. Oh the romance, the passion. I want it. Why should the warm-blooded, hairless monkeys have all the fun. I know they pay for passion with their vulnerability, their soft hearts so easily bruised, their perishable bodies so easily broken, and it may be unreasonable to be so greedy, but I want it.

I've decided to take chances for it. If that's the way it must be, if the cosmic scales must be balanced, I will take a leaf out of the monkey's tree. I will lay myself open, I will risk it all. I'll cry tears of blood and will my aching heart to stop. I'll pay the price if I must, but I will feel it, I *will* love, or I'll rip this whole town to blood-soaked shreds.

For clarity's sake, I need to state the obvious: I am not human.

I have dropped the name Basarab from all but legal documents to protect my anonymity yet remain fiercely loyal to my tribe. The House of Basarab are a proud and ancient Clan that has given Eastern Europe much of its nobility and many of its Voivode, or Princes. My coat of arms depicts three horizontal fangs encircled by a dragon swallowing its own tail. The humans believe the coat of arms represent the legend of Vitus Bathory the Warrior King who, in the year 900, with three mighty lance thrusts straight to its cold heart, killed a mighty dragon in the swamps of Ecsed, Transylvania. The truth is that the three fangs represent the three Houses of Vampire Nobility: The Basarab, The Drugeth and The Bathory.

I am honoured to carry the title of Count, as have those of my blood line for centuries. The most spectacularly visible of my ancestors, and one you may recognise, being Count Draculesi, whom is reported by your human history to have lived between the years of our Lord 1431–1476, and is yet still known by the infamous title of Vlad the Impaler.

My noble House has suffered its share, as do most human aristocratic dynasties of inbreeding, insanity and eccentricity. Count Draculesi, as an honoured Member of the Order of the Dragon, and Voivode of Wallachia, as am I his descendant, was given great latitude and pardon. Unfortunately, he so revelled in his power, invulnerability, sexual mania and blood lust that he put at risk the future survival of the entire Vampire Nation and was put to death, with much difficulty, at the hands of the Warrior Hawke

Order of the Drugeth Clan. The nefarious Draculesi legend is an ignominy I have to bear.

Rogue vampires are rare; the evidence they leave can be explained away as the stuff of human perversion, nightmare, legend and fancy. We vampires only have one law – *Do Not Kill Thine Own*(except in self-defence). Consequently, we are a lenient race, endlessly patient, hopelessly tolerant, but we have our limits. Like dynamite – completely safe, until it isn't.

I make my home in Chelsea, part of the Royal Borough of Kensington and Chelsea. The name in Old English means 'Landing Place on the River' or 'Chalk Wharf'. I prefer Chelchith from the ancient Saxon, meaning 'Cold Port' or 'Haven'. For me it has been a wickedly cold haven and continues to be.

There is something about this place by the river that nourishes the imagination, or soul if you prefer. Perhaps it is something in the nature of the land itself that drew the gardeners and then the artists and writers – Rossetti, Turner, Hunt, Sargent and Swinburne, Carlyle, Meredith, Stoker.

Chelsea was at the heart of the Pre-Raphaelite Brotherhood, but it's way too expensive for artists now. They've all long moved on, further north, first to Notting Hill and then on to Camden Town. Chelsea is now an expensive, bourgeoisie address. Think – New York's Upper East Side – but I still like it.

I have dwelt at 52 Cadogan Gardens since I built the house in 1899. It is a neo-Gothic mansion. I'm a sentimentalist; the architecture reminds me of my time in 12th century Paris. At about the time I undertook the construction of this, my current abode, a Mr Mackmurdo was building a house for a Mr Menpe: number 25. I only mention it because, while Mr Menpe, owner of number

25 was enjoying the novelty of having a home much celebrated at the time for its elaborate interior, in the Japanese style, the project was being, in some part, funded by myself through the careful acquisition of a quantity of its owners and its owners friends' paintings. These included a Mr James Whistler, among others. The slow release of these paintings over the years onto the highly lucrative art market has paid rich dividends and played a part in securing my current comfortable financial situation.

I'm always on the lookout for new promising artists and I have found their mysterious, early demise can add thousands to my portfolio. My kind has evolved the outward appearance of humans, our natural prey, and we can pass very comfortably amongst them. I move relatively unnoticed through the city's late night 'showings' staged in abandoned warehouses, low rent gallery openings and art college exhibitions. I think of it as convergent evolution, wherein striking morphological similarities between two otherwise separate species can be explained by their both performing similar ecological roles.

Whilst the greedy monkeys eat anything and everything that breathes or grows, we homoreptilia just eat them. It seems fair to me. Vampires are like Crab Spiders (Amyciaea Lineatipes or Corinnomma) in that we mimic our prey. In the spiders' case: ants. In Vampires': humans. We both fool our prey into believing we are one of their own species, and this gives us the opportunity to basically charm them to death. Like Crab Spiders, we too have chosen our prey for two very sound evolutionary reasons. One, they are very, very numerous, and two, there is not a lot of competition for their meat. Both ants and humans are found by most other animals to be both distasteful and dangerous to hunt. Indeed, everything about my physiology has adapted so I can, as needs must, move among my prey undetected and unsuspected. This I have done for many years.

Camouflage is Nature's craftiest trick.

My chosen killing fields are found in the Thames Valley, in the bustling heart of my beloved home – London. This city has evolved into my ideal habitat. Beneath my feet, wherever I hunt, is the comfort of sanctuary and quick escape. The London that homo sapiens enjoy is built over the London through which I pass, in utter darkness, silent, gliding, smooth as a water snake, which, by the way, is a closer relative of mine than any mammal.

Centuries ago, this city was criss-crossed with a network of rivers that ran down from the surrounding hills to disgorge their water into the Thames. Unfortunately for the native flora and fauna, as time passed, this once lush valley became infested with humans. The once clear waters of those rivers became open trenches full of sewage, carrion and chemicals. To protect themselves from their own filth, the humans (squeamish creatures that they are) began around the 1700s, to systematically cover those natural corridors with brick and stone, creating the tunnels and caverns that first drew me and keep me close.

These humans, whom I cherish and despise, truly are the most despotic of creatures. The once sacred Walbrook River that ran through ancient Londinium, where Roman soldiers would worship at the Temple of Mithras, is now just one of the reeking subterranean corridors that form part of my underground labyrinth. Other hidden rivers include The Fleet, The Tyburn and, one of my favourites: The Westbourne. The latter now runs in a pipe from Hampstead, through and under Hyde Park, across and above Sloane Square Tube Station and eventually, into the

Thames, providing me direct access to and from the heart of the city.

They all belong to me and my kind now.

Could it get any better? Yes, and it did. I still celebrate the birth, in 1819, of that deceptively diminutive engineer, Joseph Bazalgette. His system of intercepting sewers freed humans from the reeking pestilence they'd made of the Thames and saved more lives than can be counted from what can only be named 'death by shit'. The tenacity of that creature is cause for human pride, and he furnished me with a network of tunnels of which I, at that time, would not have dreamed possible, freeing me from any fear of exposure or capture and furnishing me with the perfect hunting grounds.

Bazalgette's network of sewers were designed and built for a population of two million – a huge number. Almost unbelievable. By the time they were finished in the 1870s, London's population had already reached four million. With continual tweaking and shoring up, much of his original network is still coping with the Tsunami of shit produced by London's creaking 8 million (and climbing even as I write) inhabitants. It can get really crazy down there. Pitch black and airless, pockets of toxic fumes, haunted by unexplained noises and phenomena. Nobody notices the odd vampire aquaplaning through the crap.

So here, in my beloved London I remain, to the present day, and at the moment, here I brood and seethe. You see I have, or, had until recently, a housekeeper and her name was Jackie Pearce.

CHAPTER THREE

Jackie

Jackie first came into my employ five years ago, a little after her 18th birthday. The first time I saw her was when she arrived for an evening interview for part-time domestic cleaning, three days a week and no references necessary.

She had pushed a small Xeroxed flyer through my door-mounted letterbox, as she had through many other doors in the area, offering her services and promising hard work, sparkling surfaces and honesty. This I took as an invitation, and acceptance on her part, of my personal attention.

I remember that interview so clearly, the way some people would remember seeing that particular stray at Battersea Dogs Home; the needy eyes, the eagerness to please, the guileless innocence of the simple-minded. Yes, it was all there to see, mistreated but willing to trust again, hoping for a little fairness, perhaps even love against all the odds. I was smitten.

I wasn't aware until I opened the door and saw her faded T-shirt, cheap jeans, trainers, red headscarf tied around her thick head of cheaply dyed hair, how much I'd missed a pet, something to play with and take care of. A warm-blooded creature that would make my house feel like a home again after all those years alone. There she stood, my charmingly chubby Amy Winehouse wannabe, looking like nothing I'd ever imagined and yet everything for which I could wish. Jackie.

She encountered me that day, as 'Mr Edward' or 'Eddy' to my friends. I have to explain something of my 'situation' at this point or we will become estranged.

When I have eaten properly and taken especially good care of myself, I become 'Eds', the young Master Edward De Vere of the house; in my twenties, perfectly normal, in fact, quite good looking. Perhaps the young Eds can appear a little world weary for one so young, but then, I can do nothing about my eyes; they have a jaded quality. When I catch my own gaze in a mirror, I can't help be convinced they will give me away. They haven't of course. Humans rarely trust their five senses, let alone their instincts in this age of artifice. Perhaps it's my lack of modernity that softens the edges and apparently adds 'geek charm', which helps young Eds appear not too … how shall I put it … creepy.

If on the other hand, I haven't eaten, haven't taken proper care of myself for months, (it gets hard to leave the house sometimes, and I tell you, existence on my timescale can be exhausting) I then appear as Mr Edward, assumed father of Eds. The family resemblance is striking and I rarely have to manufacture details. Humanity's tendency to presume is reliable.

But to be clear, these periods of fasting are brought on more by creeping self-contempt and pity than by any world disdain. 'I hold the world but as the world, Gratiano, A stage where every man must play a part, And mine a sad one.' as the sweet swan of Avon put it.

It goes without much further explanation that from time to time, I fall into a deep malaise. Choose to remain in exile for, perhaps, years. During these self-imposed periods of disconnect, I drink a lot of wine, and surrounded by empty bottles and cigar butts, I lose myself in music, books and art. I forget myself entirely and bear the gnawing hunger as penance. I suppose the human equivalent could be the Catholic monastic orders and Opus Dei – self-flagellation with a 'discipline' or knotty whip, except I don't fool myself that anyone *up there* could care less how much I torture myself.

I prefer to liken my periodic retreat to the hermetic lifestyle, one of a human mystic or ecstatic in search of a heightened inner reality or altered state of consciousness. Basically, anything to break the boredom.

It's easier now than ever before to drift into the ascetic routine and ultimately, hibernation. With the help of Amazon and ebay I need never leave the house. New poets and thinkers of all nations as well as classics; Goethe, Dostoyevsky, Kemeny Janos, even Transylvanian history as yet undiscovered by me, is just an engine search away. I recently obtained a reprint in Spanish of Bernardo de Aldana's apologies for losing the Transylvanian Castle of Lippa in 1552 to the Turks.

They all come to me; the books clatter through my oversized letterbox and fill the house. First the bookshelves and then every available surface. Eventually, they form towers under and around sofas and chairs and tables. I indulge in tobacco, firstly for the oral pleasure – ask any anorexic if you don't understand. And secondly, to disguise my personal odour.

Human science has separated reptiles and amphibians, although they accept the two are distantly related. We vampires possess the attributes of both species. Except when it comes to reproduction. In this area, we have the best of both worlds. Our females require internal fertilisation; I count my blessings on that one. Then we lay our eggs while they are no larger than a pool ball. I'm safe in assuming the entire vampire female population also feels they 'lucked in'. Our precious and rare fertilised egg is laid in deep water or a damp dark place. Here it will be left to take its chances while developing to roughly the size of a human infant in the expandable and soft, permeable to nutrients, gel-like egg that acts both as womb and placenta.

Vampires or Homoreptilia are the missing link.

As my reptilian, but also, definitely amphibious body desiccates, I start to smell fishy. This is when I reach for my old walnut pipe, simply preferring the smell of smoked kipper to sushi. It is after all an odour found in most human geriatric nursing homes. I then become 'Mr Edward Senior', or 'Teddy' De Vere, grandfather to young Eds, father to Mr Edward.

It was as Mr Edward I interviewed Jackie.

I offered £5 per hour on top of the going rate, with which pigs will fly, she argued was too much. She would arrive at 9 a.m. and work until 6 p.m. in the summer and to 4 p.m. in the winter. We settled on four days a week, which quickly became seven. I couldn't bear to share her with others. She was mine after all, and belonged at home. My home is such a large house, it was perfectly reasonable.

At first I didn't feel the need to actually see her at all. I just enjoyed the fresh flowers and smell of soap and polish and musky animalness she would leave behind. Then we began to spend the overlap between her leaving the house and my waking for the evening, together, at first just an hour, which soon became two. At the end of her day and the beginning of mine, in the house, together, awake. We'd potter about, aware of each other but separate. We could hear each other. I could hear her heartbeat, her breath, farts, burps and humming and I made sure she could hear me, footsteps, music, singing. 'Gently, gently, catchy monkey,' I would whisper to myself with a hard to suppress giggle. Courting is such fun.

Before I knew it, she was leaving Shepherd's pie in the oven, breaded cod on Friday, lasagne on a Wednesday. The terrible stench of cooking animal flesh and baking filled the house, but I loved it; so pedestrian, so normal. Careful to make sure she never found any remains of my evening meal, only the dirty plate in the sink, the food always found its way into a neighbour's bin. The ever wary predator in me was placated. The old house had been so very dark, uninhabited to appearances, for a very long time. Repairs and maintenance were needed; I was due a reawakening.

I shook myself out of my lethargy and realised how desperately I needed diurnal help – a pair of daytime eyes to facilitate my renewal of identity. Appeasing the suspicions of a growing band of bureaucratic nosy parkers had been long overdue. I needed to get busybody neighbours and officialdom off my back.

I did enjoy the flowers, silly little posies here and there – a large bowl of crazy colours in the drawing room. No tasteful creams and pale pinks and mauves, Jackie liked a discordant cacophony of bright blooms that jumped at the eye, much as did her peculiar hair. The once naturally curly mop had been dyed and backcombed into a barely contained Afro. I assumed Jackie was trying for a beehive. This she wrestled under control using an assortment of bandanas, scarves, headbands, clips, i.e. kittens, parrots, glittery stars etc. Totally amazing. Her pouf sat high and proud and put me in mind of 18th-century France and the court of Marie Antoinette. Leonard Autie, Marie's hairdresser, would have been awed.

When her hair was unchained, it looked for the world as though she had first stuck her finger into a live electricity socket and then placed a large pudding bowl on her head and cut around the edge. It was quite possible she actually had performed the latter, leaving hair length slightly too short to tie back successfully and slightly too long for convenience, but the perfect length to run my fingers through and feel the surprisingly, as it looked like a Brillo pad, silky texture. So relaxing.

There were times, when I would exert my *gentle glamour* – I find this a pleasing way to describe my ability to control the human mind by making myself irresistible. Exerting just enough influence to stop complete panic, I would lead her down to the lower/lower basement where I'd pull her through the hole at the base of the mouldering brick wall and down into my dark cold crypt. She would lay next to me in my resting place. In the soothing darkness I'd snuggle against her musky body heat, stroke that springy hair and smell her rice pudding breath. A vague memory of lying in the sun, the heat of ancient rock beneath me radiating stored solar warmth into my bones would envelop me. This false memory, this physical déja vu was a strange and precious sensation, as I've never in actuality experienced anything like it. Darling little Jackie.

At other times, we'd play chase. It was such fun to coral her about the house and she could move surprisingly fast on her chubby little legs. Breathing fast, sweating fear and adrenalin I'd let her slip out from under my grip and run while I slowly counted to ten. Not fair seeing that I could have heard her heart pounding from the basement if she'd been on the roof. But she'd never found the initiative to breach the battlements, so to speak, and climb out onto the eaves. Jackie was reliably unimaginative. She could generally be found under a bed or in a cupboard.

But we had such times. Sometimes, I'd release some of the control I exerted over her weak mind and let her scream a little; not enough to really alert the neighbours but enough to make it feel real. When I'd catch her, I could hardly stop myself from sinking my teeth into her creamy pulsing throat and ripping her to shreds like a juicy, tender steak. I never did. Never would have. She was my girl and, well, I'll admit for this record, as I have promised myself full disclosure, I had feelings. Perhaps not the love for which I yearn and grieve, but a form of it. Close anyway.

Still do.

But she hasn't been here for a week. Saturday is here again and she has left no word.

I try to picture her at home in her dingy little bedsit at the Elephant & Castle and usually when I try I can, but not now. In the past, I have reached out with my mind and generally, I find her asleep. Rightly so. She's exhausted when she's not here. This is a big house – lots to do.

I can't picture her in her bed, or on the phone, or in her flat. I can't picture her anywhere.

I was annoyed when she didn't turn up for work on Monday, and no word. Then Tuesday came and went. Even from the basement, I could feel there was no one in the house while I slept. By Wednesday, I was worried. She could have been run over; damned cars everywhere. She could have been backed over by a silent sodding Prius and not known it was coming until she was under the wheels.

I know she was physically healthy, robust even. I can detect even the smallest beginnings of disease in humans and Jackie was fine on that score, but looking back, she had been 'off' for a couple of weeks, absent minded, preoccupied. Sitting in the dark, quiet house I admit to myself that I had become complacent. More than that, I had stopped paying attention or caring. In truth it had been a long time since, in the modern vernacular, I could be arsed with much of anything. Now, sitting here, mulling it over, preoccupied isn't how she'd been acting at all. She had been worried. Anxious, edgy, nervous, and not just about her strange employer. Had somebody else been playing with my Jackie, trespassing on my property, and were they now keeping her away against her will?

Since waking around 6.30 p.m., I have spent most of the early evening pacing. That has stopped. Calmer now. I am past the worrying stage. A hollow emptiness has sucked me into an airless vacuum; I can no longer ignore the yawning void. Whenever I extend my psychic antennae to probe the ether, to find my Jackie, an echo of my own voice calling in the dark is the only answer I hear. Perhaps Jackie is dead.

I'll admit here, for the sake of accuracy, and because I am surprised and pleased, I cried. When the grief hit, I was unprepared for its power. It shook me like a rag doll until I felt weak, drained and completely empty. I have been numb for so many years, shuffling through existence. I truly thought with the passing of time I had, at last, lost the facility for emotion, that my inability to quicken and connect with the age in which I now exist was some precursor to the final sleep. I am so very old and everything that is born eventually dies. But lo and behold, what is this? The unexpected grief that carved out my heart and bowels and left me empty, begins to fill me up, to reanimate me with a white hot rage.

Someone has taken my Jackie from me.

I'd put a lot of energy into Jackie's training. Forgive me, but to be blunt, she was just house-trained. She was so reliable, we understood each other and my future plans and hopes included my darling little Jackie. As I write, I am experiencing disappointment, I'm not used to it and I don't like it.

She really had enjoyed her time with young Eds, I'd hardly needed to hypnotise her at all to feed. She didn't mind the petting or chasing; she was forgiving when the rough housing got a little out of hand. She had created a virtuous circle. She'd revived me, my appetite had returned and I'd found the will to venture out into the overcrowded city for a 'bite'. This of course kept me young and as I have said, Jackie just loved the young me.

I'd promised her a comfortable life in her own little flat; the refurbishment is so close to completion. A small 'share of the freehold', two-bedroomer off Cadogan Square. Just around the corner so she could be close but not constantly under my feet. I'd promised her a bank account, already set up, so she could buy herself as many weird hair ornaments as she pleased. I didn't mind the thought of her finding herself a mate – breeding, whatever, as they say. The world is becoming ever more complex and I have settled myself that I really do need to cultivate some 'helpers'. What better way than to raise my own little circle. Yes, I'd had a full and pleasant life mapped out for my dopey, loyal, sweet little pet.

Don't get me wrong, I feel I must make one point clear. I hope you haven't construed my enjoyment of petting, playing with and schnoodling my Jackie as in some way sexual. The thought is quite repulsive. Bestiality is not for me. Just because a human loves and pets his dog doesn't mean he wants to have sex with it. Well, most don't. I don't.

Please put whatever myths may have sprung up concerning my kind and intense teenage liaisons from your mind. I know of no other such as myself that would be interested in such relationships. What would I have to say to a human teenager? They spend all day sucking their thumbs and diddling themselves, don't they? It was certainly so the last time I looked. Umm well, come to think of it, the exception makes the rule. There may be one or two human 'chicken pluckers' that come to mind.

Also, while on the subject, a human may, if 'reeeally hungry' eat dog.In some parts of Asia and a couple of cantons in Switzerland when they are only peckish. But a stray dog and your beloved pet are two different things. I state here for the record, I would never, never have eaten Jackie. Maybe that's a bit strong. I could only imagine resorting to it in the most extreme situation. The circumstances just wouldn't arise in the modern world.

Oh my darling Jackie. An image of her, only two weeks previously, comes to mind. She is running up the stairs, her throat constricted with fear. Eyes bulging, I can actually see retinal blood vessels bursting like a spray of red confetti across the whites as she looks over her shoulder and stares at me. I'd dropped the glamour, so she could clearly see me. The fun we'd had that day.

It had taken ages to calm her down afterwards, her little heart pitty patting, fit to burst. I'd really had to put in some effort to lull her into a calming, forgetful sleep, and I'd woken her some hours later with a cup of sweet tea and a chocolate bar – a Twix I believe it was, she loved them.

Never more.

I swear to myself that this is the last time I will have a pet; they simply don't live long enough to make all the effort and inevitable pain worth it.

But before I move on and put it all behind me, as I now assure myself I will, I have a loose end to tidy up.

I pass, silent as a shadow, through the house and up the stairs, catching a glimpse of my face in the age-stained glass of the hall mirror. My blood turns cold and thick in my veins. I am wearing my angry face. People don't like my angry face. Oh dear. Few humans have seen me like this and none that have survived to tell. Someone out there, in London, my home, is going to look into these cavernous, dead eyes. Someone is going to know he or she has made a terrible … a fatal … mistake.

Someone is going to pay.

The house is silent. I move up through the stairs to the third floor where I keep my dressing room. I shower and put on some fresh clothes.

Nothing has been touched in the bathroom. Dirty towels on the floor, skin and scales forming a crusty cap around the shower drainage hole. I've grown used to not picking up after myself. That will have to change.

Combing my hair, I move back through the empty house to the ground floor. A light is flashing on my computer.

Another cryptic communiqué, no doubt; I've been receiving them sporadically for months now. I sit down at my desk and press a random tile on the keyboard and the screen lights up. I wince. Electric lights are so bright. My eyes adjust and I click to mail.

I don't receive much post. The same thing, no actual message, just: From: TRITON. Subject: ?

I know who the question mark is from – a vampire called Marcos that I know from long ago. An incorrigible human fucker but one of the good guys, I suppose. Perhaps, but a ditherer and it looks like nothing's changed.

I am in no mood for enigmatic vampire bullshit tonight.

If I respond to every 'reach out' from distant vamp relatives, I'll never have a night to call my own. That may be exaggerating – never a century may be more accurate. Nevertheless, the sentiment remains.

The question mark reminds me of why we fell out of touch. Too noncommittal for my taste.

Well Marcos, if you want something from me, it's time to poop or get off the pot. Life's too short. That makes me chuckle; my life is relentless. I click on 'trash' just as I have done for all the others. I have other things on my mind right now.

I find one of my old coats, the one with a nice patina of grime. The original rough gabardine is now smooth, even shiny in parts with ground-in grease.

In the pocket, I place a Zippo lighter and a pair of pliers, just in case I get lucky and can finish this tonight. Death can only slake my thirst for revenge to a point. True satisfaction demands adequate foreplay. The human nervous system can only take so much pain. I find sometimes a 'lighter' touch works better than just going 'hammer and tongs'. There'll be no rush … the night is young.

I check myself in the mirror to make sure I don't look the way I feel.

I'm regaining some composure. The face that stares back at me is more hollow than before Jackie's disappearance, but passable.

One evening, years ago, while staking out my dinner in Soho, I caught the eye and fancy of a drunken whore. She wouldn't leave me alone, kept calling me Withnail. She said she would 'shag me silly' and put 'things' up my 'bum hole' 'because that's what you posh boys like innit' for a minimal fee. I didn't eat her; I have nothing against people speaking as they find, or perpetrators of victimless crimes, moral or judicial. Anyway, I had no idea what she was talking about, assuming Withnail was some strain of human disease.

I'd googled it when I next had access to a computer and a photograph of the actor Richard E. Grant popped up, dressed as this fictional character Withnail in a film *Withnail and I*. Sure enough, there is a resemblance. I think I'm better looking; opinions divided, I'm certainly taller.

I put on gloves and hat and turn up my collar. I will pass. I run back up the stairs and rummage through the overflowing laundry basket until I find my old jeans, and rifle through the pockets. There it is, my Oyster card. Nearly forgot.

The last thing I need tonight is an argument with a bored Jobsworth about correct change or a malfunctioning ticket dispenser.

I turn the blue rectangle of plastic in my fingers and wipe it clean of the now dried and crusted blood smears. I genuinely enjoy my Oyster card. After all, it is my ticket to freedom. Jackie had bought it for me and kept it topped up; she always paid with cash. I smile, remembering her earnest whisper, "Cash is King, you know what I mean Eddy. Just in case. What if the conspiracy freaks are right and it really is a surveillance-tracking system?" Advice and concern from my darling half-wit. The memory starts the blood vessels rupturing in my eyes again. Calm … calm … I take some slow deep breaths and regain control.

Heading back down to the front door, patting my pockets again. Everything I need. Check myself in the mirror again. I am ready. Now I just need to push through the growing inertia encountered of late whenever it comes time to leave the house.

Can a vampire develop agoraphobia? I'll have to look into that.

I wander into the drawing room and down a half decanter of whisky. Just need a little snorter for Dutch courage. Give myself a good, hard slap on the cheek and that's it, I'm out.

CHAPTER FOUR

The Elephant

My most recent and dearest accomplice in the hunt is the London Underground. As I slip into an almost empty carriage, I can't help but remember how time consuming tracking a specific quarry could be before its creation.

In February of 1860, work began on the first part of my beautiful labyrinth of underground corridors, or as it was then called, the Metropolitan railway. It was to run between Paddington Station and Farringdon Street via King's Cross and was in no small part due to the relentless support and campaigning of my good friend Charles Pearson, solicitor to the City of London Corporation.

We first encountered each other in an alehouse off King's Cross. He was slumped over his tankard and, at first appeared a quick and easy meal. Thankfully, I took the time to listen to him as he lamented to the cadaverous-cheeked but sympathetic stranger that, having hit another brick wall with the short-sighted fools in Parliament, he despaired that he would never get his beautiful underground railway built. The commercial heart of London was doomed to remain a congested mad house.

Over the course of the evening, he convinced me of the merits of the visionary designs for the City's railways, involving underground channels that could carry the workforce in and out of the centre of the City and herald a new age of a cleaner more humane metropolis.

Remember, I had watched in awe as resourceful monkeys excavated the sewer system. I knew what they were capable of and had already determined to influence and encourage their development in certain areas whenever I found the opportunity. Charles quickly won me over to the achievability of his visionary idea. He truly was an exceptional human. I encouraged and supported him, stoked him up when his fires were cooling with rants, describing the appalling slums city workers 'needs must' inhabit and the ever-increasing congestion and pollution on the roads of our beautiful city. Industrialisation had raised new questions; we needed to find new innovative answers.

I watered and tended the dream of the tunnel system that took root in Charles Pearson, and with a little help from me, it blossomed into an obsession. For years he defended the dream against the relentless grind of the small minded 'nay sayers'. Eventually, they wore him down, but not before he had prevailed. He was quite grey by the time he pushed the first route through. It took three years of construction, and he was dead before that first Paddington to Farringdon line opened in January 1863.

I mourned the loss of such a man, but the success of his dream silenced the detractors.

In 1864, there quickly followed the line between Hammersmith and Paddington and from there it grew.

The ingenuity of the monkeys and their relentless technological advances awed me. New tunnelling shields and electric traction made almost inconceivable designs requiring deep level tunnelling, a possibility. During 1890, Stockwell to the now closed King William Street Station opened, and the rest is glorious history.

Now my deep underground city of railway tunnels stretches for miles, plus intersecting caverns, disused storage vaults, natural channels and my beloved sewers. They, whoever those clever monkeys might be, like to say, "If it's too good to be true, it probably isn't," but I say, there are exceptions.

It is winter and having endured a ride in a stuffy carriage crowded with human commuters, it has long been dark by 8.20 p.m. when I emerge at the Elephant & Castle tube station. The human travellers have thinned out a bit since peak rush so the journey hadn't felt exactly like ten pounds of 'Turkish Delight' being squeezed into a five-pound sack, but close enough.

I have my old army coat on and its stink alone guarantees personal space. I keep my wool beanie with brim pulled down to cover my face in shadow. I look and certainly smell like a bum. I try not to make eye contact – no reason to risk an annoying encounter with a sensitive. I can make light of the small chance that a human will recognise me as something 'other' but it does happen and when it does, it's explosive. I am in no mood for that kind of a scene tonight.

A few years ago, during an excursion to the New World, I'd been caught out. Boarding a train on the New York City subway, I'd become complacent. Preoccupied, I let my guard down, sat directly under the unforgiving fluorescent light and let my gaze rest on the two other passengers in an otherwise empty carriage. As it turned out, one was a de-frocked priest, a boozer and a fornicator but nevertheless a true believer, and the other, an addicted, homeless sensitive, driven to the brink of madness by his own supernatural clarity of vision. It's a sad truth that many human sensitives find relief in substance abuse. They should be Shamans, but instead they just get smashed. Four hundred and sixty-eight stations in operation, 232 miles of routes and we three came together in the synchronicity of chaos – wrong place, wrong time, no escape. It had got messy.

Climbing to street level, I slowly make my way through the interior of the tube station. Occasionally, I lean against the cream-tiled walls and take in a long draught of polluted air, tasting the pheromonal signatures. Absolutely nothing. I make my way to the red-tiled exterior that leads out onto the roundabout and roam the immediate vicinity, shuffle about, using my eyes but mainly my nose until I become frustrated and impatient. There are just too many criss-crossing scents to distinguish just one. Directly outside the tube station I can identify the olfactory remains of at least a dozen acts of violence and scores of sexual encounters all overlaid with a veneer of vomit and defecation.

I stagger around the edge of the old, tiled facade until I reach the red-brick corner where a number of refuse skip bins are lined up and I sit for a while on the cold, greasy paving slabs. Pressing my back against the damp, piss-soaked wall, I centre myself. I need to concentrate on Jackie and shut out all the noise and distractions. I retrieve the two empty cans of McEwans Export Strength beer from deep in my pockets and position them so they are visible to passers-by, crack open a third and take a deep swig. This should guarantee I won't be bothered by do-gooders. I enjoy my old army coats; they're like Doctor Who's Tardis – they might not look much but there's more to them. I keep all sorts in its sticky pockets. Right now I just need to sit for a while and give myself a chance to pick up the freshest trail I can find and work through Jackie's steps from the last time she was here.

I used to come to the Elephant when it was still known as Newington Village. In the 1500s, it had a draw – the Newington Butts, an archery range that attracted men and boys from all across the area at the weeks' end, to practice their archery skills. Think of a really good paintball range, except imagine you need to be good at paintball to eat and maybe even defend yourself and your family. At that time, there were no police, no phones to call them on if there had been. No ambulance, no hospital to whisk you off to. Any passing thug could decide to 'pay a visit' and might even decide to move in. Self-defence was important. Supplementing your protein intake with game made a huge difference. Fathers and sons had the perfect excuse to get off the farm for a day, and Sunday night was easy pickings. I wasn't interested in the innocent drunks, but I was interested in the cut-throat pickpockets and lecherous small boy 'buggerers' bent on burglary; the Butts attracted a mixed bag. You don't get as much of that here now. The Elephant just ain't what she used to be.

Some believe the Elephant got its name from La Infanta de Castilla, referring to a series of Spanish princesses. Just a theory – I guess these history students have to find something to do with their time other than smoking spliffs and shopping for corduroy. The English, they argued, had stubbornly refused to get their unlinguistic tongues around the original Spanish, and had bastardised the Castellano until it became The Elephant & Castle.

I enjoyed the idea of the English mangling yet another language to suit their purposes, but I know the Castille legend simply isn't true. The only princesses remotely connected to the place were Iberian and lived at least 300 years apart. The whole 'Infanta' thing is a stretch. What I do know is that from around the 17th century, the old conjunction of the ancient roads to Kensington, Walworth and Lambeth had provisioned me with a rich supply of tradesmen, merchants and itinerant lone wanderers. Weary travellers, of course, needed a blacksmith to re-shoe their horses, which in turn became a coaching inn, to water and feed their ever-increasing numbers. Many of those tradesmen being aligned to the Worshipful Company of Cutlers, whose coat of arms features an elephant with a howdah in the shape of a castle on its back. These Cutlers used ivory for the handles of the knives and forks they manufactured, making Newington a thriving hub of ivory trading and gave rise to the name of the coaching inn – 'The Elephant & Castle'.

A painted sign depicting the deeply-rooted symbol of a castle on an elephant's back hung for many years above the coaching inn door. It would swing and creak on its iron hinges through the winter winds and blister in the summer sun. For the illiterate rustics travelling the trading route, it made a powerful visual image when describing their destination.

The Elephant isn't a regular haunt of mine these days, but I occasionally still come here for dinner. Reminiscing about less monitored, less polluted, sweeter smelling times is all good and well, but right now, hanging around and snorting human stink is making me queasy. I've almost given up when I pick up a mere hint of Jackie's pheromonal signature. Sometimes, that moment of released tension in resignation is all my senses need to open up, silence my chattering mind and give me something.

I rise to my feet, circle the station entrance a couple of times until I'm sure. Yes, there she is. I'm off at a jog along the New Kent Road, past the Superbowl Shopping Centre, under the overpass and straight on past Meadow Row. I keep going along the New Kent and take a left into Harper Road until I pass the Rockingham Estate. The Rockingham fills an entire block and I turn down Bath Terrace, which runs to one side of it and follow that until I come to Math House, which stands opposite the Rockingham and next to the Uxbridge Arms. The latter a bleak dive of a pub that has been painted a stomach-curdling shade of week-old liver.

I look up at the Estate – hideous architecture, tiny windows. Humans would always bewilder me. What kind of a species, designed to run for miles across the African plains, locks itself up in a series of 8ft by 10ft boxes – like battery hens. No wonder they occasionally turn violent. I shudder and turn my attention back to Math House. It isn't well maintained, to put it mildly.

There has been a break-in at one of the ground floor flats and the window remains cracked and is missing a few large shards of glass. A piece of marine plywood has been nailed to the inside. Someone hadn't bothered to remove the rotting net curtaining from the window before undertaking this piece of carpentry. Swathes of black mould-stained fabric spill out through the broken glass and sway in the breeze like an exhausted hand beckoning any passing bulldozer, "Hey, over here. Do the world a favour. Demolish me!"

I look about and listen for activity. The house seems quiet enough. The smell of Heinz beans and the sound of a muffled TV coming from somewhere in the back. The front door opens easily enough with a turn of my universal skeleton key. It isn't much of a lock, but there really is no need for heavy security here. What a dump. The paisley-patterned carpet is threadbare and smells like it has doubled as a bathroom more than a few times over the years. The stairs creak but there is no need for stealth. No one gives a damn.

Up the half landing to her room. My poor Jackie – I should have resolved this situation for her a long time ago. Purple and green should never be seen. Well then, shut your eyes. The flat is clean, still tidy, no signs of a struggle, no lingering odour of panic. Nothing transgressive happened here, apart from crimes against good taste.

I slump down on her thrift-shop couch, a brown and beige acrylic, boucle nightmare. If ugliness could kill she'd have disappeared a long time ago. I shut my eyes and take a deep breath. The atoms of scent sweep across my tongue and further back across my vestigial gills and I literally drink in the atmosphere. The closeness of Jackie's things make me feel so sad and careless to have lost her. I hadn't even known her address. I knew I could find her whenever I wanted, but the truth is that when she left my house she ceased to exist for me. I let out a resigned sigh of impotent regret. As always that's when one tiny speck of scent rises up through the myriad of infinitesimal particles and kapow! My eyes spring open. 'Hello.' I think I say it out loud.

Someone has been here, someone who doesn't fit … and recently. I taste the air. They hadn't actually entered the flat, but they had been close. I move back out onto the landing; it is stronger. Exiting the flat and then the house, I am surprised to find there is more of the discordant scent outside.

I wander about, testing the air with my tongue, pulling it through my almost closed lips with a bubbling of saliva, like a wine taster. I follow the scent until I come to a spot behind the three putrid wheelie bins pushed up against the brick at the front of the house, in the small front 'garden'. Someone loitered here. I must have missed it amongst all the other stale odours on my arrival. I'm not sure how I could have done so because this trail is fresh and intriguing. I draw in closer and fill my lungs. The ground is sticky with old bin juices but I kneel down and rest my cheek against the tacky paving slabs and continue to zero in on the trail. There it is again, and I can't contain myself. 'You're mine now, you fucking poacher.'

Although I was taught not to play with my food, these days I do. I give a lot of thought to the selection process. From that part of the meal – the planning, I take great pleasure. Traditionally, extraordinary people are not on the menu, but rules are made to be broken. The exceptional, the remarkable, the unusually attractive – these people tend to be missed. Also, through experience, I have learned 'the good', under which heading come the caring, the loving etc., tend to engender like feelings and again are missed by those whose lives they have touched. The cruel, weak, selfish and downright murderous tend, if missed, to be missed with a sense of relief, and certainly with no impatience for their safe return.

I have learned that the wicked are my accomplices in their own unremarkable and perfectly explainable disappearance. Close relatives tend to furnish all manner of plausible scenarios for their burdensome encumbrant 'just wandering off' to any authorities that enquire, i.e. police, parole officers, creditors. The nearest and dearest of the cruel tend to put as much space between themselves and the unpredictable actions of such black sheep as possible. All in all, perfect.

I prefer to eat low lives. I've lived long enough that, in human terms, I might not be a vegetarian, but I've developed ethics sufficient to opt for free-range arseholes when possible.

I used to avoid eating interesting people, no matter how evil because there were so few of them. These days when I wake up from one of my longer rests, there are always so many more humans than seems reasonable. In fact, so many people, it can't go on. The planet's crawling with them. For the love of Nature, something's gotta give. It always does. But for now at least, there's a glut, ergo I get to have, what I refer to as a slap-up meal at least once a year.

Mensa Card-holding poet, with latent psychic potential and a cracking sense of humour who also happens to be a colossal paedophile and torturer, is now on the menu.

I look forward to my 'treats'. I save a good bottle of wine to have with dinner. Yes, I can drink fluids other than blood. I am of this planet, for God's sake.

I divide my special meals into courses. With each course, I like to incorporate a theme, sometimes including a change of venue. London is riddled with old basements and deep, mysterious underground vaults that really give me the chance to let my hair down. A soul can scream and scream and make themselves sick in those man-made subterranean caverns. No one's gonna hear.

The person I am chasing now is definitely interesting; for all I know, fascinating. But that is not going to save them. Oh no. Tonight will be a doozy. I take a right back onto Harper Road, past the ethnic shops, bright fabrics, African spices and past the Rising Sun pub, then down the New Kent again. I take a sharp turn into Rodney Place and carry on past Gilfords Bakeries. It has started to rain heavily, but I've locked onto a unique pheromone fingerprint and it will take more than perpetual London drizzle to shake me off.

Onto Burge Street, passing a particularly dark alley, I pause. A prickling sensation runs over my scalp. A reliable

'Be careful Eddy' from the oldest part of my reptilian brain. My amygdala is talking to me. In humans, the amygdalae is quite small; in vampires it's huge. I take a couple of steps back. What is this about? I feel a little peeved and torn because I am almost certain that what has caught my attention is nothing to do with the trail I am following, or the job at hand. But I just can't move on. Damn my curiosity.

Back tracking a little further, I peer down the soggy chasm. It reeks of piss, and weirdly, it isn't human..... nor cat, nor fox... Interesting. Looking back down the street in the direction of my trail, I run my fingers through my rain-wet hair and give myself a hard punch in the head to try and shake the impulse to investigate. It doesn't work. With a ragged sigh of resignation, I take a couple of steps into the alley. The ground is a soggy carpet of pulped circulars, old newspapers and the odd used condom. Dear God, can nothing dampen human libido! No wonder there are so many.

Vertical London brick to either side of me reaches up five storeys and frames a long rectangle of grey and mauve. The London sky is never truly black any more. Light pollution has given me a skyscape with colour, at last. I reach the dead end of the alley and press my forehead against the greenish brick. 'What the fuck am I doing?' The hairs on the back of my neck stand up. I become very still, the energy coils tight and ready inside me. Someone is walking over my grave. That wouldn't normally bother me – it takes a lot to make me shiver. I am being watched. From the corner of my eye, I catch movement behind an upper floor bathroom window. The merest rustle of curtain and a figure instantly darts back into the shadows. But in that instance, I catch a glimpse of eye. And what an eye – yellowy and menacing.

The furthest end of the alley has purposefully and copiously, been marked with urine by a large predator, and not one that I recognise. I draw in the smell. Of what I have no idea, and file it in my olfactory memory under 'unknown', that fact alone makes my eyebrows rise. I've been around a long time and here is something new.

Looking up at the window, I consider scaling the wall and paying a visit. Curiosity physically pulls me a little way back into the alley to stand directly under the window. Looking up, my body presses against the brick wall. My chin rhythmically hitting and pulling away, my nails distend, I find purchase in the mortar.

I can't do this now. Whoever or whatever lives in that dark back room in Burge Street will just have to wait. But I make a mental note to start a broad internet investigation into reports of strange phenomenon or bizarre sightings around the Elephant as soon as I get a chance. It appears to be an area that has some interesting residents.

I come back out onto Rodney Place and keep going. The scent I picked up at Math House is tantalisingly close and seems to be fresh on the air. I begin to feel I am being drawn on. Was someone waiting for me to show up at Math House? Perhaps watching from a window in one of the unoccupied Rockingham Estate flats. I turn my mind back to the ugly tower block. It is possible. The thought strikes me as incredulous, but my instincts are beginning to kick in. I take a quick turn into Walworth Road, finding it difficult to stop myself moving too quickly for discretion.

There are people about and I don't want to draw attention but there it is again. Just ahead. I could swear I catch a flash of movement, very fast, not what I expect. A little unnerved by the creature in the alley, and now this surprising and careless preternatural speed, I become wary. There are too many people about at this time of evening, caution compels me to keep my camouflage in place. I can move so quickly that most humans wouldn't register I'd passed them, other than to shiver as a sudden cold breeze brushes their skin. But it is a needless risk. The scent I have followed from Bath Terrace is very, very fresh but always just ahead. Something niggles … my reptilian brain whispers coded clues but the answer remains just out of reach.

I speed up a little and press on, past the Old Vic Theatre and on towards Waterloo Road. Ahead, the scent moves away, very fast, too quick for a human. This hunt is not going as planned. I don't like surprises. Rattled, I turn into Larcom Street and notice the scent concentrating and give a sudden snort of laughter – half amusement, half fear. I know where we are headed.

Larcom Street dog legs, and at the corner, sits the Parish Church of St John the Evangelist. The grounds have long been sold off and these days it sits, surrounded by terraced houses. All that's left of the churchyard is a ravaged triangle of damp earth at the front of the church, a skimpy thong of a glebe, that sustains one huge, ancient Oak tree. That impoverished churchway is surrounded, like the rest of the building, with a brick wall topped with iron-spiked railings, designed to keep the vandals out. The beautiful, original, stained glass windows are hidden from view by a shroud of security mesh and above the manse door, is a roll of razor wire that would look right at home in Beirut. The cream stone of the church walls are stained black with diesel fumes.

I stop and stare at the church, and slowly move around the perimeter. The large front doors are shut and I feel no echo of recent movement. I stare at the triangle of yard. In the small barricaded church glebe, littered with dead supermarket flowers still in their cellophane sleeves, empty crisp packets, and a few burst balloons, the Oak stands proud, apart, and unto itself.

I drift back against the wall of a house, bathed in shadow, and watch as a 1990 Ford Mondeo swings around the corner and parks with a whine of gears. The black-cassocked vicar jumps out and locks the car door. He's carrying a bundle of sweaty sports clothes under his arm like a rugby ball. He's quite young, stout, and red-faced; he has the earthy smell of a healthy animal that's been running. He dashes across the road and disappears through the manse door into the church. He's late; his football match went a little over time.

I continue to watch. Nothing extraordinary happens, so I move in closer.

St John's isn't one of the oldest churches in London by any means. It was built around 1823, but it's of interest to my kind because it was originally built on piles and, although renovated over the years and repaired after being bombed in the Second World War, those subterranean spaces still exist. There remains an escape route deep beneath the church's foundations which connects through a series of narrow dark water channels to a number of tube and sewage tunnels. Jumping the black railing, I follow the scent to the south of the building, hugging its blackened stonework until I arrive at the familiar half-sunken door.

The frame of the door is very low, as though it were built for the seven dwarves and although small, the door itself is solid and incredibly heavy. Plus, it hangs on rusted hinges which makes it difficult, if not practically impossible, for a human to open. Its purpose and its erection is a little mystery of architectural whimsy for the type of local human history buffs that care about that sort of thing.

The door appears nowhere on the original or revised plans for the church. I suppose, one day a human will order it opened just to satisfy curiosity and they won't find much. Just steps leading down to a dead-end corridor, and they'll assume it was something to do with repairs to the original foundations.

The door moves with just a nudge. I'm strong but even for me it's too easy. I instantly know it has been opened just moments before my arrival. The fresh scuffs and tracks through the black dust and the grime of ever-settling London air pollution confirm it.

Moving into the musty interior, I descend the five steps and pull the door closed behind me. The corridor is not as low as the door would suggest. Immediately, on descent of the stone steps, the corridor heightens and there is no longer need to stoop.

I'm greeted by the now overpowering scent that increasingly just doesn't sit right. The source is just ahead but it now has a tang, a muskiness with just a hint of ... Something hits me both figuratively and actually ... death. Whoever I have been following has used a decoy scent to set a trail and in so doing has effectively hidden their own airborne signature. Much as shark hunters will trail a bag of chum to draw out the ocean predator, I have been drawn on ... lured, played.

But those thoughts are a flash of realisation that coincides with flashes of sparkling lights before my eyes as something incredibly powerful smashes, what feels like a mallet, over the back of my skull.

Reeling a little, I lurch forward. Thoughts flash through my mind. There must be two of them because nothing, no matter how cunning, could have doubled back on me. Crouching low, I turn, ready to spring but hesitate momentarily at the sight of my attacker. The yellowy eyes I had caught watching me from a window near Jackie's flat, back at the alley off Burge Street, glow with a weird phosphorescence. There's no light but as I am a creature of utter darkness, I can see clearly. The being, perhaps five feet four, is dressed in a filthy old rain coat that hangs to below the knee. There's a discernible hunch on its back and I wonder what the old rag of a coat is concealing. From the pocket, a woolly hat peeps out with a deep rim, I assume it wears it when on the street and can pass as a particularly ugly and exceedingly repugnant, but otherwise unremarkable member of the ever-growing homeless walking wounded. I had thought the ploy of adding a touch of stink to keep the humans away was my invention alone, but yellow eyes is playing that card with aces. My proximity to the creature in the enclosed space of the tunnel is achieving the difficult and dubious feat of activating my gag reflex. I suddenly wonder how many more, foul-smelling untouchables shuffling unnoticed through the city are not what they appear.

My view of the world is shifting and it hasn't done that in some time. Tectonic plates of long held belief grind across each other as my complacent consciousness adjusts to the new.

Whatever 'it' is, it isn't hiding now; it wants me to see it and it definitely isn't human.

'What the hell are you?' I manage to blurt as it leaps with a speed and snarling ferocity that brings alive every survival instinct in my body. The yellow eyes have now been joined by their cousins, a set of yellow, two and half inch canines and a row of incisors that jut from its now stretched, black lips like a string of deadly razor wire.

I know this creature is of the monkey genus, definitely mammalian. I'm pretty sure it's a twig from the same branch as homo sapiens.

Somewhere back in the mists of time, I'm talking seven million years, probably in East Africa's Rift Valley, the place the hairless monkeys like to call 'the crucible of human evolution', there were several divergences and I can tell you, they weren't all pretty. My own ancestors originate from that same cauldron of life with its deep lake that repeatedly rose and fell over the millennia, hiding in its swampy depths my species' breeding grounds.

I have no idea what niche this creature's ancestry filled, but I do know that about two and a half million years ago, there were suddenly so many of the tasty, hairless, physically helpless humans to prey upon, that I'm not arrogant enough to assume my ancient ancestors were the only avenue evolution took to harvest a new abundant food source. I also happen to know that many of the fossil remains of humanity's extinct ancestors, sandwiched between the seven-million-year-old Sahelanthropus Tchadensis and modern homo sapiens, are not the dead ends that scientists believe them to be. Those skulls that just don't fit are offshoots that represent the genus of whole new branches of evolution that continued to develop and diverge.

The Thals, as my species call them, or Neanderthals that humanity has decided disappeared about 28,000 years ago, are a case in point. The human archaeologists have said Dorit's Cave in British Gibralter is the site of the Neanderthals' last stand – a full stop to that story. A mile or so along that same coast is another opening in the rock, much smaller, and now almost entirely submerged. This cave leads to a much more extensive network of caverns and tunnels that spread deep into the rock like a circulatory system. Arteries, arterioles and finally, capillaries, branch out from the aortic corridors that lead downward from the heart of the initial cathedral-like cave. Here, stalactites drip down from its vaulted heights, and stalagmites rise upward from the cave floor to meet each other, forming magnificent columns of rock-hard calcium carbonate. Gravity-defying helictites, formed over the course of millions of years, that would crumble at the slightest touch, hang suspended, forming a scintillating canopy of alien sculptures over the concave rock of the arching dome. That is a cave worth exploring. But knowing the descendants of the Neanderthals, as I do, it will have been expertly disguised, blocked and hidden by now.

That undiscovered cave is the true site of the Thals' Last Stand – the last place the Neanderthals inhabited while still willing to emerge into the sun, before they broke ties with the daylight for good. The poor, hounded devils had found a deeper cave than Dorit's and chose to live further and further from the chattering, voracious monkeys above ground. Eventually, to put it mildly, they changed. That, as yet undiscovered cave is most sacred to the Thals and they would have hated the idea of desecrating it. Mother Earth provided their ancestors with sanctuary and by stoppering it up – in effect, blocking what I know they would consider the natural flow of life force or Qi as the Chinese would describe it, they insulted her. But the Thals know as well as I, that humanity is determined to crawl, dig and probe every inch of this planet. So I assume the Thals will have surrendered to logic by now and thought it prudent to cap it off. I know some of them well and prefer to keep out of their way. They aren't as easy prey as the surface dwellers. They aren't as nutritious either – not much vitamin D, but I digress. That's another story.

The humans don't like surprises. There are 'none so blind as those that will not see', and I suppose we monsters should just thank our lucky stars.

My current situation is leading me to draw the conclusion not all the hidden 'twigs' of human evolution have taken so thoroughly to the troglodyte lifestyle. Or have remained as recognisably human as the Thals, and this *thing* in front of me is the evidence. I have no idea what I am dealing with and the adrenalin rush that sweeps through me instantly distends my own set of impressive teeth. I can see my appearance gives the creature momentary pause.

A noise from deeper in the tunnel breaks the impasse and with a sudden rush we are on each other … wrestling and smashing each other into the cold stone of the corridor like two pint- sized titans. Holding back the other's teeth by gripping our hands around the other's neck. Fortunately, we enjoy roughly the same arm reach.

It is unsettling to unexpectedly grapple with something so unfamiliar and genuinely dangerous. I allow myself to be flipped and pinned to the floor rather than be on top and feel it's extremely flexible legs encircling me like an orang-utan on steroids. I quickly discover there is also disadvantages to having it gnashing above me. Thick, creamy saliva is dripping off its formidable teeth into my eyes and it stings like fury. Working my knees up between us and against its chest, I tense my stomach and gave a mighty push. Its grip slips from my throat, taking a good quantity of my skin and flesh with it.

We are both immediately back up on our feet and crouching, circling each other in a parody of an old Star Trek duel between Kirk and Spock. Something about the creatures pointy ears brings to mind Spock in the throes of Plak Tow blood fever. The 'alien duel' music rattles around my head and so I have a little singalong under my breath and realise I'm smiling.

The jolt of surprise I've experienced, having been precipitously thrown into mortal combat after so many years, is wearing off and the adrenalin rush is beginning to give me a buzz. I'm perverse like that. The constriction of the creature's pupils tell me it is feeling a little unzipped. I know I have to be careful of a genuine smile around humans. I've been told my smile has a snake-like quality. It is satisfying to know even this *thing* isn't too keen to mix it with me. Its large pupils have narrowed to pin-pricks, and the old, dependable, mammalian recoil response to an encounter with the cold-blooded has kicked in.

It speaks. 'What's amusing to you, Vampyr?'

The voice is throaty and the last word, a raspy snarl. I get the impression it doesn't much care for my sort.

'You have me at a disadvantage, creature. What are you and what the hell do you want?'

'You were stalking me. I saw you back at the alley. You were hunting me and you found me, and now, I've found you. We will settle this, not when you choose Vampyr, but now!'

I pull back in time to avoid a swipe from a hand furnished with lethal claws. 'I found you, that's true, but I wasn't looking for you. I have other business at hand, with which you are interfering.'

A moment or two pass. Just the sound of our laboured breathing fills the narrow corridor. We continue circling each other and take the opportunity to catch our breath during a twitchy Mexican standoff. I begin to hope its heart isn't really in it, I know mine isn't.

'I'll kill you, Vampyr. I'll end you if you choose to make us your business. There's plenty for everyone if we're discreet!

Why do you greedy, belly crawlers always have to be so blatant – so gauche. The Elephant's crawling with police.'

That takes me aback. This is the closest I've been to a life and death struggle for years, and now I am to suffer inter-specie insults to boot. 'You've made a mistake, creature, I am here for an entirely different reason than you assume. Tonight is the first I've known of your existence, and whether we have any reason for hostility is yet unknown to me. Back at the alley I lifted a rock and discovered a queer fish beneath. Happenstance and idle curiosity, I assure you, and if you recall, I left well alone. Now, you ugly fluke of a twunter, is the time for you to return the favour and fuck off!'

Teeth still deployed, we continue to circle each other, but the *thing* is definitely losing some of its original gung-ho conviction. There is a keen flash of intelligence in those yellowy, cesspit eyes. It is considering.

'I won't have a killing spree on my doorstep, Vampyr. We now have the police and media to out-manoeuvre with surveillance and the damn CCTV appearing on every other lamp post. It can't happen. Do you understand what they are capable of with their technology, you stupid, arrogant lizard? If we go down, I'll make damn sure you bloodsucking parasites go down with us. Control your own, Vampyr. Control the immoral, debauched dregs you call family, or I will!'

The words 'CCTV' and 'technology' are forced through thin, black lips as a disgusted hiss. This creature is mightily pissed off, physically formidable and although I'm in the dark, appears to know exactly what I am. Luckily, for all its bravado, I can smell it is afraid. Rightly so.

I've obviously been spending far too much time indoors. I am receiving information at a rate of knots and

I'm struggling to process it. Having grown comfortable with my despondent, but settled state of ennui, I'm exhausted and ready for a nap. A clawed hand reaches out, and with great speed, swipes another slice of flesh off my cheek.

I raise my fingers to my face and touch exposed muscle. I can feel the whites of my eyes turning red.

'I have a mind to make you my business, creature. If you had left me be, I may well have settled my current problem by now and perhaps yours with it. You have made a mistake this night.'

I lunge forward, my hand strikes out with lightning speed, too fast for human eyes. A direct hit through the chest, a killing blow, but I pull it back with a piece of rib and flesh but no vital muscle. I'd aimed straight for the 'jam tart' but the creature responded with a reflexive feint. Impressive. The thing gasps, spits a green stinking spit ball in my face and disappears with decisive celerity. Not as fast as my kind, but I can't help a grudging respect.

I stand for a while, leaning against the brick work, allowing the adrenalin to abate. My whole body aches. My cheek is stinging sharply. I heal fast but the price of sensation is pain and I hurt.

'Damn it!'

With a resigned sense of failure, I catch my breath, descend another set of steps and follow the passage to its abrupt, echoing cul-de-sac. At my feet is a massive flag stone and carved into its centre is a small, engraved Egyptian hieroglyphic ideogram depicting a pair of human legs. To the uninitiated it would look like two small ticks, but to a vampire, it is the ancient determinative denoting movement, or more specifically, escape.

My fingernails distended during the scuffle so I ease them between the tight joints of masonry and dislodge the heavy stone slab enough to get a finger and then a hand between it and the surrounding paving. Scraping them into the joint I lose a couple of nails at the root, it doesn't matter. Nails are always the first thing to grow back. I get my hands underneath and lift the stone clear, pulling it back into place behind me as I lower myself through the opening and enter the first of the underground tunnels.

Here the scent is very strong and I follow it without much enthusiasm. Things aren't going my way tonight.

Splashing my way through the dripping, stygian gloom until at an intersection of old pipe and earth tunnels, I find it – the chum bag. A bloodied, hessian potato sack tied with a bit of string sits atop a small island of sewerage, plastic and detritus that has snarled up and gathered on a tor of ragged masonry. Squatting down, I open it and shake out first a human hand and then a tongue. A quick sniff and lick of the two items confirm they were taken from the same body, and fresh. Not Jackie.

Well, there is my chum bag. The scent is now unmistakably tainted with the sour stench of decomposition, but there is no doubt the dismemberment is very recent. The body parts had been very fresh when the chase began. I examine the stumps of the two appendages. They had definitely been removed from the living.

Turning the hand around, holding it by the wrist, I observe it. Long, sensitive fingers – the hand of a musician perhaps. Not a very successful one, judging by the ingrained dirt and chewed fingernails. A female hand. I give it a shake. Nice to 'meat' you. Holding it by the ragged wrist, I turn it over again. There is nothing else of note. The hand still in mine, I wander around, letting my hyper-observant vampire eyes guide me. I don't want to miss something important just because I'm frustrated and angry. But there is nothing.

I lean against the tunnel wall and casually brush some hair out of my eyes with the hand. Nothing compares to the soothing properties of a woman's touch at times like these. I drop it back into the potato sack along with the tongue and a stray brick, and throw it into the deepest part of the sewer line. The trail has gone cold and there is no point hanging around any longer.

My head hurts and I'm confused; the feeling is uncomfortable to put it mildly. I am suffering from sensory overload. I have undergone an experience best described by correctional facilities as a 'short sharp shock'. After years of 'dicking around' as they say, I have no idea what the hell is going on. Where has my head been? Recent events suggest wedged firmly up my own arse. It makes me feel uneasy and foolish to think how totally secure I considered myself only days ago. Complete master of my domain. King of my castle. This is how a vampire dies – through sheer arrogant complacency.

I pull a zip lock plastic bag and a half-used roll of electrical tape out of one of the pockets of the army coat and undress, putting my clothes in one and taping them to my torso with the other. I have to leave the coat here – too bulky. Luckily, I have another half dozen stowed around my house. I give my head a rub. I'm shaken up and I had forgotten how that feels. Easing myself down into the effluent, I slide into one of the natural, chalk stone run offs. It is hardly wide enough for a human-shaped body to enter. Allowing my shoulders and hips to dislocate makes it easier. A steady spring of rust-coloured liquid runs into the tunnel, the bottom is covered in a type of slimy weed that allows me to writhe and slide through it with very little effort.

The stale air is fetid with black mould and fungal spores hungry to eat into the lungs, sinus, digestive tract and skin of surface dwellers but for me is pure ambrosia. I find the atmosphere calming. The muscles in my stomach begin to undulate while my arms stretch forward to guide, my legs help propel and power me through the airless ooze. Deep under the Thames, I stop for a while to gather my thoughts and dip my face and head into the water that half fills the channel. Originally fed by a natural underground spring, probably miles from here, calling it 'water' by this point is misleading. It has become a rich bacterial soup. I hold my breath and clear my mind. I can hold my breath for a very long time but eventually, I roll onto my back and refill my lungs. Without much effort I find I can push my head into the black mould that grows like a poison garden on the roof of the tunnel. It is spongy, deep and soft as a fertile womb and covers my torn face and neck with a healing poultice of microbic life. I surrender to primordial oneness with the deep earth never warmed by sunlight or sanitized by its murderous UV light. I revel in its suffocating embrace, a pleasure only shared by creatures of the dark, crazed human spelunkers and the dead. The communion becalms and helps me to marshal my thoughts.

I make a decision. I need to go home, recoup and return to the fray better prepared, mentally and physically. I can feel electrical charges firing through my blood and brain; I am waking up. The healing process has begun and re-activated my physiology. My species' response to attack or danger is to 'boot up' and every part of me tingles, hums and buzzes with chemical alchemy.

Semi-hibernation slipped upon me so gently that I hadn't even realised I'd been half asleep, for a long time, for years, in fact. Roaming my Chelsea mansion like a somnambulist, dreaming a long and boring dream, now I've been shaken awake with one hell of a start.

At this moment in time, the only two things I know for sure are: one, I don't know anything and, two, I'm bloody hungry.

One name comes to mind – Martin Wuornos.

CHAPTER FIVE

Martin Wuornos

To the world, Martin Wuornos gives the appearance of a quiet, even shy man. Softly spoken, in his late twenties, brown hair, medium build, just under six feet tall. Women find him attractive.

Martin is the owner and proprietor of Wuornos Butchers – free-range meat, in-house pies, sausage rolls, stews – baked fresh every day. He bought the premises three years previously with a business starter loan. Young, single, his own business, he is quite a catch. Women warm to his mild, self-contained manner, his work ethic, his ready smile.

What the women who chat and sometimes flirt with Martin in the butcher's shop don't know is that when he was twenty years old, he acquired his butchery skills during a two-year prison sentence spent in Albany Prison on the Isle of Wight.

During that sentence he took part in a rehabilitation scheme: 'Retraining for Life'. Martin chose the course titled: 'Butchery Skills – A Career in Food Supply Retail'. He was tutored in how to portion a chicken, how to portion and bone out carcasses of larger animals; whole sides of pig and beef, slaughtering techniques and effective hygiene. Martin made a diligent and quick student.

Two years in prison turned an undisciplined amateur thug into a man who could now see clearly what he wanted and needed from life, and he had a plan to make it happen.

The butcher's shop on Walworth Road wasn't much of a moneymaker when he'd put his offer in. The low turnover helped him pick it up at a bargain price. He built it up, put the hours in and now it ticked over nicely. He wasn't going to get rich, but then money isn't everything.

Martin had worked hard to save up the deposit for his shop; it wasn't easy, but his nest egg had been supplemented by takings from the slow sale of the 500g of pure diamorphine he'd smuggled out of Bangkok, Thailand.

He'd embarked on his Asian odyssey just before the arrest that resulted in his two-year jail stint. The trip was funded with monies gathered during a spree of burglaries and thefts with violence, committed throughout the previous twelve months, he was nineteen years old. At that time Martin had no criminal record. He had never been caught or charged with any of the offences he'd committed during his short life, which were numerous. As well as the crimes committed to fund his drug-muling scheme, there had been a long string of indecent and sexual assaults, most of which included grievous bodily harm.

When it came to not getting caught, Martin just seemed to have the luck of the devil.

The trip to Bangkok was a brainwave. He needed money, had no qualifications or education to speak of. He had trouble concentrating and was always a disruptive element in any educational programme. At sixteen he'd dropped out of school. His alcoholic mother wouldn't have given a damn, even if she had noticed. He left home around the same time.

He could take care of himself and took to sleeping rough. It was a dangerous, uncomfortable, lifestyle but preferable to daily laying eyes on his mother.

Dysfunctional but far from unintelligent or lacking ambition, the itinerant lifestyle didn't suit Martin.

That first trip overseas was an eye opener. Bangkok was a place he could live. If you could pay, you could have, or do, anything you wanted.

On his return to the UK, he managed to get through customs and back into Britain on sheer beginner's luck. He always seemed to be just ahead or behind someone of 'interest' to border control. The drugs had been strapped to his stomach with a smooth prosthetic cover that looked and felt like a fat pot belly. In one of his bags was a 10,000 volt Z-Force III stun gun.

Immediately on his arrival back in London, he made his way to a squat in Brixton. A row of three abandoned houses, in a dangerous state of dilapidation, in which he'd been living for a short time prior to the trip. The end of terrace house was particularly foul. A cracked sewer pipe and rotting roof beams ensured it was avoided by even the most desperate. In this house, under the kitchen floor boards, he stashed the drugs and the stun gun before heading out for a night on the town. Martin wanted to celebrate.

After picking up a troubled, pretty and very drunk sixteen-year-old called Hannah Rice outside a Whitechapel pub, the evening's celebrations turned dark.

The girl, Hannah, now a woman, still bore the scars of that night. The fact she'd survived at all was a miracle.

Her screams drew the attention of two off-duty police detectives, who, by sheer luck, after a hard and disappointing day, had stopped to unwind over a few drinks at the Crown and Shuttle. Before setting off on the ten-minute walk for a Brick Lane curry, they'd serendipitously lingered at the corner of Shoreditch High Street for a quick smoke. That was when they heard, what sounded like, muffled screams.

Detectives Hooper and Sugar cautiously entered the side alley of a nearby, boarded-up restaurant to find Martin Wuornos pushing a gag back into the mouth of a young woman with one hand, while crushing her windpipe with the other. The gag had worked free during a bloody and brutal struggle. From somewhere, Hannah, with multiple fractures to her jaw, had found the strength to scream. She had the survival imperative of the young on her side. Unfortunately, she had already been subjected to a fierce but, Martin's lawyer would later argue, unintentional and uncharacteristic attack.

The two police officers instinctively knew that the man they overpowered and cuffed was bad news. They had been in the right place at the right time for one girl, but there was something about Martin that set alarm bells ringing in the two police officers' heads. Martin Wuornos tickled the vestigial lizard brain hidden deep at the back of the human skull. It is evidence that vampires and men were once related and is often enlarged in detectives, professional gamblers and career soldiers. Neither officer had been pleased to hear of Martin's early release.

Martin was not sweating when they wrestled him to the ground. He resisted arrest with the controlled, trance-like fury of a Viking berserker until he realised struggling was pointless. Detective Sam Hooper and Detective Deborah Sugar were both East End Londoners, born and bred. Both had grown up on the Estates. They worked as a tight team and both had divided loyalties. They each had family 'inside', or on their way to going 'inside'. They both had family in law enforcement, army, or security. The latter job description covered a wide spectrum of 'dodgy'. They knew that in the heart of every Englishman fought two dogs of war – one a heathen cur, bent on mayhem, longing for the savage freedom of drunken anarchy – and the other, a ferocious hound, guarding the ideals of valour, honour, truth and loyalty. Which dog won just depended on which got fed the most.

Call it intuition, or whatever you like, but both police officers instinctively knew there was more to Martin Wuornos than the average dysfunctional and violent scumbag. Here was another kind of 'strange' altogether.

On the night of his arrest, Martin abruptly stopped resisting without a word of protest, and studied them with the unblinking thousand-year stare of a lobotomised pig. The officers considered Martin to be a 24 carat creep. Such opinion was not admissible in court. The law demands probable cause, evidence, and a pattern of behaviour. There was nothing they could do; they didn't make the rules.

In court, Martin's defence claimed the girl had offered him 'no strings sex' for thirty-five pounds. Martin had agreed. They'd found a quiet spot to complete the transaction but once inside the alley, the girl had demanded to see the cash before they got down to business. As soon as the drunk Martin produced his wallet, she had grabbed it and attempted to run. A moment of temporary insanity, fuelled by drugs and booze, had led to his hitting her once or twice more than he'd intended. He was deeply ashamed and remorseful.

Unfortunately, the girl had a history of truancy, vandalism and petty theft. It all undermined her plausibility and muddied the waters. Character assassination aside, the jury found it hard to look at Hannah. Her scars were still very fresh. Martin was found guilty.

Two years later, Martin emerged from prison a new man. He'd been diagnosed with hyperactivity and ADD and now took Ritalin three times a day. He'd gathered all the skills he needed for a new life, not least the time to think and plan.

Martin didn't enjoy his time as a young, good-looking man at Albany and he had no intention of ever returning. However, he had needs, and they had to be met. It was time to take control of his life, as his counsellors had advised.

On returning to Brixton, he couldn't believe his luck. The row of derelict terrace houses still stood. Under the floorboards of the ground floor kitchen the drugs and stun gun were just as he'd left them two years before. The three terraced houses were marked for demolition. Yellow tape, warning of danger was stapled to the boarded-up windows and doors. The council had moved slowly through the application for redevelopment, struggling with counter appeals on questions of heritage zones and protected architecture. Eventually, the property developer gained his permission to go ahead. The three houses were due to be demolished in the next two weeks. Luck was still on Martin's side.

During the next four years, life became difficult, but he'd managed to land a job on the meat section of a large supermarket. Organised, calm and systematic, he worked his way up until he was made one of the food chain's youngest section managers.

Getting the job was the easy part; holding onto it, juggling parole officers and keeping his nose clean took its toll. Those years had nearly been too much for him, but he kept control. He found a way to keep it together. Getting through those long days, smiling and keeping his tone low, became easier once he'd learned to keep the main part of his being – his mind – elsewhere. While his body went through the motions, he was either reminiscing over the last kill or planning his next.

By this point, his kill kit had evolved and now consisted of the Z-Force III stun gun, a 1.5kg hammer, two sets of handcuffs, one set of thumb cuffs, two serrated butchers' knives, two rolls of black, heavy duty refuse sacks and a change of clothes. The purchase of the stun gun had been inspired – sheer genius.

He took some crazy chances during those years. Every kill was opportunistic, rushed, the time and place always left to chance. He never got the opportunity to really savour the act, to truly feel the way he wanted, needed – to be completely in control.

Everything was so difficult before the shop, but now he lived life on his own terms. He could hardly wait for the following night.

He had met Karen while having his six-weekly haircut. He liked his hair short, really short; hygiene mattered when dealing with meat.

He was thrifty and always asked for a trainee. After all, he didn't want anything fancy. He tended to use different salons. They were great places for meeting and watching women. A place women felt safe and comfortable sharing; and boy, did they share – did they like to talk! The information he'd got out of some of them during the time it took for a short back and sides beggared belief. Take Karen, for instance …

He started to chat with her while she washed his hair. Gentle flirting, exchange of personal information. Situation: single, available, one kid, no close relatives. The pregnancy and subsequent arrival of her now four-year-old son had caused problems. Her parents had her later in life; they were older and strict, and couldn't accept she was keeping an out-of-wedlock child with no father on the scene.

She left home when she was four months pregnant and headed for the Big Smoke – London. She'd craved the anonymity, the lack of judgement. Bad times had followed, and now, better times. She loved her son, the best thing that ever happened to her. Loved her job, loved the people she worked for and with at the salon, and had nearly finished her training. Her son was almost ready to start school, and she was having a new lease of life. At last, she had some energy and even some spare cash to spend on herself. She was ready to give the dating thing a go, even though all her friends told her it was 'murder' out there.

Karen would have accepted in a heartbeat if Martin had asked her out on a date. Would she like to go for a drink one night? Maybe they could get a pizza? He hadn't.

He knew her routine. She would be closing the salon tonight around eight p.m., depending on how quickly they could get the last customers out. He'd been watching her since she cut his hair. He would never use this salon again. She had been telling the truth when she said she had no relatives. She did have some friends though. She used a babysitter who lived in the same block of council estate flats. Another young woman, a solo parent with her own child for the government to raise with his tax money. He'd watched that 'one' come and go to different flats, picking up kids, dropping off kids. All paid in cash no doubt; undeclared income. She'd be on his list too if it weren't so risky. He would have to give that one a pass and concentrate on Karen. She would be punished for them both. Everything was ready down in the basement. He could feel the stirrings of an erection, just thinking about it, but he would just have to be patient. Not much longer now. Leaning forward, he turned the volume way up on the television. He knew it annoyed his neighbours. He almost wished the 'pencil neck' would knock on his door and complain. He had been looking for an excuse to smash that 'loser's' head in.

He had worked hard to keep a grip, must not lose his temper. He needed to be careful not to tell that 'Nelly' living next door what he really thought of him, and what he'd really like to do to him. Patience … just one more night of patience. He would have enjoyed making 'Mr. Do Right' listen to Karen scream tomorrow night. All night. That would make him think twice the next time he thought of slipping one of his snotty letters under the door complaining about the strange smell from the drains, or Martin's TV waking their whining baby.

It was a nice idea, but it couldn't happen. By the time Karen recovered from being stunned with the Z Force, she'd be gagged and hung from a meat hook by her cuffed wrists, her toes just touching the tiled floor of his basement, and no one could hear anything from down there.

When he'd bought the business, the basement workroom had been adequate, but for his purposes, it needed a little revamping. The floor was retiled with a steeper run off, and larger drainage outlets fitted with filter guards. He had some large steel fridges and freezers installed, picked up at a liquidation sale. New steel surfaces, two large heavy duty butchers' blocks and a row of heavy gauge meat hooks were suspended from steel beams in the ceiling, each strong enough to hang a 750 pound carcass of beef. He had a hot water hose with jet gun attachments. The basement had thick, double brick, concrete reinforced walls. It was a hygienic, efficient butchering space – the perfect 'kill room'.

He didn't need or want any baking facilities in the shop; he had his pork pies and sausage rolls baked off site. He wasn't a chef. But he supplied the meat and they sold well. He'd invested in a bone grinder; and a local garden nursery centre couldn't get enough of it. They swore it made the seedlings fair spring up.

He leaned back into his chair. All was right with his world, and at long last, he was in control – as it was meant to be.

***

Martin Wuornos got to his feet and clicked the remote. The TV screen went black. No need to antagonise the loser next door. He stood in the dark, just the glow from an over-range fume extractor lighting the flat. He thought he heard a noise from below. He stood silent. Yes, there it was again …

Someone was in the shop.

He went to the kitchen and opened the top drawer, selecting a meat-tenderising hammer and a chef's multi-purpose knife. Someone had picked the wrong shop to rob. Incredulous at his own good luck, he tiptoed to the stairs. There were times he just felt the Universe rushed up to meet him and bowed before him. All things come to those who wait. This was just what he needed.

CHAPTER SIX

'Hank Marvin'

I'd been watching Martin Wuornos for a few months now. It hadn't been pleasant viewing.

Friedrich Nietzche wrote: 'Whoever fights monsters should see to it that in the process he does not become a monster. And when you look into the abyss, the abyss also looks into you.'

He had a point.

It was a dirty business finding prospects to invite for dinner and dirt tends to stick. Luckily, I am already a monster and the abyss and I are old friends.

Location-wise, Martin's shop is expeditious. My only problem with stepping forward our introduction is that he is also someone of 'special' interest. I'd planned a 'special' evening, where we could take our time and really get to know each other in depth.

I wanted Wuornos to see the real Eddy; it was only fair as I'd already come to know him intimately. I understood him better than he understood himself.

I'd been looking forward to our evening together and I wouldn't have chosen him for an emergency snack, but he is so handy.

I have a few other prospects in the wind, earmarked for just a quick hello. I'd much rather visit one of them, but what can I do? None of them are close and none has been as thoroughly vetted as Wuornos. I don't want any more surprises tonight.

Also it's a Tuesday, so if Martin's stuck to his routine, and that boy does so enjoy his routine, he'd be found at his home about now.

He'd be watching some mind-numbing television show, or on the computer visiting one of his favourite sado-porn sites, or talking to like-minded friends with similar hobbies in secret chat rooms.

I'm not going to have the luxury of time, and Wuornos really does deserve some quality time. But with that one regret, I've made my mind up. It's time to introduce myself to Mr Wuornos. There's nothing for it but to get out of these tunnels and eat.

I head back the way I came, through the underground channels until I'm back in the vaulted conjunction of drains and sewers that converge under St John's Church. Unfortunately, my coat, shoes and the bag of body parts have disappeared, washed away down the sluice. I soon give up the search; they've gone the way of all the other flotsam and jetsam that finds its way to the City's bowels.

No more cursing myself for an idiot, I just have to get through the next few hours. If I can do that, whatever else the night has in store, I have a good chance of surviving it. Sans army coat, I feel pretty exposed; my feet are bare. I look like hell and there are CCTV cameras everywhere according to 'yellow eyes'. I know my appearance will bring attention. I need a coat.

Emerging from the church, I try to keep my head down and sway from side to side. Occasionally, I lean against railings or walls, doing my best impression of a drunk. It isn't difficult; my cell turnover has super-accelerated and I am feeling woozy and a bit light-headed. I lurch out of the church grounds and onto Waterloo Road. From there, I hit the dimly lit back streets, moving quickly but discreetly, until I take a left up a narrow avenue lined with a few ailing trees and emerge onto Walworth Road. Walworth Surplus Stores is close by, close enough to make it my next stop. It doesn't take long to get there.

I take a few moments to check out the street and ensure no one is hanging around. I pull myself up the brick work onto the roof and head for the small roof window at the back. I have used this skylight many times to access the stores supplies. A metal mesh covers the glass, but that comes away without much effort, and I flick the trick catch, lift the window and let myself in. I've disabled the alarm before the warning beeps have finished their annoying countdown. This Age of Technology has heralded a world governed by sound-triggered behaviour modification. 'Seat belt on' beep beep, 'walk' beep beep, 'don't walk' beep beep, 'higher' beep beep, 'lower' beep beep, 'bit to the left' beep beep. Pavlov would have loved it.

I quickly pick out a coat and a hat. Looking through the shelves, I find a pair of army boots in my size and behind the counter, some refuse sacks and marine tape. Dressing quickly, I shove a couple of bullseyes into the till and check the security camera is still just for window dressing, the light flashes but it's not recording.

I exit the same way and secure the old skylight shut. I always leave as little damage as possible. I like this store; it's orderly and well stocked. I can slip in, pick up everything

I need and get out quick and easy. I don't want it going out of business, that's for sure. There aren't many places like it left. With a bit of luck, apart from the cash in the till, the owner will hardly notice I've been here at all. We have an understanding. As long as I leave roughly twice the pound value of goods taken, he turns a blind eye and doesn't get curious – a rare quality indeed.

Back on the street, lightheaded, I stumble onward. My pulse is pounding in my own ears as the effervescent blood courses through my veins and leaves my extremities tingling and stinging. It feels as though I'm crawling with fire ants. My vision lurches in and out of sharp focus. For periods of time, I can only hear the rush of my own blood. At other times, the sounds around me become so loud they cut through my skull and my knees buckle. Pressing my hands over my ears furnishes no relief. It's a struggle to stay conscious and keep one foot moving in front of the other; I'm sleepwalking, but always in the right direction. A primitive force has taken control of my body, but it's alright. I know where I'm heading and I know better than to fight it. My higher functioning self, my ego and conscious will is, for the time being, a passenger, just taking in the scenery.

The physical confrontation at the church has slammed my body from first gear straight into fifth. I've entered a very precarious and risky stage of the 'renewal'. My amygdala, the larger part of my brain, is now in complete control. My survival has been threatened and there is no room for mercy or restraint. This is not the way I'd have chosen to reawaken. I've slipped into automatic pilot, my body is in overdrive and it needs fuel fast. Nothing else matters. God help any innocent that tries to get between me and my dinner.

Jackie's disappearance has thrown my orderly existence a googly. In truth, I'm beside myself with worry. Someone, or something, has decided to inconvenience me and they've taken her. I'm a little afraid and a lot furious.

I've entered turbulence, as we all do from time to time on our, hopefully, long-haul flight of life. All I can do is fasten my seat belt and hope for the best, but I feel a responsibility to do right by Jackie and am surprised at my own sentimentality.

I miss her.

I look up at the bruised sky, punchy and purple with diesel fumes, the stained concrete, the multitude of shiny metal cars produced with planned obsolescence. Nowhere for the eye to rest free from evidence of the busy, busy monkeys' industry. I feel a moment coming on:

'I have of late, wherefore I know not, lost all my mirth, and indeed, it goes so heavily with my disposition; that this goodly frame, the earth, seems to me a sterile promontory; this most excellent canopy, the air, look you, this brave o'er hanging firmament, this majestical roof fretted with golden fire: why, it appeareth nothing to me but a foul and pestilent conflegration of vapours. What a piece of work is man! How noble in reason! How infinite in faculty! In action how like an angel! In apprehension, how like a god. The beauty of the world! The paragon of animals! And yet, to me, what is this quintessence of dust? Man delights not me; no, nor woman neither.'

What can I say. It has been an emotional evening. I am managing to keep upright and maintain a brisk if stumbling pace, but shudder after shudder runs through me and I tremble; I need to hold it together just a little longer.

Back on the street, I carry on up Walworth Road until I hit the roundabout and head down to the tube station. I keep to the shadows until I reach Borough High Street and stop to check it out. It's early morning, about 2 a.m., and the street is deserted. I smile as I see a mangy fox dart across the road, hardly a hair left on its sorry little stump of a tail. I give a short, high-pitched whistle through my vestigial gills and the fox stops in its tracks and stares at me. We lock eyes for a moment, and drawing in the night air to taste my scent, it takes off and drags itself up and over a brick wall as if Satan himself is in pursuit.

I move on down the street, keeping to the shadows and doorways until I stand opposite Wuornos Butchers. From the upper windows, the flickering, blue light from a television casts a fish-tank glow. Martin is in domicile – so dependable. I cross the street and stop directly in front of the shop door. I can hear the television upstairs, the volume is way up. Martin is being antisocial tonight. Tut tut. He'll bring attention to himself that way, but then I've noticed his mask of respectability tends to slip a little just before a kill. My change of plans for Martin might just be some young woman's lucky break – the break of a lifetime you might even say.

I pick the lock on the security shutter door and roll it up. It is very quiet; Martin keeps it well greased. He likes to enter and exit without making a lot of noise. That suits me.

I also pick the lock on the glass door and enter the shop premises, closing both doors behind me. I am immediately assailed by the cloying stench of farmyard flesh laced with a more exotic meat. Little do Martin's customers know what is in those delicious pork pies. It appears there may be more ignorant cannibals living in Lambeth than should bear close scrutiny.

Standing with the shop door behind me I remain for some moments, listening, probing the space for any discordant note. There is none. All is as I'd hoped. I move through the shop and stand at the foot of the stairs leading to the flat above. I make no attempt to be quiet, just the opposite. The television has been abruptly switched off. I can feel a pensive presence above. He is listening. Movement follows. Finding a weapon? Nervous but excited and still confident. 'Martin,' I whisper. 'Martin,' I repeat, a little louder. Silence from above, but I know he has heard.

I move to the stairs that lead down to the basement, to the butchery proper. I descend and step onto the cold, tiled floor, closing the heavy soundproofed door behind me and turning on all the fluorescent strip lights.

Down here the smell of bleach is overpowering, almost too much for my hyper-olfactory senses to handle. Martin has created his own abattoir. I look around and take in the orderliness of the space. A place for everything and everything in its place. I always take the time to admire efficiency in fellow predators. I can hear him now, moving around in the shop. I let him be for the moment and examine the meathooks that hang from the ceiling. Very good.

He is now moving toward the stairs. I know he is looking down and can see the closed door to the butchery, so I open it, just a little way, enough for him to see the movement and allow a thin shaft of cold light to spill out and stripe the stairs. Silence. Now that has given him pause. Martin's butchering facilities are laid out so conveniently that I am savouring the same kind of joy I get from buying a bag of fresh stationery from a good bookshop. After all, it's the little things that make you happy.

I begin a systematic search, opening drawers and cupboards until I find what I am looking for. Wrapped in brown greaseproof paper – Martin's kill kit. Something is missing.

I murmur his name.

'Martin?'

I can hear his heart beating a little faster now. Less anticipation. More fear. The smell of it is exciting me. My teeth are distending – I'm so bloody hungry. I strip off my coat and then the rest of my clothes, folding them neatly and covering them in some plastic wrap I tear off a commercial size roll suspended by metal brackets on the edge of the heavy-duty steel butchers' block.

In the unforgiving fluorescent light, I can see that my body is changing – camouflage redundant. I am long past the charm offensive phase of the hunt. I am in full predator mode. I stretch and flex; joints and tendons pop. My jaw aches and so I stretch my mouth open. Muscles loosen and I feel as much as hear my jaw unhinge with a little muffled thud. Such a relief.

Anyone else, anyone in their right mind would be calling the police about now. Not Martin. He would never willingly invite the law into this sacred place. This is his temple, his inner sanctum – the Holy of Holies. Here in this fane, Martin alone is the high priest, judge, jury and… executioner. There is nothing to come between him and his deity. This is where he offers his blood sacrifice in exchange for access to the only state in which he can experience pleasure, the only state in which he can find the release and relief of orgasm … Control. Ultimate power over life, death and dignity. It's driving him crazy that someone is down here, touching his things. I stifle a giggle, but I know he's heard. I listen to him retreat back up the stairs to the flat. I know what he's going for. I giggle again. The sound of opening cupboards, unlocking boxes. Here he comes again. More cautious this time. He is breathing heavily; he smells so good, his sweat spiked with fear and adrenalin. Delicious.

I can hear the electrical hum of the reason for his strategic retreat. He went for 'ol reliable' – the stun gun.

He starts making his way down to the basement. The stairs creak and groan. I wait till he is half way down before I start unscrewing the fluorescent tubes.

I leave just one tube partially connected, sputtering and arcing. I like the patterns the cold light sprays across the reflective surfaces – on, off – on, off.

Martin leaps into the butchery brandishing the stunner, jabs it into my ribs and lets me have it. It tickles a bit. He fumbles with the light switch and I sweep in. I yank the gun from his hands, twist both his arms behind his back and snap a pair of his own handcuffs over his wrists. Dragging him backwards, I lift him up and hang him on one of the meat hooks. Such a manoeuvre Martin would have carried out on many a reluctant late night guest, except that Martin would have sweated and struggled with his quarry while to me, he feels as insubstantial as a rag doll.

I'm betting there haven't been many women hauled down into this slaughterhouse who have screamed as loud as Martin is doing now. Thankfully, the girly-boy shrieking quickly gives way. The snivelling and mewling, spittle dribbling down his chin starts almost the instant I spin him around and we come face to face. He really is a craven little weasel of a monkey. I've had school girls for dinner who've kept their game face on longer.

This isn't the Martin I'd come to know. Where is the cold predator, the vicious, heartless sociopath now? I thought these human aberrations were supposed to be emotionally stunted, lacking a fully functional limbic system, disconnected from their feelings. Martin certainly seems to be fully in touch with his feelings right now.

I had hoped for more grit, a bit of pluck, but it is what it is and I'm hungry. With the razor-sharp tip of a filleting knife, I run up the seams of his T-shirt and pants until he is hanging naked and pink. There, that's better. Let the dog see the rabbit – and all that malarkey.

'Hello Martin.'

That's what I try to say. My mouth is no longer fit for enunciation. I don't think he understands. The gnashing of my widened, unhinged mandible starts him squealing again.

I decide it's best to let actions speak louder than words.

CHAPTER SEVEN

'O radiant Dark! O darkly fostered ray!
Thou hast a joy too deep for shallow day'

G. Eliot

I feel a lot better now. My skin tingles but has stopped stinging. My body sizzles with life … I feel giddy … I've drunk a bit too much, a bit too fast, but I'm enjoying the buzz.

I head toward the river, after about ten minutes of dodging in and out of back streets. A quick turn down Old Paradise Street brings me to the Albert Embankment. I carry on down to Lambeth Bridge, past Vulliamy's dolphin-entwined lamp posts. As I remember, they went up around the 1860s and the dolphins arc actually supposed to be sturgeons, but they're the weirdest-looking sturgeons I've ever seen. I stand for a moment to take in the view across the river – the Houses of Parliament and behind them the London Eye. The sky glows with light pollution refracting and reflecting back colours from the chemical cocktail that is London air. Nothing strikes as sad or ugly now. Everything is magical and just as it should and always had to be.

The night is so very beautiful.

On each side of the river, the entry to the bridge is guarded by two obelisks topped with a stone pine cone. There's an urban myth that the pine cones are actually pineapples and were placed there as a nod to John Tradescant the Younger – a Lambeth resident, who with painstaking care, managed to grow the first pineapple in Britain. Looking at the slate sky, streaked with petroleum blues and mauves, and feeling the ubiquitous drizzle of London rain on my face, the idea of pineapples growing here, in the heart of the City, beggars belief. I suppose that is why I choose to believe it, because that is just the kind of eccentricity in which the English specialise and celebrate. The Tradescant urban myth has the ring of peculiar truth.

The juxtaposition of baby pink and blue paintwork against the industrial iron grey of Lambeth Bridge is a work of genius and perfection. I look up at the stately street lamps silhouetted against the city lights, a row of tall phantoms shrouded in the cool, damp air that fizzes with carcinogenic compounds, and fall in love with *my* London, all over again.

Below me the brown-green water of the Thames is running fast. The tide is rushing out and perhaps moving at near its peak of around eight miles an hour. The river laps and pulls at the far, shoal bank with greasy, greedy fingers.

Humans have always found need to cross this stretch of the river. Before the bridge there had been the horse ferry constantly plying between the Kings residence at the Palace of Westminster and Lambeth Palace - town house of the Archbishops of Canterbury. Dated 1367, there is a record of the sum of sixteen pounds paid 'for passage to and fro across the Thames to the Manor of Lambeth of Simon, Archbishop of Canterbury and Chancellor, where the Inn of Chancery is now held, and for the wages of the keepers of the said barge'. Before that, there was an ancient British ford just a little further down the river at Stangate, used by the Romans to make their crossings.

The Thames is the main artery that pumps life through the ancient settlement of London; it slices deep into her meat but it does not sever.

I slip over the wall and leap to the underside of the bridge in one fluid movement. My hands grip and release the lattice of steel girders that criss-cross the underbelly of the five-span steel arch and I swing across like a five-year-old on the playground monkey bars.

In the duffle bag over my shoulder are the remains of Martin Wuornos. I don't notice the weight. Halfway across the bridge I stop and drop it into the fast moving water of the Thames. He creates a hole in the river for all of half a second. I give him a wave.

'Jo utat Kivanok!Bolond menyet...' I'm Hungarian and terribly superstitious so I spit three times into the water before I carry on across to the far embankment.

I feel good, and the night is delicious. *My* London glows and heaves with possibilities. I let myself down onto the shingle beach on the north side of the Thames and make my way along the bank to the little set of concrete steps that leads up to the pavement directly in front of the MI5 building. I saunter, nice and casual, until I find what I'm looking for. I vaguely remember there is a manhole cover somewhere nearby, just under the northern end of the bridge where the spill of street light can't reach and there is no damned CCTV. There it is, situated in a fortuitous little blind spot. I throw a stone, too fast for human eyes to register and shatter the nearest street lamp, just in case. It winks out without so much as a plink. I lift the old iron circle and ease myself through and down, pulling it back into place quickly behind me.

I breathe a sigh of relief as my feet sink into the ooze … I'm back in the sewers. I haven't killed anybody that didn't deserve it and haven't brought any unwelcome attention to myself. It could have all turned out so much worse. Reluctantly, I dump the coat and the boots. Stripping again and using the plastic bags and tape I'd picked up at Walworth Surplus, I strap my essential clothes to my torso and start down the tunnels at a smart lick. Without the need to keep up the facade of humanity, unhindered by decorum you could say, I make swift progress.

Taking one of the main sewer lines that, along with several others, feeds off an arterial conjunction that runs under the Old Royal Horticultural Society Playing Fields, I slide, swim and writhe my way back toward Chelsea until I reach the comfort of familiarity – my old stomping grounds.

I emerge from an electricity conduit onto a section of the London tube line that runs direct to Sloane Square Station. Once on the track, I make my way to the length of track where a spray of water from a cracked mains pipe will make do for a shower. There's a trick to this, a bit like trying to hose a cement truck down with a water pistol. It takes me a few minutes, but I manage to rinse off most of the crap and dirt, concentrating on my head, neck and hands. I dress and run a comb through my hair. I'm as unremarkably tidy as a barefoot man in the heart of a city can be. Without the benefit of a proper bathroom or a shoe shop, I'm done. Checking I haven't dropped anything identifiable, I set off at a run.

There is a lot to think through. I need to get to my computer and look into what the hell is going on around the Elephant & Castle. The creature from the church had definitely given me the impression that Jackie's disappearance isn't an isolated incident. Far from it, that perhaps in fact, it is connected to, and part of, a killing spree that has been sweeping through the Elephant and making life very uncomfortable for the area's more exotic residents – almost impossible in fact. There had been a whiff of desperation about 'yellow eyes'. I've been left with the impression that the creature from the church feels it is being driven out of its home and has assumed the situation is being created by, or at least has something to do with, my brethren. I have some sympathy for how it could draw that conclusion. I've had to prematurely move on a few times, and from some very comfortable situations indeed, due to vampire shit storms. Specifically, shit storms created by one particular vampire who follows me like a bad smell, but then, none of us can choose family.

Ten minutes later, still hugging close to the tunnel wall, I can see light from the station. I've made good time, but then, I can run very fast. I check my watch on approach. The electric light of the station platform starts to stab into my eyes and I wait for a moment to let them adjust. I follow the minute hand until it reaches seven to the hour. Here he comes, the night watchman, right on time. This new one is like clockwork. Thank God for OCD. My emergence from the tunnels has to be timed just right to avoid detection. Just as the watchman passes, with his back to me on his rounds, he momentarily obscures the edge of the tunnel, shielding me from the unblinking eye of the security camera. I slip out, and up onto the platform. The station is closed, but unlocking and relocking gates has become second nature, and I'm soon strolling homeward.

I need to rest, heal and plan. Events have taken 'a turn' as they tend to do. I just need time to think over how to 'act on' not 'react to' my new situation. I'm itching to get on my computer and do some digging into what exactly is happening out there.

One thing is certain – none of this is chance. Someone or something is targeting me. I have faced the fact that Jackie has been pulled into the middle of something that has nothing to do with her and everything to do with me. Someone wants to hurt me, or perhaps just rattle me. I have no idea which, but I feel bad. Is my sweet little Jackie just collateral damage? I wonder if she suffered?

You can't live as long as I have without having numerous real and imagined vendettas brewing against you. My mind races through all the unfinished business in my past. I can feel the paranoia kicking in. Thank the Lord, it's about time. I won't stand a cat in hell's chance of getting out of this alive unless I embrace an unhealthy dose of it.

So now, here I stand in Cadogan Gardens, staring at number 52. I lean against the wrought iron railings that surround the tree lined square, onto which the front of my home faces. Is it safe to enter? I should take nothing for granted. Behind me, the central garden is dark and rustling with life. Even here in central London, gassed, poisoned and uprooted, Nature continues to fight back. I can hear and see a couple of foxes; they've made a den somewhere over in amongst the azaleas. I identify noises from squirrels, a couple of moles, plenty of rats, a few mice and all that crawls. Birds nestle up in the trees, leaves fall, and twigs crack. My eyes narrow and study the garden. One snap of twig, a crisp break, is made by something a little heavier. I continue to stare for some moments, but all has returned to a snuffling, rustling silence.

With a sigh, I turn back to the house. Time to grasp the nettle.

I am awake, intrigued and also a little afraid. I smile – a real smile. That's OK. No human here to see. I am alone, completely alive and it is oh, so dark. It feels good.

CHAPTER EIGHT

'Her face was sad and lovely with bright things in it.'

F.S. Fitzgerald

A quick reconnoitre on entering and I'm satisfied that I am alone in the house and head for the shower. The steamy water runs over me for a long time before I towel off and dress in some track pants and a super-fine cashmere sweater. Some things about this crazy world of theirs are good.

Silent and alert, I descend the central staircase to the ground floor. On the way to my study, I grab a bottle of Glenfiddich. The mellow buzz never lasts long with my kind but I find the flavour and the ritual of boozing helps me relax – perhaps just association with good times and fine meals. I sit down at my computer. After a few liberal slugs, the whisky begins to take the edge off my hyper-vigilance and allows me to focus on my research. I'm open to, and grateful for, any help I can get marshalling my muddled thoughts tonight, so I pop a few valium, just for shits and giggles, and wash them down with another good snort.

Tonight I will lick my wounds, literally. It helps while luxuriating in self-pity and contempt for my complacent arrogance. My inability to execute a simple course of action, ergo rescue or avenge my dear Jackie, rankles. I'd had a trail, yes, it was a decoy trail, but someone was laying the bait and I'd lost them.

I've had Jackie's abductor or murderer, or at least an accomplice right under my nose, almost in my grasp, and I'd fumbled the catch. I'd been sucker punched, sliced, diced and had the stuffing kicked out of me by some sort of troll. All in all, it had been brought to my attention that I'd disappeared up my own rectum. I am lucky to still be breathing.

So here I will sit and watch as my scrapes and wounds heal and my ego festers. Tomorrow night, I will find the individual who has interfered in my life and perhaps ended dear Jackie's and there will be bloody hell to pay.

The hand and tongue were not Jackie's, so who had they belonged to? I can still see them in my mind's eye; perhaps I should have brought them home for closer examination. I still don't think there was much more they could have told me. They were female, they were not Jackie's, they were very fresh, and there is a chance the donor may still be alive – just. A human loses a lot of blood when they lose a tongue, let alone a hand. Unless you know what you're doing they bleed out, go into shock, and die pretty quickly.

I can't shake the feeling that the hand and tongue were a message of some kind, a message especially orchestrated for me. I don't believe any of this is random or coincidental. Someone had waited for me to come looking for Jackie. They wanted me to know they are not human, that Jackie is gone and was … and this part really niggles … inconsequential to the game they are playing with me.

The thought continues to torment me that the body parts would have been Jackie's if she were still alive. If my tormentor believed a game of 'Is she? Isn't she?' with Jackie's life would get my full attention, would really sting, that's the game we'd be playing. Obviously, torturing me with the threat that my darling Jackie's life hangs in the balance does not make for satisfying entertainment. The stakes must be much higher.

If Jackie's abduction had just been the appetiser, the main course is going to be damn hard to swallow. Who the hell's hand and tongue were in that bag? Everything about the wild goose chase I'd been led on, now begins to strike me as purposefully disrespectful and mocking. Someone is goading me. For instance, the old hessian potato sack, where the hell did you even find such a thing these days? I thought everything came in plastic. Details are important; there had been an element of degrading the victim.

My inner pragmatist is starting to consider practicalities. I can't deny it any longer. The nuisance value of this message really infuriates me. How long will it take me to find another pet? I am heartbroken, don't get me wrong, but the sheer inconvenience is enough to make me see red. Jackie had that mixture of innocence, stupidity and guile, all married to an instinctive self-interest which gave her a capacity for complete self-deception not easily found.

I have made the mistake in the past of adopting a moral human – a human with the traits of courage, loyalty and intelligence that I so admire. My only excuse is that I was very young. I cringe at memories of youth. For centuries I was a sophisticated child. I called myself an agnostic. In truth, I was unable to see the wood for the trees. Since then I have come to believe I should never try to rationalise this world. I have no answers for seekers of truth, only more questions. I am a scientist, so I understand the need to find an explanation for every phenomenon. The need to analyse events based on empirical evidence, statistics and probability. To find the comfort of physics or random meaninglessness; to dissect and lay the mystery bare.

I have tried, still am trying. I'm stubborn but I am no fool.

I have hundreds of years of empirical evidence to draw upon and my terrifying verdict is: everything means something, something means everything. The human biologist Paul Krammerer paid a heavy price when he peeked behind the curtain and formulated his theory of Seriality. Krammerer tried to make some sense of the synchronicity and coincidence that surround us. It drove him insane. Sadly, he took his own life before I had the chance to meet him and discuss his ideas on the source of these 'waves of seriality' that influence and shape our destiny. I have my own theory and I feel the humans too are edging closer to the unbelievable truth.

I no longer take lightly the chance that I may be connecting with, and therefore becoming part of a predetermined plan for a human. In effect 'hitching a karmic ride' with a human surfing a 'wave of seriality' that is heading in a direction I really don't want to go. No, I won't make that mistake again.

My Jackie was a gloriously amoral primitive. A sweet-natured simpleton, who at a push, wouldn't have thought twice about all manner of questionable deeds and doings as long as she wasn't confronted with too much blood and gore. She had been the perfect companionable pet, utterly pedestrian and I needed that appearance of normality. Instinct, far wiser than my cognitive mind, had spurred me on. Even in my sick weariness I found the energy to cultivate a buffer between myself and the 'big brother' world in which I find myself.

The prospect looms of an existence totally controlled and monitored by ever-present government, CCTV, electronic and computer surveillance. The tracing and correlating of money trails and assets. Intrusive police investigations unbridled by law or decency. The humans are rushing toward a fascist authoritarian nightmare, the general populace being the weaker nation to be conquered, displaced and subjugated. I need to 'tech up' and clean up the trail of bread crumbs that may lead to my undoing. 'Yellow eyes' from Burge Street is already feeling the pinch and I have no reason to be smug. Our exchange in the church begins to feel like a portent of my own precarious situation. Cleopatra isn't the only Queen of 'denial'. I've been putting my head in the sand for way too long. I need the camouflage of the banal more now than ever before in my life. Real fury is beginning to boil up again and I force myself to lower my heart rate and breathe slowly. My body will heal much faster if I stay calm. But the damned itching of regenerating skin and nerve is driving me nuts.

The screen illumination from my computer is the only light in the house and its glow casts pale blue shadows across my hands. I turn the brightness way down; my eyes can't handle looking directly into an electric light for long. Most humans wouldn't be able to read the screen at the level I set. First things first, I type in a range of searches. 'Missing persons', 'Elephant & Castle', 'Murders', 'Unsolved mysteries'. I widen my searches to include Lambeth, Camberwell, Bermondsey and Peckham. Sure enough the creature was right, there is a growing number of missing persons from those areas and the frequency of bodies turning up along the Thames Embankment is increasing. The police are being cagey on the details.

Someone is being very careless.

One case in particular catches my attention. The police are being very discreet about profiling a certain type of victim, but I can read between the lines. There is a serial killer on the loose, perhaps not working alone. A growing bewildered frustration from the police that will soon galvanise into determined action, if it hasn't already. The monkeys do not like to be made fools of.

The emerging pattern appears to involve young women, hardly women at all in most cases – girls. Some young boys too, but less so, perhaps not even part of the same pattern. Mainly homeless runaways. Most of the victims are girls of the type that are difficult to trace, even more difficult to pinpoint the time and place they went missing, and if they are missing by choice. Girls who came from broken, abusive homes, the wrong foster care, often victims of neglect more than brutality. These were the young women who had no one looking out for them, no one who cared if they lived or died. From the look in their haunted eyes, themselves least of all. The perfect victims.

The part that must be baffling the authorities I suspect is the length of time the pattern spans. Some reporters are digging up cases as far back as the 1930s; hopefully these overzealous lateral thinkers are considered flakes. The evidence is only forming a pattern that screams 'serial murder' now because the frequency of disappearances is increasing. Bodies are piling up. Someone is leaving a sickening trail of carnage.

From my perspective, the long view you could say, any increase in unsolved crime cases can be explained by the fact it has become more difficult to disappear now than it was thirty years ago, let alone seventy years ago. The police are quicker to assume that if you're not showing up on the grid, you've been the victim of foul play rather than to assume you've gone abroad on a impromptu holiday. But balancing that out is the fact that it's much more difficult to discretely dispose of a body, and I should know. Until they can get their eyes on a body, the police are nervous about shouting murder. But now it looks like someone has gone rogue, taken that reckless, self-destructive nosedive to oblivion and given up making any effort to cover their tracks.

I assume and sincerely hope the police are confused and will continue to be. Unfortunately, it is all beginning to make perfect sense to me. The creature I'd encountered in the basement of St John's Church had a right to be angry. Someone is definitely making life more difficult for us all, and if the pattern continues and becomes any more extreme, I suspect will succeed in making life in London impossible.

There's more …

Something has happened, something momentous, and my hands shake a little as I type in one of the missing persons' names. She is one of the most recent disappearances. She is quite lovely. The poorly focused snapshot immediately caught my attention. I think I recognise her, those eyes. She sings out to me and, defibrillated by hope, I feel my cold heart jump in my chest even though I know she is more than likely already dead.

There have been times, over the years, when I found the whole idea of truly good humans laughable and had decided the best cure for my fascination and attraction to them was to be found in familiarity; it breeds contempt.

I mentioned before I have adopted humans with integrity in the past. I 'rushed in where angels fear to tread'. It makes me smile, knowing all that I know now. I really had no idea, couldn't conceive, that 'angels' are real. They are flesh and blood, and right here among us. Humans may not share the preternatural physical gifts with which my race has been bestowed, but they do have some eerie supernatural hocus-pocus of their own in play.

I tell myself I will never make that mistake again. Indeed, told you. The truth ... the chance to find out would be a fine thing.

I've already made it clear I don't claim any knowledge as to the meaning of life, or have the inside track on profound, esoteric secrets and mysteries. But I've lived long enough to know one thing for sure – there's something freaky going on with the monkeys.

There appear to be three categories of homo sapiens that defy the normal rules with which I can predict human behaviour.

Of course we all know there are humans who are, for want of a better word, evil. They want to inflict harm. Why? Because they enjoy it. I've watched them and they are not insane. They are not misunderstood or aberrant or delusional or damaged. They're having fun. The fact that they seem to enjoy extraordinary streaks of good luck when it comes to getting away with murder, bears some consideration when it comes to creating a unifying theory of our earthly reality. I think of them as dinner.

There are also humans who are 'good' as in 'And God blessed them ... and God saw everything that He had made, and, behold, it was very good'. They exist and are wholesome. They often never enter a church, the world being their temple in which they worship. They give thanks and supplications for humble pleasures and little joys. Their eyes are open to the multitude of wonders the earth daily showers upon them. They rarely have wealth of the kind humanity recognises as such. They tend to like boring pastimes and jobs like gardening, fishing, street sweeping being a favourite.

They have some recognisable traits. I find them very loveable, although humanity often doesn't.

I want to press them close and rub against them. Sniff them and taste them. I want to swallow them whole and drink them in. I want to crawl inside, deconstruct them and see what makes them tick. I want to feel and know their secret contentment. I want to possess them body and soul. But they are a bit like eating Chinese food. I feel empty almost immediately and the cravings start again, too soon.

They are elusive fuckers, that's for sure.

There are times, times like right now, I really think I must have a death wish. Perhaps I've taken one too many blows to the head, and here's why. The real problem with my keeping one of these for a pet, is no matter how deep in trance I place them, even when they've been blessed with a barely functioning IQ and the fact retention of a gnat, I can't suppress their memories for long. I also have great trouble controlling their behaviour. Something to do with living very much in the moment, I presume. These guys know that being chased around the house or grounds in a terror sweat, screaming and pleading for life is not fun, not for them anyway, and it is not love. They seem to have an innate understanding of love, the emotion or force I crave, and perhaps that is also part of their fascination for me.

No matter how many treats I lavish upon them after a session of play hunting, no amount of money, or expensive, beautiful possessions makes looking the other way acceptable. Or maybe they are born with no common sense, no survival instinct. Nature is red in tooth and claw but they can't or won't accept that I am but part of Nature and I have needs beyond my control. They generally seem immune to bribery or threat or my will. Try as I may to suppress my inborn nature, it will assert itself eventually.

What's bred in the bone will out of the flesh, and eventually we 'fall out'.

So that is my conundrum with category two: the 'good'. I can't live with 'em, can't live without 'em.

Luckily for some, they pass through this world mostly unnoticed and often tragically quick. Perhaps that has been the fate of the young woman I am now looking at on my computer screen.

Don't be fooled, monsters among you. Do not be lulled into a false sense of security by my words. The 'good' are the most unpredictable, tenacious, relentless beings. Wicked, beware!

And I should know, because, as I mentioned, I fight an attraction to the 'good'. I've tried several methods to purge myself of this weakness. Methods ranging from aversion therapy, canine shock collar therapy, psycho analysis, behaviour modification, Ludovico technique, covert sensitisation, conversion therapy to plain old 'cold turkey'. I've given up. We are what we are and 'the heart wants what it wants – or else it does not care...'

As far as the common or garden 'good' go, I can sniff them out pretty quickly these days. I'm still acutely drawn to them, but I no longer suffer from the arrogant confidence of youth and I give them a wide berth. The determined meek are an underestimated force.

Now we come to the third category. During the span of my existence and my intermittent, guilty but reliably regular truffle hunt for the good, I stumbled upon something entirely different, something extraordinary:

Angels ...

Or at least, one Angel.

Here I must be very careful.

You see, they are truly dangerous.

Never mind ridiculous Prof. Van Helsing and all that fictional shoot 'em up nonsense, these are the real deal. When one of these 'special ones' becomes aware that I and my kind exist, if I let one 'see' me clearly for what I truly am, they inevitably try to destroy me and my kind, utterly, or die trying which, of course, they inevitably do.

After six hundred and more years upon this spinning blue orb, suspended by forces I can only pretend to understand, in the cold and barren infinite vastness of space, they are the only force I've encountered that makes me at all anxious for the continued survival of my species.

These Angels are delusional, of course. Soon after encountering me they become fixated with supernatural hooey. The trouble is they are so stout-hearted and resolved, that they inevitably pull me into their delusion and make me question my very nature and right to live.

Rarely, these shining ones, pure of heart and true of deed are born into vulnerable, beautiful, mortal flesh. Rarely, but it happens. I've stumbled upon such a creature twice before. Both encounters produced the same effect of re-igniting a dead, or at least dwindling, fire within me and rehabilitating my jaded spirit. They made me want to engage with life again and gave me motivation to 'tune in' to the age in which I live. Days spent with them become precious because inevitably, there are so few of them, and yet moments spent in their company stretch out into vast timelessness in my memory.

These angelic beings, although they exude an enduring, other worldly charm, always seem contemporary and perfectly aligned in time and space. They are 'present' and live life entirely in the moment. The experience of their company is sublime and difficult to capture with words. They invigorate. They make me want to live, or at least care about not dying. They make me treasure the moment, and fear eternity, and that feeling hasn't happened for me in a long time. They're just so damn refreshing, and here I am, parched and dying of thirst.

During the course of the passing millennia, I have attempted to adopt two of these. I will insist on calling them Angels for want of a better word. I realise my narrative is becoming confusing. Let me try to explain but be warned, this is where it gets a bit flaky. I believe the two were but one ... the same soul ... different incarnations.

My eyes move back to the screen and the familiar, angelic face shining out of a grainy passport photo. She is just one more name on a long list of the 'missing – presumed dead'. I doubt this photograph has ever been used on a passport, but it is much clearer than the unfocused snapshot from the newspaper article, and there is no doubt I recognise that face.

My breath catches and sticks in my chest like a stone. Eventually, I let out a long sigh. Just imagine you're on a hike and you suddenly notice a Unicorn casually grazing among the sheep in a muddy paddock, or you are taking a bracing walk along the windswept shore when you stumble over a beached mermaid tangled up in seaweed, plastic from six packs, used syringes and styrofoam. There would be the shock of recognition, the stunned pause while your conscious mind catches up with your body – your body that knew immediately and reacted with a shuddering thrill.

I can always find the 'bad' monkeys. Like the stink from one putrefying rotten apple in a barrel, the 'bad' monkeys inevitably bring attention to themselves. You can smell them; they tend to leave an acrid trail of corruption wherever they pass. You can't miss them. They like flash and their egos demand an audience.

The 'good' shuffle through and off this mortal coil, the 'coyle of fuss and bustle' – with the lightest step. Anonymous and humble. They leave the merest hint of daisies and white chrysanthemum. The more people, the fewer they seem to make. So precious, so fragile, they take some sniffing out.

But discovering my Angel took no effort on my part. It was one of Krammerer's mysterious waves of seriality that bore me to her and her to me in one of those miracles humans call coincidence. Such a happening is always a fluke, down to chance with its strange patterns and plan. It never does me any good to search for her.

And now here she is – such a waste. Are you still alive? My heart quickens with the possibility.

The computer hums and I am transfixed. Michelle Blake is looking back at me with the merest hint of an uncertain smile – an enigmatic Mona Lisa. Vulnerability is evident in every sweeping curve of her face. If only she could have been born to a wealthy, powerful family … launched into the world brimming with the confidence of the cherished. Just think of the difference she could have made. But it never happens. Now I know you're thinking, especially the rich, particularly the politicians amongst you, that this seems too severe a statement. I'll be the first to admit that I've lived long enough to 'never say never', so I'll just say I've never seen it, and leave it at that.

There is a point to my navel gazing – I'll get to it. Twice I've contrived, using all my charisma and guile, to make 'my Angel' my companion. Both times I could keep her with me for no longer than a few days. And twice, for my troubles, was nearly ended.

I am an addict, it's a lifelong struggle, a battle never completely won, but in general, I have sworn off the 'good' for once and all. I leave them alone without bitterness or regret. You've probably guessed that the woman on my computer screen is the one exception – my weak spot, roughly the size of the San Andreas Fault. Given the right confluence of circumstance, she could well be my undoing. Perversely, my weakness pleases me and is my greatest joy. I find it exciting that my Angel exists and can disarm me with such ease. She is the hypocentre of destructive seismic activity in my cold heart and gives me a knee tremblor. Excuse the pun.

Her existence whispers the possibility that a God exists, perhaps the Devil too and countless secrets to discover between the two of them. Existence and all its unexplained synchronicity becomes again, a magical, beautiful, dark and dangerous mystery for me to ponder.

Or perhaps it's just that depravity craves innocence. That said, make of it what you will.

My gaze unbidden travels across the room to the oil painting of a young woman dressed in the style of the late Tudors. The slightest hint of an enigmatic smile plays on her lips. I chose to call her Angel. Although it wasn't her given name, it was the perfect name.

Further away, across the hall, another painting, the same woman, this painting much older, one hundred and fifty years older in fact. The same face, the same smile, perhaps she was the original. Her given name was Michaela Angelica. For all I know, she could have been reborn a thousand times before. Perhaps she has existed in one body or another since the monkeys climbed down from the trees and hauled themselves upright. But for me, Michaela Angelica was the first. How I loved those two miraculous monkeys, and although they were born one hundred and fifty years apart and it really does sound crazy, I swear they were the same soul reincarnated.

My eyes flick back to the screen and a single blood tear surprises me by splashing onto the plastic keyboard. The girl is calling to me, reaching out for my help through the pixels and lines of computer code. The same angelic face … Can it be true, will I get a third chance? They say it's the charm. I stop breathing for a little while. I think my pulse stops for some moments.

Don't get pedantic on me and start thinking about zoophilia and my thoughts on sex with Fido. This is different, couldn't be more different. Angel is my *amore e passione,* my *szivem.*

I settle down to dig a little deeper. Information is patchy on her. Her name in this incarnation is Michelle. Extraordinary – no middle name. Michelle Blake. Blake, so harsh. Nordic Viking roots from the North of England. It doesn't suit her. She looks pale in the photograph.

Removed from unfit mother, foster care, no mention of father, compulsive runaway, another two or three foster homes. It looks like the compulsion to run stopped briefly during her stay in number two foster home. Reading between the lines, foster mother number two struggled to cope after the sudden and unexpected death of her husband due to heart failure, caused by unexplained blood loss. I can't find any more details on him. Foster mother number two is sectioned due to nervous exhaustion and clinical depression. Michelle is back in the system and eventually re-homed. Compulsion to bolt returns. I can't work out if she had been placed in one or two more homes after that. It doesn't matter. Something drove her out of those placements and onto the streets. What does it take to drive a damaged child out of a warm shelter, with a door to keep the 'nonces' at bay, and onto the mean streets? My familiarity with the streets of London at night makes me wonder how bad it has to get. I take note of the foster parents' names … something to look into later.

Education: patchy – no surprise there; no formal educational certificates. It's hard to know exactly what I'm dealing with in Michelle, but I'm beginning to form a profile. There are a couple of references to arson, mention of small fires at foster homes, culminating in the burning of an abandoned industrial building. The words: problem, troubled, unmanageable, keep popping up.

'Give me a child until he is seven and I will give you the man.' She'd been removed from an unfit mother, but not before she was emotionally and developmentally scarred. Bureaucracy had swept in to save the day. As usual, too little too late. Thrown into the foster-care system when she was no longer a beautiful, malleable baby but a damaged and difficult, little person. Difficult to fix, difficult to love, difficult to place, she had become one of the growing number of rejected, invisible children tossed into the 'too hard' bin.

I swing back in my chair and let my eyes glide over the ornate plasterwork of the ceiling. I feel I know her already. In a nutshell, she is a poorly educated, penniless, emotionally unstable (assumption), pyromaniac (evident). Well, it could be worse. She could be dead. The thought is surprisingly painful.

I have to keep in mind this girl, Michelle Blake, may not be my Angelica reborn. Perhaps I am looking at a mere physical doppelgänger, but the clincher is, could discovering my long-lost love at this time, in this situation, possibly be mere coincidence? My mind races. No other living being knows about my Angelica. My obsession isn't something I shout from the rooftops.

Who would take the trouble to study me so studiously and lay me bare? Who has come to know me so intimately and peered into my soul so as to expose my secret hopes and desires? And crush them. One name comes to mind.

So the stakes are going to be high in this game I've been invited to play, much higher than I would have guessed.

Looking up at the windows, I can see a pink tinge infusing the electrically luminous blue-black of the London sky. The clocks chime a dismal six times. Time for me to go below. How long does my Angel have left in this incarnation? Perhaps the game is played out. She is already dead and I am too late.

From my left, I sense, rather than see, movement. Nothing sneaks up on me, except another … and there she is. She has made herself fully visible and stands at the foot of the stairs. How long she has been here with me, I couldn't say, something I find very unnerving. She is getting better at this sort of thing and I am rusty. I really should have known. It has been so long since we were together and now here she is, and it is difficult not to stare at my childhood companion Elisabethae Batthyanyi, my cousin, the Blood Countess.

She looks as if she has just stepped out of the painting by Dante Gabriel Rossetti, the one titled 'Lady Lilith'. He found the perfect model for the subject – my Ezserebet. She is my Lilith – the evil temptress, seducer of men and murderer of children.

Rossetti started the painting using his long-time muse and mistress, Fanny Comforth as the model. But then he suddenly changed the face to that of a mysterious woman who went by the name Alexa Wilding. The resemblance to Ezserebet is too complete for coincidence.

I'd caught sight of Betty coming out from Cheyne Walk in Chelsea on a foggy night in 1869. I hadn't seen her for many years and I certainly hadn't yet seen the Rossetti painting, which he had only finished in 1868. She disappeared so quickly that night, like a spectre in the mists. I searched for a while but then assumed I'd been mistaken, just my imagination playing tricks in the gas light. It wasn't until a couple of years later that I saw the painting and remembered that Rossetti was living at Tudor House, 16 Cheyne Walk when he'd painted it. I'd taken the time to look into the identity of his mysterious model. Alexa Wilding was supposedly a dressmaker and would-be actress. I assumed Betty used the dressmaker part to explain her fine clothes. She loved fashion and exotic fabrics and was never one to hide her light under a bushel.

As for the actress part, Betty is the consummate method actress. She will be who or whatever she or you, depending on her agenda, need her to be.

As expected, my investigation into the woman 'Alexa' turned up inconsistent results. Depending on who I asked, her age could range anywhere from mid-twenties to mid-thirties or even forties. Dates were always a little off, they were so easy to fudge before computers. There was evidence of her living with children, assumed her own, but the records didn't support that assumption.

Moving in on a family like some hideous cuckoo was a strategy Ezserebet had practised throughout the centuries. She liked to have human servants and when she grew tired of the adults she would eat them, keeping the children as daytime slaves and using them as a red herring. The perfect camouflage of motherhood. Alexa was described variously as the mother, sister and at other times, aunt of the children that were known to share her abode. Poor little chicks.

Nothing about Alexa added up. She apparently died at 37, always a favourite watershed for Ezserebet. The perfect age to disappear and change identities before her unfading beauty would start to draw attention.

I've never asked her, but I know the painting is of Ezerebet. I don't really need or want the fact confirmed. It is a cardinal sin for a vampire to leave such blatant evidence of our existence and longevity. I'd take a wager that once Betty heard Rossetti intended the subject of his next painting to be 'Lilith', she couldn't resist. She's unapologetically vain.

How could she help but be …

I had assumed after such a transgression Betty would have fled London and headed back to her beloved Transylvania.

The story goes that seeing Ezserebet, aka Alexa, from his carriage window, Rossetti stopped the horses, jumped to the street and, getting down on his knees, begged her to be his model – his and his alone – for an extra gratuity. He never stood a chance. When Betty wants something, she tends to get it. As soon as Ezserebet had made the decision to let herself be 'seen' by an artist such as Rossetti, the deal was done. He must have gone crazy to paint her and to possess her.

I, myself am momentarily hypnotised by the luminosity of her face, paralysed by her stillness. I hear my voice before I realise I've spoken.

'Betty … Oh beauty. Till now I never knew thee.'

My words hang suspended in the shaft of pale morning moonlight that separates us. Dust motes caught in the mauve darkness dance on the air currents, suspended in what feels like a curtain of time through which only we can see each other as we truly are.

For me, Betty momentarily appears to have a strand of seed pearls wound through her copper hair. Aristocratic blood red lips form a sensual, cruel mouth. The staircase shadow creates the illusion of the folds of a long gossamer robe with pennent sleeves, through which I can see she is actually wearing thigh-hugging, dark jeans and torn T-shirt beneath a skintight leather jacket. In the place of softleather shoes are a heavy pair of motorcycle boots. The drabness of her clothes only serves to emphasise how unbelievably, other worldly beautiful she is. Her voice, rich with accent, runs through me like warm syrup and as always, her words turning me back into an awkward boy.

'Hello Edward, you really are such a bloody idiot, and don't start calling me fucking Betty again. Call me Izzy. Now come here my csillagom, dragam, I want you.'

CHAPTER NINE

Ezserebet

Year of our Lord 1359

When Count Thurzo Rakomez, Lord of the Castle Csejthe, returned to Western Slovakia from fighting the Ottoman Turks along the Transylvanian border in the year of our Lord 1359, he brought home with him two acquirements of great import – gains of war that would change the very nature of his lands.

The first acquirement gave rise to much pride and celebration.

The Count returned with a reputation as a great warrior and travelling with him was a fearsome retinue of loyal, hardened troops.

Count Rakomez was now known as The Black Bey or to some, The Black Knight. He had gained a reputation for savage ferocity on the battlefield and was conferred the title of War Lord, an honour which commanded respect and bestowed much prestige on his Princedom and its people.

The contingent of mercenary warriors he gathered and took with him to push back the Turks returned with him to Castle Csejthe as loyal subjects, blood brothers in troth to their victorious Lord. Amongst the soldiers who returned were the brothers Szatm'ar, mysterious Transylvanian warrior knights who fell in and joined forces with the Count as he moved through the province of Sedmohrad. Having pledged to join Count Rakomez and sworn allegiance and arms unto death in his blood feud with the Ottoman Turks, the Szatm'ar brothers returned with him to Western Slovakia at the end of his campaign. They took up residence within the castle walls, as his personal guard, some would argue presumptuously, commandeering chambers within the Lord and his Lady's personal quarters, and there they remain. The continued presence of such warriors guaranteed the province protection from the Ottomans, and respite from the raids and pillaging that had plagued and impoverished this forested corner of Slovakia. The relentless fear of looting and attack is now a thing of the past.

The second acquirement was a cause of confusion and some antipathy – his new bride.

In an unusual move for a nobleman of the times, the Black Bey married a woman of unknown ancestry – Elisabethae Batthyanyi, from the province of Sedmohrad in Transylvania, also known as Wallachia. She came to the Princedom without benefit of pedigree or title, but she did provide a dowry. To her honour, she came with considerable wealth.

A band of swarthy gypsies in servitude to his Lady had followed the Lord's soldiery as they travelled toward the Castle Csejthe. The gypsies, acting as keepers of the Lady's dowry, surrounded a sturdy cart, heavy with caskets and trunks, said to be filled with Byzantium gold.

In an unprecedented and shocking move for the times, Elisabethae had chosen to retain her own name, and there persisted a rumour that she is a Forest Witch.

For fear of punishment and in the name of loyalty to their Lord, the peasantry lay aside such evil speculation and tried to open their hearts to the Lady Batthyanyi. After all, a Forest Witch can be nothing more sinister than a knowledgeable herbalist, a healer versed in natural remedies and practitioner of folk medicine.

Persistent whispers of disappearances, unexplained deaths and secretive burials accompanied Count Rakomez' warrior retinue as they journeyed back from Transylvania. That said, these were the times of cholera and fast moving infection. To live beyond forty years a feat of constitutional heroism achieved by few, such scurrilous rumours were disloyal and to repeat them became punishable by torture and death.

We move forward in time and Count Rakomez is now long dead, cut down in his prime by a mysterious illness of the blood that slowly took every vestige of his once formidable vigour and left him a brittle husk. The Lord of that now decrepit castle was a brave man, unafraid of dying, but in dread of a bad and ignominious end. His greatest fear was realised. It came to pass that he succumbed to frailty and lay dribbling and incoherent, mired in his own filth on his death bed. There were whispers he spent his last days heavily sedated, drugged with extract of hemp seed.

The year is now 1407. The neglected but partially habitable Castle of Csejthe, located in Western Slovakia, with a fiefdom of seventeen villages, has walls so thick and impenetrable that they will continue to stand into the millennium. Deep within the castle walls in the shadowy depths of a windowless chamber sits Ezserebet Bathory – the woman of unknown background and indeterminate age whom the Lord of that hamlet brought home with him from the wars some forty years before. She is the Lady of the Castle and mistress of all the forests, lands, villages and peasantry that surround it.

Two of Lord Rakomez' loyal warrior retinue, the brothers Gut and Keled Szatm`ar remain. They have become, or perhaps always were, it is speculated, the Lady's creatures. They fawn, they take part in perverse and sadistic sexual congress with the Countess. They guard and protect her, relaying messages and orders to her troop of heathen gypsies. They procure young women, and dispose of bodies.

Ezserebet sits and reads by candlelight. She is terribly bored, caught in that vampiric malaise, the ennui that robs her of the impetus needed to propel her forward and back into the world she so misses. The guttering candle flame sends fans of pale light over dark, arched brows that frame black lashed, luminous, jade green eyes. Sometimes those eyes are so dark they almost appear mossy black, but tonight, shots of a pale peridot radiate out from the large pupils.

If anyone else had been in the room that night, those eyes would mesmerise, but she is alone. Her dark, red hair shines like burnished copper and has been brushed to a glassy sheen and pulled back tightly from her face, held in obedience by a gold and ivory Japanese comb, set in a coiled and plaited abundance at the back of her long, pale neck.

She is acutely aware of her carelessness of late, bordering on recklessness. She has been pushing fate to force her hand. She can find no will of her own, has entered a time of nihilism, and she knows of old that the only cure for that is a brush with death and danger. Her eyes turn toward the nihonga she painted in Japan many years before. Those had been exciting days spent with her

Samurai Lord. How he adored her. But he aged as humans do and proved weak and eventually, inevitably tedious.

She must move on but she would not leave her beloved Hungary. Whatever the fools who surround her believe, she is more noble than any human lord. She comes from a long line of ancient blood that carries the strength of the natural and rightful rulers of this snivelling peasantry. In Ezserebet's opinion, the feudal system that prevails in these lands reflects the natural order. She is of noble vampiric blood lines and to tyrannise and feast upon those talking sheep is her right.

Her name is Bathory. It translates to 'good hero' in the young language, but in the more accurate, ancient Hungarian, 'b`ator' translates to 'brave hero'. Goodness is for the weak and the superstitious. Her bloodlines are not good, but they are brave, and bravery and iron resolve will carry her through this time of upheaval and trial, as it always has. She is the Blood Countess. She is fearless and almost immortal, and she will do as she pleases.

Although her ancestry is her rock and sustenance, it is also her burden. The blood of Batthyanyi confers not only strength of body, beauty of flesh, daring and fearlessness. Her Clan is also drenched with lunatics, sexual fiends, torturers and sorcery. All manner of corruption runs rife in Bathory blood.

Her honored father was and remained, afflicted with the Bathory curse. From youth, he was known to fall prey to irregular bouts of seizures and fits of rage. Ezserebet's earliest memories of him were of feasting with her father in the deep underground halls of their Transylvanian castle and involved witnessing, at her father's hands, the impaling, roasting, hanging, breaking on the wheel, starvation and whipping of the peasantry. Her two pleasures – feeding and sadism would forever be inseparable.

And as for the gypsies – her dear father had been infected with the peasants' prejudice and considered them sub-human. He would never feast on them but satisfied himself with cutting off their hands and ripping out their tongues for the pleasure of the sheer savagery. It was the one area in which Ezserebet and her father diverged in ideology. The fact that the mewling, genuflecting peasantry considered gypsies Godless creatures elevated them in her mind, to a useful diurnal resource – a branch of the human species with which she could stomach close contact.

Over the years, she had rescued a number from her father's attentions, with the aim of grooming and ultimately enslaving a small retinue to her will and into her service. This she had achieved. The ones she selected were indeed Godless, ruthless and unclean in their habits, but also resourceful and most importantly, fiercely loyal.

She would beat a strategic withdrawal soon from Csejthe Castle, but she would always return to the secret, deep subterranean corridors beneath this magnificent ruin. She needed no human deed; the castle belonged to her now, and would remain her property in perpetuity.

And Hungary would continue to be her home. She would not travel far from these lands. The humans may try to rally and rise up against her and her kind but it wouldn't work. She could easily expunge memories of witnessing her 'crimes' from the porous brains of the weak-minded fools. The feudal system, together with the glamour she could exert over feeble human intellects, made it impossible for any to testify against her. The peasantry had no legal rights and as for the gypsies, the human populace considered them no better than animals. No testimony from that quarter would ever be admissible within a court of legal commerce.

Now that she had married into a human line of aristocracy, she would begin to merge her vampire nobility into the human ruling classes of Hungary until she was sure the Vampiric race were untouchable. Diseases of light intolerance and aversion could be hereditary among the humans and this would become the cover under which her blood lines would rule. These damn humans would come to realise they were her property to do with as she pleased.

She would surround herself with kings, princes and cardinals. Her ancestor Vitus from the Bathory Clan of vampire elite would be proud of her manipulation. Through wealth and political machinations, she intended the humans would remain her kindred's servants into the new age, but for now, to her shame, she must flee. The Castle Csejthe would be her home again one day and these meddling humans would be sorry. But tonight, the revolting peasants below weren't looking for recourse from the law. The old primitive blood lust was rising in the village and she must bow to greater numbers.

She would retreat. Gut and Keled had already prepared for her escape. Her loyal kinsmen had brought her The Black Bey so she could start her infiltration of the human aristocracy and they had done well. But even the handsome and dangerous brothers Szatm'ar of the Warrior Hawke Order, begin to wear on her nerves. She needs variety, novelty and she misses Herronimus, but she would not run to his arms for shelter.

Herronimus has his own problems. His great-great uncle, Vlad, had apparently gone completely berserk. It had always been on the cards. Drunk on Turkish blood lust, he had lost all control and according to messages sent to Gut and Keled, the Warrior Hawkes were having trouble obeying orders to put him down.

She must keep her thoughts to herself. Her response to the news is insensitive and politically dangerous. She has sympathy for Vlad. Many a time has she considered donning armour, and with the help of Gut and Keled, riding down into the village and slaughtering the entire populace. But Gut and Keled's first loyalty is always to their Oaths of Honour to the Warrior Hawke Order; to uphold against and protect the Vampire Race from all threat, be it external or internal. That includes exposure by rogue vampires. They are becoming tiresome.

At least having a 'nut job' like Vlad in the family might wipe the smug, judgmental smirk off Herronimus' face. The next time she runs to him for help with family problems, he won't be so haughty.

Almost directly below where Ezserebet sits, deep in the dungeons of the castle, the remains of young women lie unhidden, in various stages of decomposition.

On her desk is a glass of fresh blood from the last of her victims. The girl is still alive … just. Ereszebet can hear the girl's weak pulse; she still has the strength to occasionally pull herself back to consciousness and give a weak sob, and call out into the darkness for help. Not that anyone could hear her if she screamed at the top of her lungs, which she already tried some weeks ago. It didn't help.

The peasants from the village below may be 'weak in the head but they are strong of the leg' as the saying goes. You couldn't beat them to death with a stick, but Ezserebet had been willing to give it a try. She gave a little guffaw and reflexively looked around the room. No one there with whom to share the joke. How dreary.

The wooden tub in which she bathes, whenever she can fill it and never with water, sits empty. It is stained with a dark ring mark and streaked with a rusty residue that the trained eye would recognise as evidence of her perverse penchant. She doesn't care who sees, she'll do whatever she likes. Blood makes her skin glow and she will have it. Her beauty is wasted in this wearisome Carpathian wilderness and tonight, she lacks the will to fill the tub.

Moving out of her chamber and towards a window in the bailey wall, she looks out on the blissful night. Below she can see torches and hear the imbecilic girning of the fools below. She must make haste, damn their impudence, how dare they intrude on her contemplation. Yes, they and their weak-minded progeny, and their progeny after them, shall pay for the impudence of their ill-bred ancestors. But for now, the time has come to embark on the strategic retreat she both welcomes and resents. She silently calls for the brothers Szatm'ar … it doesn't matter where they are, they could be across an ocean and they would hear her summons and find her.

Below in the village, the peasants that she so despises, are restless and fearful. During the early evening of that day, a band of travelling tinkers passed through the village on their way to Austria. Weary and hungry, they had prepared to settle for the night. On hearing the name of the Countess Batthyanyi, the tinkers, heartless cut-throats and fraudsters that they are, turned white as ghosts, extinguished their fires, packed up camp and made ready to move on with haste. Restless and uneasy they will not stay even one night in the forests surrounding the Castle Csjethe.

Before they took their leave, they traded hard liquor to the villagers and shared tales of the Lady Batthyanyi with those who came into their camp to barter and drink.

There is a red-haired woman, the Blood Countess, her name, Ezserebet of the Dragon Clan of Bathory, who is known to have left a trail of dead pre-pubescent girls strewn across the Carpathian Mountains. This Lady does own an evil reputation. Wherever this Countess does appear, so do young bodies gather, mutilated by the most heinous marks of torture. Pierced with needles, skewered with red-hot pokers, hands and tongues removed and all manner of amputations, starvation, scalding and floggings – all so extreme and vicious. Yet, those marks of violence are unable to cover the multiple bite wounds that cover the young bodies, as though they had been feasted upon by some fanged beast.

The stories have spread throughout the village like a virulent disease, creating a fever of fear and hatred. Since the Lady Ezserebets' arrival in their midst, an unusual number of their young women have disappeared. Some have been found, all dead, with strange markings over their pale, wasted bodies.

The Lady Ezserebet must now be, as far as the elders can calculate, more than sixty years old, at the most conservative estimate, and yet she still looks just twenty. She makes no effort to conceal her relentless youth and undiminished beauty, and gives no thought to convention, decency or prudence.

It is now clear that, at best, their Lady is a powerful and evil Forest Witch, well versed in the black arts and blood sacrifice. But they fear the worst; that the Lady who has dwelt amongst them and within the walls of Castle Csejthe these forty years is no mortal woman at all, but a diabolical creature of utter darkness.

The village and its surrounding small holdings are not a place of abundance. The fruits of plenty, that protection from the marauding bands of opportunistic Ottoman invaders promised, have turned to ashes in their mouths.

Since their Lord returned from pushing back the Ottoman Turks along the Transylvanian border, the village has been battered and ravaged by frozen, brutal winters. At such times, the populace is forced to constantly and wearily forage for fuel to fight off the bone-aching bitter cold. But there is no respite as the snows melt. For the merciless winters are followed by torpid, rainless summers through which the peasants starve, their crops attacked by root diseases, potato blight, plum pox, bunt, and loose smut. In their hollow-stomached misery, they are tormented by plagues of earwigs, lice, mosquitoes, ticks, aphids and fleas.

Down in the village, a small crowd has gathered around a drunken, but yet convincing, speaker. He is the father of the latest of a long list of missing children. His daughter, Kristiana, just turned sixteen, has taken a position as handmaid to the Lady of the Castle.

It was hard to resist the chance of a paying position inside the castle walls. Although Kristiana's father hadn't encouraged his daughter, to his shame, he had not stood in her way. He reasoned she would be one less mouth to feed, and perhaps she could bring food for the little ones from the castle kitchens. He had once been respected as a man of some education. During his time as a squire, his master had him taught his letters ... he could read. Perhaps Kristiana could improve her lot by close contact with those that were her natural betters.

When she had sat at his knee and asked him whether he wanted her to go into service at the castle, he had shrugged, and his weak spirit had found an avenue for exculpation in silence. Her siblings were hungry and he was powerless to provide. He stood before his neighbours a broken and shamed man, the full weight of his guilt resting heavily upon his stooping shoulders. He would no longer cringe in his freezing cottage to save his own hide.

The man stands on the packed earth of the village square and holds forth. He speaks of the darkness that has enveloped the province and now, his own heart. Pointing up toward the pine-covered hills, where the just visible turrets of the Castle Csejthe jut upward behind the tops of the conifers like shards of dark glass, he dares to say aloud what everyone knows to be true.

'She, up there, has taken my Kristiana and used her in some unclean way to nourish her never dulling youth. Who is she, or I now wonder in truth, *what* is she? Whence did the creature come? Never did our Master, and a fair Lord he was, talk of her family. Never did we see even but a one of her kinsmen come visiting.'

At first, the fearful villagers listen to the man from behind closed doors and windows, nodding in silent, craven agreement. But as the night becomes inky dark and presses upon them with its stifling dread, increasing numbers of folk venture out, and with their numbers their courage grows.

'We are all guilty of weakness and cowardice, and have proven our own shameful selfishness. Let us act now for all that is holy, and perhaps for our very own souls! Let us act whilst we still have some strength in us, whilst there is still a chance to cleanse this valley and allow our children to grow to maturity and ... perhaps know the pleasant and fruitful times that some of us can yet remember – the pleasant summers of our youth ...'

Here he paused, almost choking on his words, and struggling to master some inner convulsion of emotion and disgust until he pointed up again to the castle.

'Before the creature that sits like a spider in her web can again steal from us the only precious thing we have left.'

At this point, he could continue no more. Racked with sobs, he took to muttering, 'Kristiana! Oh how could I let you go there, my darling child.'

A consoling murmur ran through the crowd which now consisted of the entire village, save for infants and the senile. It was as if the starless, black eye of the night sky stared into their fearful, superstitious souls and threatened them with the portent of evil retribution. But tonight they would not be crushed by some nameless, creeping apprehension. These simple humble souls had been pushed beyond stoic endurance. Something had to happen. Torches were lit.

A tremor of uncertainty thrilled through the crowd as another voice from amongst the listeners took up the theme. It was the voice of the young priest, not the holiest of fellows himself, yet he wore black and wielded the mighty power of Papal authority over his ignorant and deeply indoctrinated flock. He had never seen the 'creature' that was the Lady Batthyanyi, although he'd heard much talk of her striking Transylvanian beauty.

Since the death of the old Lord, no member of the clergy had been given leave to set foot in the castle, that crumbling seat of power was as yet a mystery to him. The Lady paid no tithes and gave no alms. To the priest's mind, this was her greatest sin. These uneducated fools were obviously wrong to talk of witchcraft and sacrifices in connection with ruling nobility, but the Lady needed a lesson in respect, and to be taught the value of a priest's allegiance and protection. She would learn she needed the Church as her proxy and a conduit of communication and largesse between herself and her serfdom.

He resented her lack of tribute to him in the form of alms or the buying from him of 'relics' – dove feathers and crosses made from straw and blessed by the Church, that she could hand out to the peasants on holy days to secure fealty and affection. A Lady such as herself should be purchasing 'indulgences' from him. He had a pile of the 'indulgences' – certificates, pre-signed by the Pope that were gathering dust in his bureau. These certificates could pardon the sins of her living relatives and pardon the sins of those already dead and languishing in purgatory, or worse ... condemned to hell. In these times of bloody war, and given the proclivities of the aristocracy, a noble woman should constantly be buying 'indulgences' for her male kinsman. Did she care nothing for the souls of her ancestors?

The priest had come to believe he had been sent to the arsehole of the world and although, in theory, even the poorest peasants would find a way to pay – pay to be christened, pay to be married, and pay to be buried in holy ground, they could only do that if they had money. The peasantry certainly didn't welcome the idea of not getting into heaven, but what good were his admonitions and brimstone-bubbling sermons when he was surrounded by snivelling, starving fools. His opportunity to redress the balance of power in this rotting hamlet appeared to have risen.

Some in the crowd noticed from the slight slur of his words that the priest too had been imbibing, but he drew his scrawny frame tall and spoke with all the authority of the Catholic Church behind him.

'Brothers and sisters, let us go now and reclaim some of our self-respect. Let us put our case before those that should be our natural betters and as our heavenly Lord tends his sheep, should by all natural laws, tend to their inferiors. God will, I fear, punish those that would show contempt of their natural dependants, and a neglect worse than the poorest among us would show our own livestock!'

The priest's intention was, using force if needs be, to claim some of the back-alms he felt were owing. He'd had enough suppers of nibbling sour goats' cheese and gnawing through stale, grainy bread.

To his surprise and horror, his words had an electrifying effect on the mob. Like a single organism, the peasants heaved and sighed and surged. They moved as one, exhaling a collective groan of consensus and resolve. Another voice from somewhere in the epicentre of the throng, this time louder and with the local guttural accent, called out:

'Let's burn her out! Let's blast her underground warrens with cleansing fire and be free of her!'

A shout of approval rang out. The tinker's 'fire water' had run out and a jug of the locally distilled, eighty proof, rough spirit was passed around amongst the throng to fend off the coming night's bitter cold.

Now there was a reckless courage rising and spilling out from the gathering. A palpable tightening and flexing of some mass muscle of vengeance. The time had arrived for action. Memories of their hesitation and cowardice, stung with the sharp jab of shame, and set light to the tinder dry anger that had been brooding and growing, just waiting for the catalytic spark to ignite the touch paper and explode into action.

While the priest shouted for patience and restraint, declaring that he should be allowed to lead them up the hill and take their demands to the Countess, the assemblage moved in the direction of the castle as if a single, writhing animal. The priest found himself roughly pushed aside, He tumbled into the dirt, but was quickly back on his feet and running abreast of the mob, snapping at their heels like a confused terrier. He shouted for their trust to be placed in him and the Holy Church, to take a warning to the Countess and secure recompense on their behalf. This had gone badly wrong for him. The vulgarians were now insensate to reason and they moved through the trees until, en masse, they came to a standstill before the castle gates, and shuddered like a racehorse in the blocks, waiting for the word.

An instinctive recoil from contact with something alien and unclean ran through the villagers. They hesitated to breach the threshold of the malevolent shadows that shrouded the massive wooden gates. The impetus of the moment was draining out of them like pus from a lanced boil and, with it, the will to action. The crowd began to shout threats of retribution that had the sour taste of bravado.

Pushing her way to the front of the horde, Kristiana's mother prepared herself to speak out. As the people spread and converged at the foot of the drawbridge, she waited. She waited until the youths stopped baying for blood and stood still and silent. She waited until the priest stopped worrying and yapping and all had settled. Not a sound, save the inhale and exhale of steamy breath could be heard.

Looking upward with tear-dulled eyes, she spoke, not in a shout but almost a whisper, a whisper that echoed louder into the silence than any scream.

'Why do you hesitate? Do you still lack the courage? How long will all you 'good' men stand by and do nothing?' There was a bitter contempt in her whisper that cut like a knife.

'Is there to be no punishment for such evil?'

The charged silence was suddenly alive with a thrill of electricity that lifted the hairs on their arms. A massive surge of energy moved them forwards and upwards like a stream of liquid, briefly defying gravity as they poured over the drawbridge and down through the gates.

That night, so long ago, passed in an frenzy of destruction. The heavy inner doors were battered to splinters and gave way. The castle interior was breached, the mouldering grandeur of the castle's upper living spaces, looted and burnt. As dawn broke, the less determined of the villagers began to drift back to their homes, leaving a core of the bereaved and aggrieved to gather the courage to follow the dark corridors down into the lower regions of the fortress foundations.

Eventually, even the brave began to falter as the depth and extent of the underground tunnels revealed itself. Progressively, the corridors became more airless. Moving through the darkness thick as malignant treacle, became exhausting. Breathing the dank miasma burnt the lungs and the tunnels continued to narrow and grow smaller until they were no longer traversable. It became clear they had not been created by or for man.

The determined among the villagers ventured as deep as possible into the cavernous depths, but ultimately, even the most courageous found the network of ever diminishing tunnels impenetrable and had to be satisfied with the pouring of pitch. It was left to the most stalwart among them, two brave young men, the most unshakable in the village, to spread the flammable liquids through the caverns and into the darkest recesses. When these two young heroes emerged from the tunnels and back into the foul dungeon from which they branched, they were in a terrible state, retching and raving of the horrors discovered below. Pale and unable to give voice to all the gruesome particulars, they made the sign of the cross and threw their torches into the caves, setting light to the pitch that would burn for seven days and seven nights.

As the years after the siege passed, smaller stones from the castle were requisitioned to build pasture walls and repair cottages. Some of the larger, heavier slabs were used in an attempt to plug and block any entry, and more importantly, any egress from the underground dungeons and tunnels. Yet the strength and formidable thickness of the castle's battlements defied deconstruction and the looming presence of Castle Csejthe remained hollowed, but unbowed.

The Countess' troop of fearsome gypsies dissipated like fog on a sunny morning. Some eerie and confusing tales reached the village of sightings of them travelling across the Carpathian Mountains, guarding carts loaded with crates and valuables, leading fine thoroughbred horses during the day but accompanied by two fearsome lords dressed in full armour at night. Always, they left gruesome evidence of unnatural crimes in their wake. These stories were whispered by the travelling tinkers who passed through the village from time to time, the villagers would make the sign of the cross and change the subject for everybody knows you can never trust a tinker or a gypsy. Both will manufacture a 'tall tale' if they think it will keep you a few more hours buying their wares.

The brothers Gut and Keled Szatm'ar were never seen again in the Province of Western Slovakia, although there were rumours of their continued fighting in the campaign against the Turks. In times of turmoil and war, fearsome, brutal warriors are extended almost inexhaustible pardon.

The Lady herself, the murderous and unconventional Countess Elisabethae Batthyanyi was not to be found in the castle when the villagers entered, or, if she were there, she remained undetected. No one ever heard tell of her arranging or procuring passage. Neither her living person or her corporeal remains were ever found. She disappeared just as she had appeared – silently, mysteriously and without joy.

The resolve of the villagers for the castle's utter destruction ebbed. The serpent's bite had been incised, the poison had been drawn and the wound inevitably healed. Csejthe's crumbling towers still stretched up to meet the corn blue Carpathian sky and its crumbling arches now framed verdant Alpine Clematis that beckoned entry into the ancient, and once again, majestically picturesque seat of power. Stillness, as of patient waiting, settled over the ruin.

It was enough that she was gone, and all returned to how it had been. The summers that followed were as those of memory– warm, fruitful and pleasing. The wild flowers, killed off by one or more of the pestilent root diseases and believed extinct, now returned. The valley was full of steppic flora and forest flowers: Turna Golden Drop, Lady's Slipper, Primrose and Buttercups.

CHAPTER TEN

'Beauty is a witch.' Shakespeare

Looking at her now, I can hardly credit my stupidity. Of course, the moment my life started to unravel why hadn't I known there could only be one monster behind it?

'Ezserebet! I knew it had to be you. You found me and made a meal of my fucking pet!'

Tonight her eyes are apple green and the pupils narrow to pinpoints as she turns her attention to me.

'Yes, of course, and it's not Ezserebet, it's Izzy now. We aren't in the Middle Ages. Do you think it suits me? Look at me, do I fit in?'

She did a little pirouette that sent a shiver down my spine.

'Do I appear suitably under-dressed, over-educated and over-privileged to roam your London as little Izzy, the poor rich kid with aristocratic Eastern European bloodlines?'

She said it all with that strange, girlish pouting demeanour she assumed from time to time. I think it may be her idea of flirting. Personally, I'd be less unnerved if she came at me with a pickaxe.

'No, it doesn't suit you, you're an interfering bint. You could never look like 'little' anything. You look like a lipstick lesbian enjoying some London R and R while in town with the Slovakian All Women's Basketball Team, and you've gone way too far this time. I think I may really have to kill you, Betty. I should have done it a long time ago. You Bathory never mellow with age, you all tend to slow putrefaction, like cheese. Eventually, you have to be got rid of.'

The veins in my neck are popping. I'm too tired for all this; the sun is close to rising and the drug of daylight is already beginning to sedate me. How Betty looks so fresh I don't know and don't care to speculate.

She leans back against the wood panelling and licks her lips.

'Have you become soft? You would think to kill me, one of your own, over a human pet and such a dull, bland morsel she was. It was only her fear at the end and the taste of her affection for you in her blood, Eddy, that put a little salt on the boiled egg.'

With one leap, I cross the room and have her wiry neck under my fingers. Dark, little crescents of blood begin to appear around my fingertips as they dig deeper into her creamy flesh, and all the while that infuriatingly smug smile remains. I press a little harder until I can feel her cervical vertebrae bending to near breaking point and suddenly, the smile is gone. Her over-ripe mouth draws down into the childish pout I know so well and damn it all, I release her neck and kiss the evil mouth that has probably been stretched around my little Jackie's throat.

Immediately, I feel her rough tongue push into my mouth and I lick and suck greedily at the sweet serum that forms and drips from her distending canines. The kiss goes on for some moments. Pressing close, our bodies fuse into one. Throwing caution to the wind, I dive into that deep oblivion that only vampiric lovers can plumb, and just for a fleeting instant, feel Betty join me. Briefly, we share a communion of complete honesty and oneness before, surprised at ourselves, we lose our nerve. We quickly swim back up to shallow water, back to the unthreatening, familiar breakers of lust.

'So, you still love me, a little?'

She whispers close to my ear and the horrible truth of it almost makes me wretch. There is a masochist deep inside me that just can't resist, but a momentary lapse doesn't mean I've completely lost my marbles.

'Get the hell out of London Betty, before we kill each other, or far worse, start this up again and wish to God we had.'

It is difficult for me to untangle the tight, little knot of my emotions where Betty is concerned. The ties run so deep, and it is hard to know where one thread begins and another stops. Right at this moment, struggling with the fact I am secretly thrilled to lay eyes on her again after so long, I'm really not sure if I want to shag her or kill her, or both, but probably both, and in that order if I'm honest. A big part of my problem where she is concerned is the first law of vampire – laws drummed into me, partly by vampiric culture, but mainly through thousands of years of evolution: 'Thou shall not kill thine own.'

Slipping out from under my hands, she crosses the room.

'Too late, I think, but you always cry over the spilt custard.'

She makes mocking, theatrical, dabs at her eyes as she moves toward my computer and starts idly scrolling through my searches.

'How long have you been here, Bets? And the vernacular is not custard – it's milk!' How she exasperates me.

'Poo! Who cares? Custard, yoghurt, milk, I hate languages! it takes me two lifetimes to learn them and then I move on. What's the point? I suppose I'll have to learn Chinese eventually. Until then, I'll just middle through. Anyway, what are you doing here? Shopping?'

She is still looking at the computer.

'Maybe we should buy some balzsamot. I'll rub it on your fenek, and I can tell you how special you are and better than anyone else. You like the sound of that, yah? You big baby! Jackie, Jackie. Oooh, oooh.'

She makes some more mocking dabs at her tearless eyes.

'Let's go back to mine and you can take me out for a slap-up meal tomorrow night, and we'll make it something a bit tastier than the dreary Jackie.'

I push her aside and sit back down in my study chair to switch the computer off before she has time to get into my bank accounts. She is around the table before I know it and closing on me.

This is all going quickly and horribly wrong. She presses in closer, her jean-clad legs that seem to go on forever, rubbing against mine just for a distracting moment before she straddles me. I remember that I should keep a bit more space between us. Too late, one sharp sting of a needle jabs into my neck and garlic shoots through my veins like battery acid.

She's injected me with something nasty, laced with powerful hempseed extract. Bets is a bit of a herbalist, the utter bitch. The only thing I can reliably predict with Bets is that she is so completely unpredictable. Will I ever learn not to let my guard down around this particular 'nut bar'. She quickly darts to the far side of the room. What gets me is that she's laughing.

Getting to my feet, I stagger against my desk and snatch up the first thing that comes to hand – a vintage Montblanc 'Mystery Masterpiece' pen. It has some weight to it and with all my remaining strength, I throw it with some force. The gold pen flies across the room, just a blur, like a guided missile and embeds satisfyingly into her left eye. I watch as she slowly draws it out with an impatient:

'Ouch, bikaszem! Good shot Eddy, bullseye yah. Nice pen.' She drops it into her pocket, but she isn't laughing any more.

My vision begins to blur and fade. I just know this is going nowhere good.

CHAPTER ELEVEN

'What girls do to each other is beyond description…'

Tori Amos

I try to focus. Waking is painful and not just physically. I'm naked and strapped up like a dominatrix's gimp, to a slimy brick wall. She's used high-tensile steel chains, bars and some sort of rods, perhaps titanium. Ezserebet is nothing if not resourceful. I give my restraints a little test. There's not much movement. So I give them a real test. I jerk and shake and writhe. All the while, I bellow like a bull on its way to the slaughterhouse.

Eventually, I surrender and slump back, letting the cat's cradle of steel chains support me as if beaten, but I felt a bit of give, just a bit, where the steel bolts are keyed into the old masonry. It will do.

We are obviously underground. My nocturnal vision quickly adjusts to the utter blackness. Betty stands before me, statuesque, like carved marble. She really has the trick of stillness nailed. She is naked, her wounded eye still just a little bloodshot but otherwise completely healed. It can only be fourteen to fifteen hours at most since she dosed me.

Thinking of her eye, I can't suppress a slight smile. It was a damn good shot under the circumstances; it must have stung. The trouble is I am helpless and she is pissed off. She has been standing there for who knows how long, waiting, watching for any sign of my regaining consciousness and coming out to play. She is stark naked and has a plan. I know what I'm dealing with – a spoilt, psychotic child. The waiting has been winding her up. I don't flatter myself that the nudity is in any way meant to be alluring, or holds the promise of sexual pleasure. Betty isn't squeamish. If there's a messy job that needs doing she's up for it, but she has never liked to get her clothes dirty.

We are in a vast underground vault, more like a cavern, lined with ancient brick, that rises forty feet high before forming an arch over our heads. The walls run with water and the place stinks of black mould and sewerage. It is truly glorious.

Betty is already in full vampire mode. The tips of her canines are evident against her full lower lip. Her nails have extended and she's lost the softness of skin and firmness of flesh that cloaks the predator within. Impatient as always, she's been itching for me to come round and now moves toward me with reptilian languor. Seamlessly progressing from ground to wall, her nails and toes finding purchase in the crumbling mortar, she scales the vertical mouldy brick until she can press up against me, anchoring herself to my body with her long legs.

She is clearly still a bit annoyed about her eye. I watch as, with one of her hands, she gingerly explores the bones around her orbital socket for any remaining sore spots. This is just to give me time to process what's coming. All the while, with her other hand she strokes my face tenderly. There is really no need for the charade, I'm not on a mystery weekend, I've done this before. I knew from the moment I 'came to', where we were going tonight. Soon enough, one of her sharp, perfectly manicured, talons finds the soft part of my right eye and begins steadily – she's in no hurry now – to skewer it. Eventually, after some extraneous twisting and jiggling, she pulls the talon away. A schlurpy noise follows and with it, my eyeball. She holds up her index finger avec my 'mince pie', like a sherbert lollipop, for inspection.

'Szep a szemed. You've always had lovely eyes Eddy … deep set, brooding.'

She's having a good look at the iris and then she leans in and severs the optic nerve with her teeth and pushes the eyeball down over her finger, so she can wear it like a ring.

'Beautiful colour.'

Having an eye gouged hurts a lot. She knows it and accordingly, took her sweet time. I make no sound, no protest and certainly no appeal for mercy. That would be a red rag to a bull. But the night is young. I hold no illusions regarding my immunity to the attentions of something like Betty. Pleading may well occur at some point during our 'date'. If it goes that far, I'm 'Friar Tucked'.

Betty's lips find mine. The shameful part for me is that it still isn't entirely unpleasant. It's been years since I've felt the thrill of agony and genuine fear. It's not exactly fun, but I can't deny it's exciting. Her lips move down, under my chin and then across my cheek. I feel her tongue, rough as a cat's, lapping up the trickle of blood oozing from my gaping orbital cavity. The tongue continues and probes the socket, now sans eyeball, and she opens her mouth to form a seal over the cavity. The better to suck the last of the blood pumping from the broken ophthalmic artery. She hoovers it up … such a greedy girl.

Her abrasive tongue starts exploring again around the four walls of the orbis and all the way down to the apex, probing at the entry to the optic canal. Despite the pain, I notice that she is not chewing at the extraocular muscles. This is a sign she doesn't want to inflict long-lasting damage. She doesn't intend to kill me, but then Bets often does things she had no intention of doing. I have a horrible feeling this is Betty's version of rough foreplay. I think we've moved past 'first base' and now I'm starting to worry.

The rough little tongue continues on its travels, winding around my ear, rasping, probing and leaving it as clean and pink as a mother cat would leave her kittens. She continues down to my throat; her lips and tongue caress me and centre their attentions just above my pounding jugular. Now I'm really getting nervous. She has such poor judgement, weak impulse control and one hell of a nasty temper. I can tell her eye still aches.

How she's survived this long is a puzzle. Her longevity goes to prove the usefulness of a remorseless, unflinching, insatiable will to survive over just about everything else, including calculation and cunning.

Her fangs pierce the surface of my skin and hover there. She wants to give me time to think about my situation. Suddenly, they plunge into the vein. She isn't gentle. She has only been drinking a few moments but those moments start to feel like an eternity. At last the drawing eases and her fangs start to retract.

During the painful eternity of her feeding, we come close to the ultimate intimacy between my species. For it to have been complete we would have fed from each other, in unison and willingly and then we would have shared all our thoughts and feelings. Obviously, Betty doesn't want that. This evening will be a one-way street and that can only mean she believes she still has some secrets for me to discover and doesn't want to spoil the surprise.

Nevertheless, in a limited way we drift away together, back into our world of shared childhood memories.

In a verdant valley, nestled in the Fagaras region of Transylvania, we two monster children are thrown together by fate. As we grow, we come to learn that we are born of a rare breed, unique and alone; we are the only two, the lost children of the night. Monster children will make the best of what they have and we have so much – a whole world of moonlight and magic. And so we create our own dark games to be played in dark gardens. It appears the world is a paradise made for just we two – a Garden of Eden, and we are the first to walk it. We have become everything to each other. We love, hate, laugh, cry and hunt, just us two, in our dark secret world, our stygian paradise.

It is unusual for vampires to have childhood companions. As I've said, we are born infrequently and the chances of two mating couples finding themselves with dependant offspring at the same time, in the same region, is rare indeed, but it occurs. Unlike the humans we mimic, my species is not a social one. We are lone predators and highly territorial. Unfortunately, the circumstance of Betty and I becoming companions emboldened both our already neglectful parents to be even more careless.

We vampires have long childhoods, and the potential to live such long lives, that vampire parents usually invest a lot of time and energy in giving us the best possible chance of survival. This involves abandoning us at regular intervals in harsh, threatening environments. If we are lucky, they turn up just when we need them most, and not a moment before, to rescue us from our own stupidity. If we aren't lucky, they don't.

Vampire parents are somewhat cold-blooded, it goes without saying. They have their own needs to satisfy.

Among them the need for periods of solitude and the need for hunting grounds that can sustain them, leading to the jealous guarding of territory. Competition for survival extends to their own progeny. If it weren't for the ultimate imperative, survival of the species, vampiric parents would, without a doubt, eat their own young while they were too weak and vulnerable to put up much of a fight. And so they make for contradictory, eccentric guardians.

Often protective and nurturing, they provide the best education available: languages, religion, occultism, sciences, astronomy, botany, biology and anatomy. The study of the latter for a hunter, as has been noted with human psychopaths locked in maximum security prisons, is of particular interest. Knowledge of the human anatomy, and in our case, also that of the vampire, is invaluable. With that knowledge you have the ability to kill quickly and, of course, very slowly. Most vampires could easily pass any human medical exam.

Betty and I spent our childhood surrounded by literature, music, and the arts. After all, who would want to share immortality with an ignorant dullard. Yet vampiric parents can be disinterested and sporadically, downright cruel. Betty and I regularly found ourselves clinging to each other for our mutual survival and came to enjoy having companionship through the millennia of our needy childhood and youth.

Needless to say, our shared adolescence was 'interesting', to put it mildly. I look back on those years as an alcoholic would reminisce on a long, destructive bender, the parts of it I can remember. Through a mist of hormonally induced chemical imbalance, I still have flashbacks of a hundred-year binge on an excess of emotion, savagery, lust and blood.

When I was still so young and vulnerable, the proximity to Ezserebet moulded my character and certainly helped hone my survival skills. I'll admit I have always and still do, find her physically attractive – my archetypal female. Whether I like it or not, Betty is the architect of my libido, the blueprint of desire carved deep into my psyche. Also it is not a subjective attraction she exerts upon me. She is unusually beautiful, even for a vampire, and it would be difficult for any male who enjoys the company of women, even just a little bit, to resist. But tonight I can resist; I had ulterior motives for being such a pushover at the house. Knowing Betty as well as I do, I know it is impossible to make her do something she doesn't want to do. In this instance, to tell me where she keeps her still warm victims.

Luckily, up until now I've been doing a pretty good job of keeping my mind blank. Betty can read me like a book and it's taken all my self control not to give the game away. Even during our communion down memory lane, I kept part of me locked up tight. If Betty thinks she can hold back from me and that such a loophole doesn't allow me a certain level of privacy, she's wrong. She is satisfied for the moment, and now I can briefly allow myself to think about the missing girl I saw on my computer search. The girl that looked so much like my Angel, the human I came to know and love so long ago and the fact that she, or her reincarnation, may well be here, suffering somewhere in one of Betty's tunnels. I have considered she is already dead, has to be, but it is hard to resign myself to another three hundred years of loneliness when there's even a tiny chance that she may still be alive. As soon as I'd realised the killings and disappearances at the Elephant had the mucky paws of Ezserebet all over them, I'd also known, for sure, she would never tell me if the girl were alive or dead. If dead, not even how she died, and if she is yet alive, definitely not where she is.

It's mortifying, but obvious now, that Betty knows I have a 'special someone' out there. How and when Betty came to possess knowledge of my Angel is a mystery and it leaves me wondering. How many times over the passing years, hundreds of them, have I believed I was alone, and Betty has been close and watching me. Biding her time, meddling and amusing herself at my expense. The thought sends a shudder through me – the woman is a true obsessive. My childhood chum has turned into an immortal, psychotic stalker.

Back at the house, I knew the only way I would ever be sure of the veracity of any information I got from my crazy cousin would be to go with Ezserebet, on her own terms, whatever they maybe, to wherever she may take me, and find the answers for myself. If I could make Betty feel she was calling the shots, if I could lull her with the illusion of power into dropping that kooky, hyper-vigilance down just a notch, I might get lucky. She might want to impress me, she's such a show-off. She would take me to her favourite place, somewhere she is proud of, and somewhere of which I am completely unaware. A place like that would make her feel superior, safe from surprises and in control. I have a feeling we are there; this place is grimly Gothic – perfect. She must float around down here like the Phantom of the Opera.

She presses in for another nibble, and by the time she pulls back from the bite I can hardly see. So weak I can barely maintain consciousness. Again I am stung by humiliation. I can't suppress or hide the erection that presses between us. When you're invulnerable, as I am, there is something irresistible about feeling completely powerless and at the mercy of a beautiful female, especially one as unhinged as Betty. No matter the circumstances, she still has the ability to pull me into a sensory vortex. She can keep me teetering on the dizzy edge of pain and pleasure for days, weeks, years. If she hadn't brought Angel into the mix, and with heartfelt apologies to the memory of Jackie, God help me, but I'd be in bliss.

As it stands, right now I need what little blood I have left to return to my brain if I am to get out of this alive. She bites down hard again and my last thread of consciousness unravels. I am spiralling down a long, dark chasm, leaving all sound and sensation behind.

I am rising again, speeding back upward toward a pinprick of red light. I slowly become aware of Bet's hand holding my lower jaw, while pouring almost fresh blood down my reflexively contracting throat. My one good eye snaps open wide and I am perfectly aware.

'You nearly killed me that time, you crazy bitch,' I manage to choke out.

She smiles and backs away, crawling down the wall like a flame-haired spider, and replete as a blood-bloated leech, she inelegantly plonks herself down on an overstuffed armchair. Of all things to add to a torture chamber, it would take a mind as twisted as Bet's to choose the piece of frippery in which she nestles. It's the only piece of furniture in the vault and it is filthy. It stands in two inches of indeterminate muck, but I can smell it had been new when she shoved it down the ancient coal chute, or whatever channel she used to access this amazing spot. The fabric, a pastel, floral design, belongs in a cottage somewhere in the Cotswolds. The juxtaposition of a naked, excrement-smeared vampire lounging wantonly between its feather cushions is something to behold – the Succubus range by Laura Ashley.

The muted rumble of traffic and tube train indicates we are still in central London, but very deep below ground level. A dank, oxygen-poor air current passes over me and I instinctively know there are more tunnels and vaults above and below. I wonder who built this vault, when and why. I can't see any clues to its purpose. Perhaps storage for weapons during the Second World War. I'm just guessing as part of my brain tries to piece together every scrap of sensory information to get a handle on my location.

The fresh blood has hit my veins and thankfully, all my brain cells begin sparking. I can actually see flashes of electro-energy arcing across the back of my eyelid with my one remaining eyeball. I feel like a human on Red Bull, or perhaps cocaine, I wouldn't know about the latter; it does nothing for me. I might as well snort icing sugar.

My thinking is still not entirely clear though. I feel I may have lost some time and can't be sure how much, the past few hours are patchy, but at last, my body is responding to threat instead of abandoning itself to playtime. I gobbled up the infusion of life force and I can feel my inner vampire making the most of it. Survival time. I am hyperaware and suddenly feel invulnerable and all on half a cup of blood. It's a wonderful side effect of a close shave with death for a vampire, this amplification of all that we were before. What doesn't kill you makes you stronger. That old chestnut was coined by one of mine.

Thirty feet up on the opposite brick wall hangs the inverted body of a young woman. Her ankles bear her entire body weight and are raw where the rusty metal of two ancient iron manacles clamp tight around them and cut deep into her pale flesh.

She is filthy and it isn't surface dirt. Her hair is matted with grease. Homeless, I assume. She appears almost still a child but her slight frame is deceptive and I put it down to lack of good nutrition, I can sense she is somewhere in her mid-twenties. I notice she is missing her tongue; a vile smell of charred flesh tells me the root has been crudely cauterised. Also her left hand is missing, the stump hanging strangled in a rough tourniquet. With an agonising groan, she musters strength to turn her head. She is not entirely conscious but yet still driven by instinct to search for the comfort given by the one source of light – a single, guttering candle. It is too dark for her to see me but in her search, she has turned her face toward me and I can see her. My 'jam tart' jumps in my chest. I can feel, rather than hear, her whispery heartbeat, which resonates in my body through the damp, fetid atmosphere of the cavern. Her barely viable pulse thrums through the mouldering atmosphere, setting my soul humming like a tuning fork.

Why does this particular scrap of humanity affect me so? How can she hold such power over me? I have no doubt now, it is my Angelica. Almost dead from blood loss and shock, she is perhaps already too far gone, lost to me again for another three hundred years or more. An expert little nick in her neck releases a regular drip of blood that plinks into a crystal bowl expertly aligned thirty feet below to catch the ruby drips, a battered tin cupful of which has just been poured down my throat.

I close my eyes for a moment. Savouring that blood is a memory I will have to relive in my quiet moments. If Angel dies tonight, I will taste her sweet metallic lifeblood over and over in my dreams, through all the years that remain to me. The flavour will leave a bitter stain on my tongue and spoil the one pleasure left to me – feeding. Damn! Ezserebet is good at this stuff. I stand in awe of her twisted genius for physical, mental and spiritual torture.

Betty continues to sit on her soft furnishing, one long leg hung over a well-upholstered arm. Her legs stretched apart, akimbo, that girl was always overly crotch-confident. The leg that doesn't hang across the arm stretches forward so that a long, daddy toe with a black painted nail can swirl patterns in the putrid, reeking water. She is surreptitiously watching me. She has seen it all – the shock, the pain, the realisation. She's loving it. I don't think Angel was here before Ezserebet bit me, but I wouldn't swear to it. I can't be sure. I'm a little confused and disoriented. I think Bets may have spiked the blood, and I don't want to speculate on what was in the syringe she shot me with at the house.

It's typical of Bets to think of dragging furniture down here, to strike a jarring note, throw a psychic curve ball. Betty must have taken some time to set this up; the juxtaposition is sheer dramaturgy. I now realise I'm starring in a theatrical production, staged for an audience of one. We vamps don't need, or particularly enjoy, human creature comforts, particularly in our theatres of death. We aren't the soft creatures we mimic. Vampires surround themselves with beauty and treasure, like the dragon on our coat of arms. It's a survival strategy, our camouflage and protection. Betty and I are subterranean, closer to crocodiles than to the chained monkey hanging from the opposite wall. Betty's gone to a lot of trouble to make a point; I'm beggared if know what it is.

If humans were to stumble across this cavern, I wonder how many individuals modern forensics could identify from the various remains found down here. Three, four, could be hundreds for all I know, and I would predict many of those victims would resemble the girl overhead. Young women, most of them younger than the one bleeding out before me; hard to trace runaways. I know Betty's profile well. She has an obsessive hunger for nubile females, her favourite quarry, and her version of Crème de la Mer. She has nurtured some strange beliefs and rituals involving their blood, her theory being that it keeps her young. Cleopatra, Queen of ancient Egypt bathed in asses' milk every day to preserve the beauty and youth of her skin; it is the closest you can get to human breast milk. Betty prefers to go one better – the torture part is just the game the whole family can play. She's growing more like her debauched father every decade. I have clocked the large Victorian claw-footed bath tub in the shadows. She's been up to her old nonsense again. Utter bollocks, the logic of the delusional psychotic. Any crusty old tramp would have exactly the same effect on us as the tender shoot I've just been drinking. Moreover, I could encase myself in a vat of blood for a hundred years and it would have no effect on me whatsoever. We are not human, and applications of lotions and potions to our dermal scales or scutes is completely ineffectual. We are predators and for us, blood is food and any human blood will do.

I feel suddenly bored with Betty. Surely she should have outgrown all this 'Tom Tit' by now. The weary monotony of inflicting senseless, unnecessary suffering on the innocent should have worn thin lifetimes ago. There really are only so many ways to skin a cat, after all.

'Where is this going?' I whisper.

'Oh Teddy, I just love how you protest and gripe when I visit, while your pleasure and excitement to see me again is always so obvious.'

With that, she gives me one of her leers, glancing down toward my now shrinking member. That boat has sailed. The whole scene is beginning to strike me as something of a ghoulish Benny Hill skit. I mumble some words to that effect, and she feigns ignorance of the reference, but I notice she draws herself up a little and gets in touch with her inner Countess. Her vanity is the only real chink in her armour. Whilst she is momentarily distracted by the distasteful thought of having been likened to a short, plump, 1960's comedian, I test the strength of my chains. This is going to hurt, but it might be doable.

I moan and let my head loll forward, slow my heart and breathing, which isn't easy. Every part of me is on high alert, aware that the capricious witch sitting before me could decide to finish me at any moment. I have to draw on my brief stint at The Curtain in Shoreditch and a couple of warmly received turns on stage at The Globe. It was over four hundred years ago, but once the greasepaint is in your veins ...

I have no faith in our childhood bonds of affection and familiarity or even her stalkerish obsession. Where Betty is concerned, expect the unexpected. I have witnessed her do all kinds of mischief on a whim that she has regretted and whined about afterwards.

A couple of hours tick past while I drift as close to hibernation as I dare whilst hung to tenderise like a ditch chicken before one of the deadliest creatures on the planet. Bets isn't jumping to my rescue. She is still pissed off ; I really rattled her cage with the Benny Hill reference. When would I learn to shut my mouth? Note to self: in future, never insult an almost invulnerable psychopath who has you manacled in a dungeon.

I close out every thought except her movements, at first just the fidgeting rustle of her thighs against chintz as she battles with impatience. At last, the sloshing of feet through black water, the clink as the tin cup touches the side of the crystal bowl, and the sound of her scratching and writhing up the old bricks toward me. Her hands are on my chin again and a second cup of blood is poured down my throat. I drink, while silently begging my little Angel's forgiveness.

'I can't believe how weak you are, Teddy. This is what happens when you drink that NHS szar – one little bite and you're all floppy and swoony.'

There's plenty more disparagement where that came from heading my way, but she is interrupted by my sudden jerk and flex. The rusted bolt rings rip out of the wall in a cloud of ancient mortar and dust. I reach out and snatch her close to me in a vice-like bear hug. Together we fall to the floor of the cavern, landing with me on top of her, along with a good amount of old brickwork. Her lovely hair spreads out around her in the black sludge like the tentacles of a deadly jelly fish.

I still have the new titanium manacles around my wrists and ankles; one of them has some brick still attached. The steel bands that were locked over my chest are hanging from the wall by one bolt a side, groaning and screeching as they swing against the stone. I'm free, but nonetheless Betty had put together some very efficient restraints and nearly all of my ribs are broken. One or two are poking through my torn flesh. My whole body hurts like hell, but what can I say ... sometimes you just have to go for it.

Immediately, we both scrabble into defensive positions while searching for any offensive advantage. Betty's hand is already clenched around one of my protruding broken ribs and she's pulling furiously. I take a swing with the chain, more a masonry flail, at Bets' head, using the brickwork still clinging to the end of my wrist chain as a mace, but she is too quick. She ducks away and then jumps on me, nails and teeth slashing. My fingers wrap around her throat but

I can feel my grip slipping as she writhes and twists under my hands.

Sudden movement from above catches both our attention. Down one of the vertical shafts that enter the dungeon through the arched ceiling, something large drops, fast, like a stone and just stops short of smashing onto the stone floor. A great vortex of air spins around us, whipped up by the flurry and flapping of a pair of huge, featherless wings. The surprise literally takes the air out of both mine and Betty's lungs. We're momentarily, but completely, distracted from trying to kill each other. The great wings are stretched out, almost transparent and pink, threaded through with a tracery of veins and ligaments. They have a membranous quality and so does the skin covering the muscular body to which they are attached. We are looking at something that is very much like a man-sized, humanoid bat.

With shocked recognition, I look into the yellowy eyes of my attacker from St John's Church. Those eyes have now taken on an owl-like quality. They burn through the blackness and it is clear 'it' can see me just as clearly as I can see 'it'. We look at each other for a second, and the creature bows and slightly turns its head to fix me with one steady eye in an oddly avian gesture. I think, or at least hope, I may have just been given 'the nod'.

Arrogantly, I had assumed the creature from Burge Street was a sadly misshapen grotesquery, undoubtedly strong, but nevertheless, another evolutionary mis-step. I couldn't have been more wrong. What appeared to be a calciferous hunch on its back under the filthy old flasher raincoat, had in fact been a pair of folded, bony, magnificent wings. Disrobed, the creature took on a whole new aspect. I am quite taken aback by its chimeric beauty. Greyish, pink skin covers a thin but muscular torso, armed with a set of vicious teeth and claws, night vision and wings. The slug from the alley and then church has undergone a metamorphosis, and turned into a magnificent gothic moth. Entirely hairless, a true creature of the night and dark places.

My surprise is compounded by the small but noticeable breasts on its chest, or should I say her chest. I now assume it is female. She draws herself up, stretches out her wings, momentarily holding the pose before bringing them down to pound the air beneath them until she rises to half the height of the cavern only to expertly descend again, toes touching down onto the sewage-covered flags with a chaste, but definitely theatrical kiss.

Unbelievable! I have another fucking diva on my hands.

Ezserebet's eyes are stretched wide. She's as 'gobsmacked' as I've ever seen her. Never have I seen the informal explicative illustrated so perfectly, her mouth hangs slightly open framing her canines as though she's received a unexpected slap on the 'moosh'. Ruby lips stretch thin, red hair trails across her shoulders and runs over her body like rusty rain. Her face is spectral pale and magnificent. She is genuinely lost for words or action. I think I can safely assume this winged creature has come as much a surprise to her as it did to me. I savour the moment, which doesn't last long. Betty shakes herself out of the shock of the new and lunges forward, toward me, hissing and snapping her maxillae. I swing the wreckage of my iron, chest restraints with as much force as I have left in me. Blood swamps her mouth as she falls backward. A direct hit. Pretty sure I've broken at least one of her fangs. That has to hurt.

I notice she has closed her eyes, her lids screw tight for a moment. Our fangs are sensitive. That snap of ivory would feel like a nail penetrating her brain. Now is the moment to launch a ferocious attack, while she is still on the ropes, but this is Betty. Killing her will not be a 'wham, bam, thank you ma'm' kind of deal. I could be here all night.

I have other things on my mind – more pressing demands. After hundreds of years of time crawling like a geriatric snail, it has sped up on me. Each second of delay could make a shattering difference … tick tock.

Taking advantage of Betty's discomfort, I leap at the cavern wall and dig my claws into the mortar, quickly crawling upward and over the ceiling until I reach Angelica, or, I suppose I should call her Michelle until she gets used to me. But that may be academic. She appears lifeless. I press my ear to her chest. Her little body is surprisingly strong; she's a resilient little thing, must come from drinking all that London water. She isn't going without a fight. I can still detect the presence of a faltering heartbeat. I rip the manacles that suspend her out of the brickwork and pull her into my arms. It is her, I know it is Angelica. Reborn, under all the dirt and blood, it is her.

Clutching her under one arm, I crawl back down to the ground and lay her as best I can on a stone step at the base of the arching walls, out of the filthy water.

From behind, I feel Ezserebet's hot breath on the back of my neck, can almost hear her jaw unhinge – all the better to eat me with. Claws dig into my back, only to be violently ripped out. I hiss, spit and turn with a grunt of pain to see her lifted upward, impaled on razor-sharp talons by the yellow-eyed, winged creature. Betty's legs pump and flay as though she's on a bike and coming up to the finish of the Tour de France.

From the corner of my eye I am aware of Ezserebet twisting herself into a backwards curve that would be the envy of any human contortionist. She can't turn her torso because of the razor claws in her back but she is inverting her body and trying to pull herself up the creatures legs in a way that would be impossible for a human. A battle royal is about to take place right above me and I want to watch more than almost anything, but the reason I allowed myself to be brought here is dying at my feet.

Leaning over Angel, I know it is all but hopeless. Perhaps if I could get her to a hospital. My mind races. Could I carry her out of here, move as fast as I am able and give no thought to hiding or disguising what I am? Could I get her to an A & E in time? Wishful thinking; I know no human doctor can save her now. She is all but gone She would be pronounced 'dead on arrival' from a human clinical point of view … it's already game over.

I weigh my options – there appear to be only two. One, I could let her go and chalk it up to fate. I'm not ready to do that, I can't do that. Two, I try something risky, something I've never done before, but I've heard others of my kind have. I could try to feed her. I know I will have to drink some of her blood, direct from the vein. Maybe it's her plasma mixing with mine that in some way makes my blood digestible and will allow her to metabolise it, and with it, my life force. I really have no idea how or if it will work. Or if it has ever worked.

Perhaps I am grasping at straws, dragging up campfire tales and urban myths I have heard over the years, and I'm trying desperately to remember the details. Perhaps none of the blood exchange means anything. It could simply be an injection of the serum/poison that oozes from the glands around my fangs. It could be that the super, recuperative properties of my cells pumped directly into her arterial blood stream, while she is so close to death, will stimulate regeneration. I know the chemical composition of my serum changes with my mood and my intent. I can make my prey docile and let them drift away from life in a warm bath of narcosis, or I can produce chemicals that stimulate the adrenal medulla, inducing a hormonal cascade in my victim that manifests a state of hyper arousal, making them intensely sensitive to pain and fear so that death becomes a painful, terrifying nightmare. I must concentrate now on what I want, bend my physiology to my will. I love this creature, I want her to live – I need her to live.

Right now it's all striking me as complete hokum, but I am desperate.

As far as I know, the stories I have heard are just children's creepy bedtime tales. They were never something I had any real interest in, that is until tonight. I have always considered tales of vampires and their unusually long lived human concubines to be exaggerations, twisted versions of an event with some historical truth that have been used as the basis of an allegory on the dangers of consorting with the livestock. Folklore and cautionary parables told to young vampires to instruct them that although desperate times may lead to desperate measures, it never ends well.

I have no other ideas; if I don't try I'll be left to wonder and I can't face another three hundred years of regret. I have to try, even though I have no clue what I am doing, or any faith that it will work.

Interspecies-metamorphosis? My intellect screams this is impossible. But then again, humans are using pig hearts in transplants. Of course, they are at least dealing with another mammal. They are basing their experiments on science. I on the other hand, am wrestling with the far-fetched chance that the possibility of biological and metaphysical alchemy between the monkeys and vampires as told in legend is actually true. I have to give it a go or I will be haunted by the chance it may have worked and I hesitated because of some archaic set of scruples with which I was indoctrinated in my impressionable youth.

But if I choose to take the tall tales literally, I cannot pick and choose the parts I believe. I'm on the horns of a dilemma; there are good reasons for a certain level of caution. What's giving me pause as I hover over Michelle Blake, are the various outcomes reported in those legends that accompany the rite of transformation. These fables I'm drawing on are vampire fairy tales, and just like human fairy tales, before Disney got hold of them, are meant to be dark, whispered warnings on the dangers of hubris. Sometimes when we choose to play with powerful magic, things go wrong. Horribly wrong.

Super accelerated cell growth, recidivism, grisly disturbing accounts of creatures that had to be destroyed. According to legend, that part was no piece of cake.

'Forgive me Angel,' I murmur close to her ear. I doubt she can hear me as I lean in and bite into her throat. I can't take much, she's already in a state of hypovolemia. My purpose is to ensure that she receives an ample measure of serum injected straight into her artery as I drink. She is all but gone. Quickly, I pull back and with a clawed finger, slice through my wrist, pressing the thick, oozing, red liquid up to her lips.

At first I think I imagine she drinks. Just wishful thinking, almost imperceptible, but then I feel a slight draw; it stops as quickly as it begins. I tear a deeper wound in the ulnar artery, pump my arm and, squeezing my wrist, force the blood to flow down her throat, but it just pools in her mouth and runs down her chin.

She has taken only one sip.

I press my ear to her chest. Her heart has stopped. She has slipped through my fingers again, just surviving this cold-hearted world long enough to quicken my jaded heart for one night. Has it been twenty-four hours? Not even that. Again she is moving away from me. She drifts away like a skiff at sea, caught by the current and pulled on the tide until she is out of sight and the chances of my finding her again on that vast ocean of time so small I will almost lose hope … almost, but not quite. Can I face the torture, another three hundred years of waiting? Resignedly, I know of course I will. What choice do I have?

I hold her hand in mine, the one she still has, and lift it to my lips.

'Oh my Angel.'

I can feel her wrist against my lips … distinguish the ridge of that most beautiful artery under the thin tissue of her skin. That is when I feel it start. The weakest throb of life, but it is there. I laugh and let out a sob of relief. My breathing stops; I cannot hear any sound except the muffled thump of her pulse. Time has slowed. In a single moment of eternity what is left of my vision since Betty plucked out an eyeball, narrows laser-beam sharp, excluding everything but my lovely new pet and I take in every curve of her face.

'You are mine, mine, entirely mine and this time I will keep you.'

Satisfied, I exhale. Senses re-assert with an explosion of sound and an almost audible whoosh as my vision expands to take in the bloody battle raging over my head. The two combatants, a spinning ball of flaming red hair, pounding wings, writhing, clawing and hissing flesh, disappear as one into an overhead chute.

CHAPTER TWELVE

'Love all, trust a few,…' Shakespeare

One last covetous, wet stroke of my darling's cheek and I make a leap for the wall, meeting it half way up. Digging in with my clawed fingers, I scale it and continue across the ceiling until I reach the shaft from which the winged creature descended. I can hear the combatants somewhere ahead, somewhere deep within the tunnels. If I can find them and secure the unexpected help of the yellowed-eyed *thing* this could prove the best chance I've had in centuries to finally rid myself of Ezserebet Bathory. In any vampire court it would stand up as justifiable vampicide, self-preservation being the best defence on the books.

They have disappeared into one of the tunnels that extend out from the overhead chute. A strange phenomenon of ricocheting echoes is making it difficult to track the origin of the sounds of battle. For a human, the maze of tunnels would be completely disorientating. Again, I can't help but be impressed with the location. I have to admit from the moment I'd woken, I'd fallen in love with the place and quickly decided to claim these caverns for myself, but first I have to deal with the present occupant.

I listen until I am as sure as I can be which of the tunnels to follow. Half running, half free-skating through muck, I'm pretty sure I'm on the right track when suddenly, all sounds of struggle cease and I become slightly flummoxed as the echoes continue, creating a sound loop, a round robin of repeating grunts and shouts. I should be able to follow the scent trail, but now even that is no longer straightforward. The smell of the creature is pungent to put it mildly and it's everywhere. The tunnels have now become a bit like entering Harrods perfume department. It doesn't take long before the fumes start to burn my mucous membranes. The creature's musk has a heavy, acrid, chemical quality and completely swamps my senses.

I stop and listen until, mercifully, the echoes evaporate and I can discern the direction of raspy breathing; it's coming from one of the smaller channels. Crouching low I take off again, toward the noise, until I almost fall over the body of 'yellow eyes'. She is still conscious but the blood oozing from her head and the dazed, confused look tells me Betty managed to land a particularly effective blow to her 'loaf of bread'.

'Which way creature, which way?'

She points limply back toward the direction from which I've just come.

'No, impossible. Think!'

Lifting a bony finger and shaking her head, in an attempt to clear it I assume, she continues to indicate back the way I've just come.

'She went that way, and if she didn't then I have no idea. Where the hell were you, you cretinous vampyr? Together, we could have taken her.'

I'm in no mood for an argument. Retracing my steps, I notice an even smaller inlet channel dissecting the brick-lined pipe that brought me to 'yellow eyes'. I listen… nothing. But there is a smear of blood on the corner where the pipes intersect – vampire blood. So she doubled back this way and I deduce from the complete lack of any telltale sounds, she is now long gone. I take a deep breath and close my eyes, wondering whether I will ever get a break where that harridan is concerned. I turn and the creature is at my side, nursing its head with one hand, but other than that, apparently not grievously injured. I have my suspicions that faced with a cornered Betty fighting for her life, and finding herself going it solo, yellow eyes took a dive.

I turn on the *thing* and get up close enough to be hit by some serious halitosis.

'Where the hell did she go, bird breath?'

She is playing the injured party. I get it, 'Infirmity doth still neglect all office', and all that malarkey, but my canines are starting to drop.

'Why are you asking me? I'm not a fucking Swami.'

I take a deep breath and count to ten. I'm in no mood for banter, but she isn't finished.

'You are unbelievable Vampyr. I did my part. I followed you here, to this stinking pit to kill that harpy of yours and finish this. She's incredibly strong, something you obviously already know but I just found out the hard way.' To make her point, she starts fingering the wound on her head. 'Maybe if we'd been in this together, as I foolishly assumed would be the case, it would all be over by now. You see I had the crazy idea that if I followed the pair of you to her lair, that when you eventually made your move, there would be two against one – a surprise attack. I jumped to that conclusion when I saw the vampyress drag you out of your own house, strapped across her shoulders like a spring lamb and haul you unconscious across the rooftops. What the hell were you doing back there?'

The creature is doing its best to control, what I now see, is her own very short fuse, I can't blame her, she has 'skin in this game'; she wants the Elephant to go back to normal and put herself where she needed to be. I let us both down. Also, although I am trying to hang on to the rage, my teeth have retracted and I suddenly can't stop smiling. I can see it's driving her nuts. My Angel is alive. I decide I had better start talking.

'The female of my kind is actually the more deadly, especially when completely unhinged. I can't believe I've let her get away again, but there was nothing I could do. The timing was bad and I had to take care of something urgent back in the cavern – it couldn't wait. I'm heading back there now if you want to come and see?'

'Oh yes Vampyr, I think I will come and see what's more important than dispatching an enemy that certainly looked as if she intended to kill you. She strikes me as more than up to the task as well. She's strong enough to throw a hog over a house and apparently, can get the drop on you any time she likes.'

We stand and give each other a long, appraising stare. This bat-like creature has obviously been watching me, perhaps followed me home from St John's Church. I thought I'd felt eyes watching me from the gardens back at the house in Cadogan Square. So far, I know she is both stealthy and fierce, but apart from that she is still an exotic alien, an unknown quantity. Whatever the creature is, it had been in the right place at the right time. Something like that could be worth talking to. I decide this is one of those times I just have to take a leap of faith.

For her part, she is giving me a cold, assessing stare, taking note of my injuries. Her eyes drift across my torn chest, the visible ribs, and for all practical purposes, my lack of one 'mince pie'. The extent of the damage and my obvious discomfort seem to calm her down. Now is my chance to shift gears into diplomacy.

'Yes, well, looks can be deceiving where Betty is concerned. Whether or not she really wants me dead is probably unknown even to herself. If you should encounter her again, I would suggest– No, this won't do.' I stop and turn to face the winged creature and extend a hand to shake. 'My name is Edward deVere, please call me Eddy. I am a vampire, or homoreptilia. My habitat of choice is the City, my prey, homosapiens. I am somewhat over six hundred years old and I am pleased to make your acquaintance.'

After a momentary hesitation, she takes my hand in a dry, bony grip and shakes it. 'My name is Tiamat, you may call me Tia. I am a gargoyle or that which inspired the idea. Gargoyle is a derogatory term by the way – I can use it, you can't. I could be described as homoraptor, or homostrigidae, as my kind mainly hunt and forage at night. My habitat of choice is likewise the City, my prey, homosapiens. Only the stragglers, I hasten to add as my kind are the carrion eaters of the city desert. We are perhaps best considered the hyena of the concrete sahara to your lion, but as you can see we can certainly hunt if we are hungry enough, and defend ourselves. I am approaching my hundred and thirtieth birthday, and if I'm honest, I am *not* pleased to meet you.'

'Well, that said, and given that I don't appreciate being trailed, I thank you for taking the initiative. You created a diversion that may have made all the difference.'

'Diversion?' Tia's pupils narrow to pinpricks and then expand out to full hunting mode.

Formalities over, I quickly continue with my thought: 'As I was saying Tia, if you should encounter Betty again, although I completely understand she is making problems for you at the Elephant, I would keep firmly in mind, no matter what comes out of her mouth, that the woman has killed more people than malaria and she intends to kill you at the very first opportunity. She won't forgive you for tonight – you have made an enemy. Don't be distracted.'

Tia stays silent but nods in a curt, decisive way that reassures me she fully understands the nature of the vampiress she is hunting.

We head back to the vault and my sleeping Angel. We drop down through the ceiling shaft. She is where I left her and as I left her, seemingly dead to all but those with heightened perceptions. In fact, I am pretty sure she has entered what vampires call the profound sleep. When one of my species has suffered some grievous, almost mortal injury, we take to the earth and slow our metabolism, the better to heal. How and when we awake is always a lottery. I've seen mighty vampire warriors take to earth with what appeared recoverable injuries, not to re-emerge for years. Then again, I've witnessed a low ranking, puny specimen of my kind take to earth with injuries that should have killed him, only to awake as fresh as a daisy the very next evening. It isn't an exact science. I assume that Angel will remain in this healing coma until her body has recouped and rearranged itself to accommodate my DNA. I will just have to be patient a little longer.

I lift Angel and carry her to Betty's chair, it's the best I can do to keep her open wounds out of the black water and muck. Tia circles her, sniffing the air and to my disrelish, examines Angel's stump and bloodied mouth with her leathery tongue. Her eyes become a little glassy and now that I know her nature, there is definitely a carrion feeder's intensity about the way she circles Angel.

'Tia, just so we're clear on one matter ...' She looks up at me as if surprised I am still in the dungeon. 'This human is my familial, and she is not, and never will be, food, whether alive or dead. Do you understand me?' Again the yellowy eyes meet mine, just one quick blink in an otherwise long, emotionless stare. I sense a moment of suppressed defiance before, with a shrug of her concave shoulders, she again gives the curt, decisive nod, which I hope indicates agreement and compliance.

'So you have revived the dying, female human. I've heard vampyrs could do such unnatural things – interesting, I thought it was just a 'Jackanory'. I've not actually seen one of these hybrids before, so it will be interesting to see what wakes up.'

Tia's thoughts are a little too close to the bone for me right at this moment. I too have part of my mind turning over what will emerge from the profound sleep but not with curiosity – with alternating hope and dread.

Before we leave I try to find some trace of, or clue to the location of my dear Jackie. I tell Tia the whole story as I search and she makes some feeble attempt to help. As she doesn't know what she is looking for, I don't expect much from her and as it turns out, she is far too distracted by all the meaty remains lying around in various stages of decomposition to be of any help. She proves herself to be honest at least; definitely a scavenger, if all the crunching and furtive squelching noises are anything to go by. At least she is no longer hungry and has stopped eyeing Angel with that obsessive intensity.

As it turns out, I don't find any traces that Jackie's been here at all. There is no fresh spoor, save for a red, polka dot scarf that definitely had been around her neck at some point; it is now black and soggy, floating on the surface of the foot of muck covering the vault floor. I can't identify any blood or traces of adrenalin on the scarf but it certainly has remnants of my housekeeper's distinctive milk puddingy odour. It doesn't seem to fit and I'm at the point where I just need to know how it played out with Jackie. If she isn't here, it means Ezserebet must have taken her to another location and she could have any number of these 'bolt holes' scattered across London.

Betty has never been known for moderation – more is always more. There are plenty of defunct underground storage spaces all across the City. There is a huge network under Clapham North underground. Perhaps I should start there. With a final howl of frustration, I rip at my hair and give up. Jackie isn't here – for all I know has never been here. I have no idea why Betty would take her somewhere else to torture and kill. We are obviously at her base of operations as this place has all the signs of a favourite playpen. She'd brought Angel here, and Angel had been her main game play. I am completely at a loss. The thought of Jackie hanging from a wall somewhere, perhaps in pain, is making my head buzz but right now I have no idea where to start a search. I have no choice but to let it go for the moment and deal with the immediate.

Escaping Betty's vault isn't difficult. We just follow her old trails until I recognise a familiar conjunction and from there it's easy to find my way back to Sloane Square. I am heading home, but this time I avoid the tube tunnels and take a longer route that allows us to emerge through a sewer manhole straight onto Milner Street. I'm not taking any more chances tonight. Getting Angel to the relative safety of my Keep in Cadogan Gardens is my first and only priority.

I decide to invite Tia back to mine; there doesn't seem much point playing the shrinking violet at this point. She'd obviously followed me home and spied on me from the central garden last night. She already knows where I abide. I'm not going to be churlish about it. I'm grateful she decided to stalk me, because her arrival at the dungeon had been helpful to put it mildly.

I lift Angel up from below and Tia pulls her out of the drain hole and holds her surprisingly gently while I exit and reposition the manhole cover. She is staring down at Angel cradled in her arms and completely absorbed as I brush myself off. I reach out to take the girl back into my arms and notice Tia hesitates. She will need some watching, there is such a force of character behind those yellow eyes. If we both survive this latest Ezserebet fiasco, I am beginning to feel she could be quite someone to know. But for now, I will need to be careful with Tia in the house. After all, she is a predator, like myself, and as such, never completely predictable.

'What will you do with her, Vampyr?' Tia's eyes never leave Angel's face while she speaks and I wonder if this is more than hunger … if she can see it too – the otherness of my little human.

'Call me Eddy, we're comrades now, as far as I'm concerned anyway. I'm going to keep her somewhere safe until all this 'Barney' with Betty is resolved and then, hopefully, she'll regain consciousness and we will just have to wait and see. It depends how the transformation goes.' I trail off, my train of thought again considering possible outcomes.

'She is more than food to you. She has something else you value. You call her Angel?' Her eyes still have not moved from Angel's face.

I'm not in the mood for any more complications tonight. 'That's right Tia, not food. I call her Angel because ... oh, it's too long a story for tonight. The name on her birth certificate is Michelle Blake. Now pass her back to me, creature, and if you're still hungry you can run along.'

Her eyes jolt up to mine and she hands the girl over, I lift her carefully but quickly out of Tia's arms, I feel very protective and suddenly jealous; it's wonderful to give a damn about something other than me again.

'Michelle ... I see. I wasn't thinking I'd eat her. She seems different in some way, unusual, and I was wondering what her value is to one of your kind.' Tia bent her head to the side as she spoke. Those strange, mesmeric, avian eyes are suddenly very large ... the better to see you with, my dear. Orange and reflective in the dim street light, I notice a lightning quick sweep across her retina of a nictitating membrane. So she has a third eyelid, like an owl, and I realise the reason for the turn of her head whenever she focuses on me is that her eyes cannot roll in their sockets.

I don't like being questioned, and I don't like the hard, shiny quality to the creature's stare. Is she excited by the idea of having something on me? Does she recognise the signs of an Achilles heel? Knowledge is power. Or could it be something else? For a vampire, I consider myself a simple soul ... I'm not into the cloak and dagger stuff, but then, it appears for the moment, I'm not calling the shots.

'Well, she's different now, that's for sure.' I brush some matted hair away from Angel's face. Her skin colour has improved ... she is definitely getting stronger. 'Let's just get back to the house and settle down. I'll tell you the story if you want to hear it. I owe you that, and then you can tell me your story.' I stop and look straight into Tia's eyes. There is a slight turn of her head to the left, the massive eyes following in that direction, but I know she is taking in a wider angle with her binocular vision than am I. Is that a sign of evasion? She is not human so I can't completely trust my instinctive 'read' of her. Life is hard enough. I don't want to make it colder than it need be and I don't need all the fingers on one hand to count the times someone or something came to my rescue.

'Full disclosure, Tia. We need some transparency in this relationship, I can't take any more subterfuge. Ezserebet has that thoroughly cornered and now that you're on her radar, you'll need me one day, so you can stop the machinations. You suddenly look more like a chicken than a gargoyle and I know how vicious and greedy chickens can be.'

For a moment, she is undecided whether to take offence. Then, with a wry smile, she shrugs her shoulders and, keeping to the shadows, we continue along Milner Street and into Cadogan Gardens without another word. Angel remains unconscious in my arms, the three of us being the only souls on the street. Nothing unusual for London – just a trio of dishevelled party people, and everyone knows girls can't hold their drink.

We let ourselves into No. 52, and behind the closed door we stand motionless in mutual silence. Minutes pass … one … ten … fifteen … until, with a glance and nod to each other, we move forward. The house gives every indication of being vacant of monsters with the exception of the three of us – Tia, Angel and myself. No humans here - a thought that makes me very happy. I nod toward the sitting room and Tia wanders in. She looks around, and with pursed lips, gives me a nod of approval.

'I'll be back shortly. Make yourself at home.'

I carry Angel through the door that leads to the lower levels and keep descending the spiral stone steps until we reach level minus three, my inner sanctum and sanctuary. I can feel the weight of her in my arms. She is real – she is here and with me now. I check her pupils and pulse. She is deeply unconscious; a human doctor would say she is in a deep coma. How long she will stay like this I have no idea, possibly months. Any less would surely be impossible with her injuries. For all I know, it could be much, much longer – perhaps years.

I lift her gently over the lip of an ancient sarcophagi and lay her down. I've collected many of these stone burial boxes over the years. This one is Egyptian and very beautiful in its monolithic simplicity. It suits Angel – a resting chamber with effortless gravitas for my ungilded lily … the Lily of the Valley, convallaria majalis, a sweetly scented but highly poisonous herbaceous perennial that prefers partial shade. Etiology has it that the Lily of the Valley first came into being and grew from the earth where the blood of Saint Leonard of Noblac spilled into the soil during his battle with the dragon. Why did I think of that? A little shiver runs through me. My relentless memory is a curse – it can taint almost any pleasure.

'There,' I whisper as I position her in the cold, stone trough. 'Sleep my Angel, I can hear you breathe, my love.' And with that, I slide the massive, stone lid back into position above her.

She is as safe as I can make her for the moment. I look around the subterranean room; her resting cenotaph is not the most obvious place an intruder would look. Just like the ancient Pharaohs, my tomb is less a pristine shrine and more a fortified, overfilled and untidy storage unit. I share one particular compulsion with humans – I am a bit of a hoarder, the difference being that my junk happens to be priceless antiquities. My sanctum is a dragon's cave stuffed with treasure to be slowly sold over the years.

Angel will be able to breathe; I've made a little modification to her sarcophagus in the form of a groove cut diagonally across the upper edge of the trough so that when the lid is fitted into position and the box is shut, the groove creates a small but adequate air hole. I know there is plenty enough oxygen for a human – I've kept snacks in it before.

My eyes move to the blocked-up well shaft ... all quiet on the Western Front. I walk over, stand on the stone cap and listen. Nothing ... silence. Tonight, it is very cold standing here directly over the cap stone. I take one step to the side and the temperature rises a little. I step back onto the well cap, and shiver. This place is too cold for Hell. 'Um ... what's rattled your chain tonight, ghost?' I press my ear to the flagstone for a response. Silence. There is a definite chill rising from the pit tonight. It could mean nothing, but I am more than edgy and with good cause.

The chest freezer hums in the corner. I lift the lid and select a bag of human blood, labelled 'Property of the NHS'. It has been a while since I've felt hungry enough to drink this szar, but I'm starving again and I don't think Tia will be willing to oblige.

On leaving, I toy with the idea of locking the door behind me, but don't. Instead, pulling the key out of the lock, I tuck it just under the edge of the Chinese rug beneath my feet. I climb the stairs until I reach street level and look into the drawing room to see Tia reclining on my leather sofa. The creature has taken the liberty of lighting the fire and removing her boots, scarf, the filthy old raincoat and a pair of black-lensed John Lennon glasses. They are the same clothes I remember it wearing on our first encounter under the Church of St John the Evangelist. She had the entire rancid outfit stowed in one of the upper chambers, only to throw it back on before we left Betty's torture vault and now, the odoriferous items are draped over my reading chair. The *thing* seems to take the ensemble with her everywhere she goes.

Her extraordinarily ugly feet knead the arm of my sofa, the sharp nails on her elongated toes leaving scores across the leather, much like a cat when it's getting comfy. I would swear it's purring. I really find the creature more than a little repulsive, but who am I to judge. I stand for a moment in the doorway watching, knowing that she is aware of me, but feels no need to acknowledge my presence. I break the silence: 'I'll be down shortly,' and head for the stairs. I need a shower.

On my way to the grand, carved wooden staircase that leads to the upper floors, I pass my study and I can't help but duck in for a quick look at my computer. It's a mistake – the computer screen is flashing. I have mail – I'm tempted to ignore it.

Sitting down, I let out a resigned sigh. Now what?

CHAPTER THIRTEEN

'Misery acquaints a man with strange bed-fellows.'
                                        Shakespeare

When I eventually get back to the drawing room Tia is asleep and I take the opportunity to have a closer look. Now that I've downed a couple of glasses of Sullivan's Cove single malt, I'm feeling princely and a little more generous of spirit. The little Tasmanian distillery only made 516 bottles from barrel HH0525 and I got fifty of them – should have ordered more.

It's really hit the spot and taken the sharp edge off my mood. I fall to studying Tia with a little more compassion. She is extraordinarily hideous ... and yet, somehow she possesses an almost heartbreaking beauty. Nature's alchemy has created a form that although alien, exerts the attraction of efficiency. Beneath her grey skin, all the way from her head to her feet, is a bone structure, both strong and symmetrical, the ghastliness of her hollowed-out cheek created by extremely high, chiselled zygomatic bones. She is striking me quite differently to my memory of her at the church and I realise, when she is awake, she cloaks herself in a glamour of grotesquery, part of her natural defence strategy, I assume. Asleep, I can see the chameleon beneath and, certainly to human eyes, she would be terrifying even in repose. But to me, she suddenly appears quite magnificent.

She has large ears and eyes; I take from that she must have very keen senses. Her fingers and toes are tipped with retractable, black, curving talons, the underside of which appear to be serrated and razor sharp – perfect for catching and holding prey. I can tell her yellow, almost orange, eyes have evolved specifically for night hunting. For a moment, in my mind's eye, I can picture her diving from the roof of a tall building, catching air currents under those glorious wings that allow her to almost silently swoop down to street level, and snatch up an unsuspecting quarry.

The memory of those wings fully extended in Betty's cavern prompts me to lean in for a closer look. Her species has developed two sets of arms, one set connecting to the side of her torso at the shoulder socket are human in position and appearance. The second set seems to have developed from enlarged scapula bones on her back and are connected to her shoulder blades by a network of tendons and powerful musculature. This second set of arms has evolved into wings. The bone structure of the wings appears to basically be the same in overall content as her first set of 'human' arms. I can identify the humerus, ulna and radius and they are much the same in dimension and physiology as regular arms, while the carpals, metacarpals and phalanges have stretched and hollowed to form a pair of enlarged, elongated hands that form a skeletal fan of strong, but lightweight bones that, when extended, stretch down beyond her feet. I can trace these arm and hand bones beneath a flexible membrane of skin that has the texture and appearance of grey 'leather look' stretch silk.

I notice that the thin, tough wing membranes connect to her torso from under the scapula and run down the sides of her back continuing almost the full length of the femur before stopping.

Her large eyelids are edged with a spray of wiry lashes and it isn't the top lid that has stretched down to cover the eyeball, but the lower lid that has closed up in sleep, like a Raptor. I see she has extraordinarily high, arched brows that, like her lashes, are a dark grey/green colour that I hadn't notice until now. Through her pale grey, opaque skin I can see a tracery of blood vessels and veins as though I'm looking at a piece of body art by Gunther von Hagens, but otherwise her body could be that of a human female Olympian – all long muscle and sinew. There is a pale, silvery scar on her left breast, where my hand almost tore her heart out under St John's Church. She has accelerated regeneration - something to keep in mind. I stand back and surprise myself by murmuring 'Exquisite!' under my breath. I am experiencing more surprises tonight than I've had in the last fifty years. I let myself drop into my favourite armchair and become absorbed in observing the patterns formed by the sparking embers.

I can hear Angel, her steady shallow breath and slow heartbeat reaching my ears all the way from the basement. She is really here, in my house – another chance to get it right. Where Angel is concerned, I will adopt a different strategy than I have in the past. Steady Eddy – that will be the new me. This time we may have millennia to get to know each other, and, no longer driven by the fear of wasting precious time, I can be patient. There will be no need to risk overwhelming her with information. My chances of making it work are so much better this time around, especially if the transformation goes well. We'll have common ground.

How can I disgust her, and why would she judge me if she is just like me, driven by the same needs, constrained by the same weakness and imperative? She will still be part human, I assume. I can't believe one little transfusion of my blood could completely alter her basic physiology, but something powerful is happening. She is still alive, after all.

'Penny for your thoughts ...'

I look up to see Tia has opened her eyes, and is looking at me quizzically. There is no mistaking that she certainly doesn't hold me in awe: in fact I detect a touch of good humoured contempt.

'Well I'll be jiggered, look at you, you've got your eye back. You look all shiny, good as new in fact.' She shifts on the couch until she can rest on her side ... the better to see me.

'Yes well, over the course of the last couple of nights events have given me a bit of a shake-up. I'm awake and firing on all cylinders, you could say.'

'What do you mean, you're awake? Haven't you been awake? You looked awake the first time I saw you.'

I shrug and roll my eyes. 'It's difficult to explain. I've been running on low battery, you know, like an energy saver switch, just ticking over, but now I'm not. As you can see, the engine's revved up. It's a bit uncomfortable to tell you the truth.'

She rolls onto her back and contemplates the ceiling for a moment. She is thinking; I can see the cogs turning. She is going to prove a tricky customer, I just know it.

'Do we have a plan?'

'What plan can there be? I have no idea where Ezserebet is. Tomorrow night I'll go back to the dungeon and try to pick up a trail. What more can I do?'

Tia repositioned and rolled on to her side again, curling into a ball and fixing me with those yellow eyes.

Now that she is awake, there is no doubting that she wilfully makes herself as unattractive as possible. The change in my perception of her is startling. If the ability to perform that trick has evolved as a defensive weapon, it works. She is suddenly unnervingly repulsive, similar to a skunk spraying stink from its anal glands. You just want to put as much distance between yourself and the odious creature as possible. I can't imagine how she would affect a human.

'I wasn't asking how *we* find the female vampyr, I was asking if you have a plan for when *she* finds *us*? After all, here we sit, with your human in the basement, like a tasty goat tied to a stake.'

Tia has a point: Betty knows where I live. I don't want to speculate how many times over the years, unbeknownst to me, thick-skinned moron that I have allowed myself to become, she has paid me clandestine visits. She has watched me, learned my routines and my secrets, gained entry to my sanctuary and all without leaving the smallest trace. Tonight she has been wounded physically but I suspect her pride will bleed more profusely than her body and be slower to heal. Will she slink off to lick her wounds for a few years? Perhaps. That has been her pattern. Perhaps not. My guess is not. Betty doesn't like to lose, but she hates surprises even more, and Tia had certainly been a big surprise.

'Are you nocturnal, Tia?'

She smiles and stretches out. 'Not by necessity. Unlike you Vampyr, I'm no slave to the night, I can function during the day. The simple option would be for us to hole up here and just wait you know. She doesn't strike me as the patient sort. She'll be back soon.'

She is right of course, but if I can help it, I don't want Betty close to Angel again, and there is something else –

there has been a development and I decide this is as good a time to share it as any.

'There was an email for me when we arrived back. It was waiting on my computer.'

Her eyes flick back to my face with an intensity I'm coming to recognise as part of her species' response to anything which strikes them as interesting and perhaps dangerous.

'You've taken your time mentioning it. Was it important?'

'Really I'd say it's more just a little mysterious, coming out of the blue the way it has. Although, perhaps not entirely out of the blue, but the timing still seems suspicious. The vampire that sent it would be the last ally Betty could make. I've been considering how to handle it.' I move through to my office and return with my laptop. 'Here, see for yourself.'

Tia looks at the screen and back to me. Her furrowed brow suggests she is weighing me up. I don't blame her. She reads the email aloud:

'Sender: Triton

'Topic: in town, midnight

'Message: Pontoon C, East Dock, St Katherine Docks – off East Smithfield Road, Canary Wharf.'

'So, who's Triton?' Tia is sitting up now, the computer on her knees. She has fully woken up from her power nap and is wondering what she's gotten herself into. I know the feeling.

'Not who... what. Triton is a boat, a sail boat. The message, I assume, was sent by a vampire by the name of Marcos. We have known each other for a long time, friends of a sort – at least we're not enemies. We're kinsmen, distantly ... I would have always assumed he was dependable.'

It feels strange to be sharing vampire information with someone, something, else, but I'm on a ride so I've decided to just hang on and see where it takes me.

'But you aren't assuming that now?' Tia's nails are tapping computer keys. She is looking through email history, but she won't be able to access much other than what I've chosen to show her.

'The timing seems a little weird. All this and then a blast from the past. I don't know what to think really. I've been going over it – it could be a coincidence. This particular vampire, Marcos, really has more reason to genuinely hate Ezserebet Bathory than I do. She annihilated his entire family, a whole multi-generational dynasty. She sailed with them for a few years and then the next thing I heard through the grapevine was that the entire Atl Clan were gone. Marcos alone escaped. Some years later I heard from Marcos. He'd recovered, refitted one of the Atl Clan ships, and was again at sea. His were a tribe of vampire pirates.' I shoot a quick look for Tia's reaction. I know this last piece of information will get one.

The corners of her mouth turn up. I shrug, knowing it sounds amusing if not ludicrous. 'Don't think Pirates of the Caribbean, think more along the lines of seafaring, bloodthirsty marauders, raiders, armed robbers, ruthless plunderers.' There is no merit in labouring the point, she'll just have to take my word that vampiric pirates are no joke.

'The Atl Clan claim they originated from the same area in Mexico as the first Aztecs, the most ancient race of the Teotihuacan, and that they can trace their ancestry all the way back to Chicomoztoc, or 'The Place of the Seven Caves'. According to the Atl, Chicomoztoc was the birthplace and sacred dwelling pits of the first vampires to walk the Earth. I don't agree with that part, but that's what they believe.

'They continued to worship the Gods of the Night, Chalchiuhtlicue: Goddess of the Sea, and Mictlantecuhtli: Ruler of the Underworld, right to the end, which of course required copious blood sacrifices and offerings. The favourite method of sacrifice for my South American cousins, predictably, entailed ripping out the still beating hearts of said offerings. They remained steadfast traditionalists in the field of maiming and murder, and were known for being tiresome stick in the muds when it came to religion. Having said that, they eagerly embraced any new technology that could help them dominate the seas and their 21st century criminal empire was cutting edge and *hi tech*.

'They conducted multimillion dollar deals – arms, drugs and stolen antiquities, using cyber financial vehicles, shell companies and international conglomerates that could hide, launder and make the money respectable. In the human world they became reputable, if mysterious, tycoons. Their perennial youth prompted the assumption that they were heirs to some successful, long dead captain of industry's fortune, or technology whizz kids. Under a veneer of modernity, they remained pagan warriors that paid tribute to their Gods in the currency of human suffering and blood ... well, any blood really ... occasionally even vampiric. I will guarantee that Marcos still practises the ancient blood rites.

'The entire Vampire Nation turned a blind eye to some of their more dubious practices. My own Order of the Dragon left them be. We believe in freedom of worship, as long as you're discreet and anyway they weren't the type of vampires that got fucked with, that is, until they made the mistake of taking up with Betty. I'm just filling in the gaps for you, for the sake of our 'entente cordiale'. Just so you know, it would be wise to be careful with Marcos and not assume he's the complete ninny he appears. I'm sure he'll still be whining and playing the victim but the Atl weren't a blameless band of swashbuckling, Errol Flynn type buccaneers that fell the hapless victims of a ruthless psychopath, ergo Betty. It was more a case of ruthless blood-hungry, psychotic vampiress finds a home among the like-minded, and if you lie down with dogs … yada yada.'

'So how do you know this Marcos? You said he was a friend.'

Tia had her back to me as she spoke. She stood at the casement window, looking out through the leaded panes into the darkness toward the central gardens, but she was paying close attention. She wanted to know details of my species' 'soap opera' as much as I would like to know about hers. I was hoping for reciprocity of information at some point.

'Those born of the Atl appeared, to a young restless vampire, to have a satisfying sort of life. That's how it seemed from the outside anyway. I first met Marcos in Pacific Polynesia and he took me home to meet the family. The Atl lived by their own set of rules, a code of sorts with a distinct way of life. Not a way of life for the faint-hearted but a life of high-stakes risk, adventure and excitement. I'd hit a rocky patch, been wallowing in a long, dark night of the soul and needed to remember how much I could enjoy living.'

'You seem to do that a lot.'

Tia still stood facing the street and garden; I couldn't see her face. She'd murmured the words more to herself than me. She really is a ball breaker.

'Well, anyway, their culture certainly appealed and even seemed romantic to this land-lubber. So I took up with them for a short while and I'll admit it blew my hair back. The novelty didn't take long to wear thin though. The excitement always seemed to involve a lot of unnecessary cruelty, which wasn't for me. I can see how it would have appealed to Betty though.

'I don't know what happened to precipitate the massacre. No one does. No one survived to tell and the way Marcos related the story, even he is pretty much in the dark.

'Marcos awoke later than usual that night; perhaps he'd been drugged. His ship had been holed and was taking water fast. The decks were deserted and covered in blood, the latter only unusual in that it was the black oily blood of vampires. He survived the open ocean – the Atl are nothing if not resourceful, but from what he's shared, and reading between the lines, it wasn't easy. I didn't hear from him for some years after the massacre. I think it took a toll, physically and mentally. He went to ground, literally, for some years. I've heard he was burnt badly, down to the bone in fact, by the sun. That's a pretty traumatic experience for one of my kind. I don't know all the details. Suffice to say, he's one hard son of a bitch to put down.'

'Sounds a bit fishy!'

Tia snorts with laughter. She looks very pleased with her little joke, and I have to admit, in part, I agree. Perhaps that's why I have kept a little distance from Marcos over the years since. It's easy to let logistics take care of disengaging from an old cohort when that cohort is a pirate. They tend to be on the water a great deal, and I don't. Now he turns up like a bad penny just when the shit is hitting the fan and Betty's the one flinging it. The issue of piscine timing niggles.

'Yes, well, as you say, a bit fishy and it remains to be decided what I do about it. Can I take the liberty of saying what I think 'we' should do?' I look across at Tia and she gives me a sceptical, lopsided grin and one of her curt nods.

'Tia, feel free to share your thoughts, but the way I see it, if it's an innocent coincidence, it could prove serendipitous. We'll have an ally, one that's quite a force to reckon with, or if, as you say, his appearance proves in some way malignant, then perhaps we have the best lead on Ezserebet we're ever going to get. How or if this ties together, I haven't a clue.' I shrug my shoulders. It really could go either way.

'It seems the decision is made. We meet this vampyr, Marcos, at the pier and see what comes of it. You say he has a good reason to hate Betty and a good reason to want revenge and suddenly he arrives. He may have been hunting her for some time and has followed the trail here. She's not made an effort to keep her presence in London inconspicuous, after all. Or perhaps he is tracking you. Or perhaps, me.' Tia pauses to let the last comment sink in. 'I will not go with you to meet him, I'll hang back – I won't say to be the wild card up your sleeve. For all we know he's already aware of me, but I can keep my distance and see how things develop.'

If I'm edgy, I can't blame Tia for becoming anxious to the point of paranoia at the mention of yet another vampire in the mix. She must be starting to feel she has stumbled into a vampire nest, and if she knows anything about us at all, she knows that is a dangerous thing to do. I know that we vamps always have hidden agendas, lots of them, and even I don't relish dealing with my own kind.

'I don't see how he could know of you, Tia, as I haven't mentioned you, that's for sure, but we'll play it your way. I've been thinking it would be best if I meet him alone anyway. What I would like is for you to stay here in case Angel wakes. Given the extent of her injuries, I shouldn't think that will happen, but the truth is I have no understanding of the process she's undergoing. The question is: Can I trust you, Tia?' Her eyes take on that intense alertness, bird-like, beady and alien. I find her impossible to read ... it's disconcerting.

'You can trust me, Eddy.' She gives the now familiar nod.

The words hang in the air. Is that a simple statement, a question or a challenge? I have to make my mind up if there is a silent question mark hovering at the end of her words. I'm paying the price for being a lone wolf and I don't have a lot of options. 'Then we're decided. I go to the pier, you stay here and wait for me to call.' I point at the house phone. 'Do you have a mobile, Tia?' She shakes her head with an amused incredulity.

'Well, I have some burners in my study. I'll give you one before I leave ... it should be good for about three days. Hopefully, there'll be no need to use it. I'll be keeping this meet short and, hopefully sweet, and will be back before you've noticed I've gone. Keep an ear out for Angel, and obviously Betty. You'll have the burner with my number on speed dial so if you need to contact me, you can.'

I walk to the far side of the drawing room and press a panel next to a bank of shelves. It opens to reveal my rack of armoury. Tia's eyes widen, and her little, secret smile returns. I'm really not sure this is a good idea. Lined up across the shelf are crossbows loaded with wooden stakes and underneath is a row of hand pistols furnished with exterior mounted barrels that hold six shots of garlic serum. 'This might help if Betty should turn up.' We look at each other. Tia approaches and reverently runs a talon-tipped finger along the rows of weaponry.

'Yes, you're quite right, Vampyr. These will be helpful should your kinswoman visit. I can't help but notice that all your weapons are for vampyr slaying and you yourself are a vampyr?' Tia's brow furrows. She genuinely looks baffled and obviously isn't as familiar with my species as she would have me believe.

'Betty is only my kinswoman in as much as all vampires are distantly related.She is just the kid who lived next door when I was growing up, so to speak. I didn't choose her as my lifelong companion, although unfortunately it's worked out that way. Childhood bonds run deep I guess. It's taken me a long time to accept Ezserebet cannot be part of my life. Unfortunately, our opinions are divided on the matter and that means a permanent goodbye is the only way she'll ever leave me in peace. I hope we're together on this. I'm not playing games with you, I've been completely straight and you are, of course, correct in your assessment of my armoury. It's all designed to kill vampires ... I don't need weapons to kill anything else on this planet. I have no challengers ... I'm top of the food chain.'

Tia's eyes harden a little. 'If you say so, Eddy. As I have said, you can trust me to do the right thing in this particular matter.'

There really isn't much more to be said.We appear to have each other's backs for the moment in an uneasy alliance and return to our respective spots in front of the fire. I sit and stare into the embers, imagining I can see fiery, little dramas playing out among the curling flames. Tia sits on the floor, as close to the hearth as she can endure without singeing her wings, and puzzles over her new burner phone and the tiny print instructions.

She is still untangling charging plugs and swearing under her breath when I gather up my coat and ready myself to head out for the docks. She doesn't make a move, just carries on tinkering with the phone. She looks comfortable but alert. She hasn't got a stitch on ... nudity is obviously her natural state. I find it a bit of a distraction, not to mention a damn imposition, but she is completely uninhibited and I will just have to go with it.

'Perhaps you could find one of the throws to perch your arse on, Tia? Just a thought. I rather like my Victorian velvet couch and that fifth-century Chinese rug you're scooting your asshole across.' She pulls her face into a grimace, both mocking and insulted. Strangely enough, I realise, as far as she is concerned, she is dressed. She covers her body in a cloak of hideousness that hides her true self as effectively as any nun's habit.

I can leave her in my home willingly and with some sort of agreement and goodwill between us, or I can throw her out only to have her break in as soon as I've left, if that is what she decides to do.

I reach the door and glance back at her. She looks up, gives me a nod and in a sardonic deadpan voice, mumbles:

'Knock 'em dead!'

I really hope it doesn't come to that. We are strange bed fellows indeed.

CHAPTER FOURTEEN

Marcos

Emerging at the entrance to Tower Hill tube station I cross East Smithfield Road and head for the Docks. There once stood a fine example of a medieval church here. St Katherine by the Tower, founded in 1147, had been a 'Royal Peculiar', meaning it had been the personal property of the Queen of England. The Queen's patronage made this little corner of London a Liberty precinct, which meant it had its own court and prison outside of the City of London's civil jurisdiction. In St Katherine's heyday, around the 1500s, it had boasted its own brewery and had a musical reputation to rival St Paul's.

The area attracted travellers from all nations, as well as seamen, rivermen, vagabonds, cut-throats, scoundrels and prostitutes. They all pressed together in long narrow lanes with names like Dark Entry, Cat's Hole, Shovel Alley, Rookery and Pillory Lane. Those alleys formed a densely populated warren of desperation, unimaginable poverty, squalor and disease, and yet there was a 'joie de vivre' about this network of rat holes on the Thames. When the Great Plague hit and decimated the human population to the north and east, St Katherine's mortality rate was less than half her richer neighbours.

By the 19th century, the Liberty of St Katherine's had become a small village, that continued to offer sanctuary to outsiders of all varieties – immigrants, the wretchedly poor, criminals, free thinkers - and the perfect hunting grounds for me. I was sad to see it demolished along with the hospital, workhouse and about 1250 hovels in the year 1825. The 11,300 souls who infested those wretched cottages were unceremoniously made homeless. Never get in the way of a clever monkey with a plan. After about two and half years of construction, the Docks came into existence and were in pretty much constant use, one way or another, right up until 1968. The swinging 60s was a party that just didn't happen for this part of old London and during the following years, the Docks were pretty much abandoned. St Katherine's wasn't making money and, apart from sex, money is the supreme driving force for the monkeys.

I look around and am struck, as always, by the jarring sight of the Tower Hotel. In about 1973, the ugliest hotel in the world, in my opinion, was built at St Katherine's and although hideous, it worked some sort of alchemic magic. This little jewel of a site on the banks of the Thames, in the shadow of Tower Bridge, was rediscovered.

I haven't been here for a while. Too much activity and the Docks' lights are far too bright for my liking, but I have to admit the marina complex is looking good in that modern, soulless, Disney World way. The area has been gentrified by yuppies from the City and is now antiseptically trendy.

I feel nostalgia for the days when this was a dangerous place to be. The most pressing worry for the young professionals who hang out here now on the esplanade that runs next to the quays and locks that offer alfresco dining, is the nagging possibility they may have been slipped some horse meat in place of organic ground beef in their overpriced gourmet burger.

During the 1700s I would regularly come here to hunt. I remember making my way down to the Docks, cutting through Black Dog Alley, emerging out on to Nightingale Lane and from there, staying in shadow all the way to Hermitage Dock. There were no police to be found in this area, and back in the day, the residents decided and dished out their own justice. The monkeys have changed the name of Nightingale Lane to Thomas More Street. It separates St Katherine's from London Dock, but I guess you just don't hear Nightingales singing down here any more.

I'm feeling exposed by all the clean lines and user-friendly streets and wish we were meeting somewhere a little more comfortable. I miss visiting this place as a hunter. Under the glare of electric lights, the air still thrums with the ghosts of the past and under my feet, I can feel a magnetic force that converts potential into kinetic energy. Standing here and letting the ether wash over me, even if I had not been alive to witness much of it, I would know this place makes 'things' happen. Kings and Queens travelling between Greenwich and Hampton Court used this landing site. The Romans claimed it and used it extensively during and after their invasion. The British tribes of the Catuvellauni, Trinovantes, Cantiaci and the Iceni chose this stretch of river to moor and establish camps from 200 BC, and long before.

Ivory House still sits in the middle of the twenty-four acre site. During Britain's Colonial heyday, 200 tons of elephant, hippopotamus and walrus tusk, as well as swordfish weapons and even fossilised mammoth tusks from Siberia, were deposited in that warehouse each year. Humans should count themselves lucky that we monsters aren't nearly so voracious and greedy, or we'd have hunted them to extinction by now.

It's typical of Marcos to moor up at St Katherine's. The Atl are, or should I say were, creatures of habit. I know it will be nostalgia that has driven him here … memories of good times, bad times and just the call of the familiar. I understand his thinking process; it's difficult for ones such as us to utterly relinquish prime territory to humans, but this location has become risky. Escape could prove difficult, perhaps impossible, from a lock-accessed marina. Marcos is a fool to be a slave to sentimentality or pride regarding this particular place. He has a short memory. He wouldn't be the first pirate to fall foul here. Just up the road at Tilbury Point on the river stood the execution docks where Captain Kidd, along with plenty of other pirates, met his end by the hangman's noose.

Pirates. The word conjures up sugar-coated movie versions of high jinks at sea. St Katherine's has created a nostalgic theme-park atmosphere around her associations with them. Tobacco Dock boasts two replica pirate ships in Wapping Lane. It's all just fun now, and every child wants to be Jack Sparrow. I wonder if, two hundred years from now, monkeys will read bedtime stories to their little monklets about twenty-first century street gangs. Their similarity to the pirate crews I remember are striking. As I recall, unpleasant though it may be, Blackbeard, who had at least thirteen wives, regularly encouraged his crew to ravage his current young bride. Becoming part of a pirate crew, like joining a modern day street gang, required the 'initiate' to demonstrate submission and obedience by carrying out some heinous act of tribute. Usually involving beatings, violence, sexual assault or murder. Under the captaincy of a minor drug lord, come pimp, grifter and thief, they served in fear and shame. How the passing of time can romanticise the truth.

The permanent execution gallows for pirates stood in roughly the same spot that is now occupied by the Captain Kidd pub. It's a jolly establishment, and has a lingering whiff of bleach about the conveniences, certainly not to my taste. Kidd was hung on the 23rd of May 1701. The rope snapped the first time, leaving him dazed, half choked, and still begging for mercy. The second attempt was successful. After hanging, as with all pirate executions, his lifeless body was chained to a post on the foreshore at Tilbury Point. The humans also used Cuckold's Point or Blackwall Point for these public displays. Usually the corpse was left out in the sun until it had been submerged by three tides, but in the case of Captain Kidd, his body was left to hang for more than two years. This practice of encasing the body in a strong metal cage and hanging it from a gallows so the sun could thoroughly do its work was known as gibbeting and thankfully was abolished in 1834.

I'm all in favour of progress and the stamping out of such superstitious 'nonsense', but then, I have an axe to grind. The fact is, in the heart of man resides a lingering suspicion that 'there are more things in heaven and earth, Horatio, than are dreamt of in your philosophy'. Human sailors had good reason to want proof that a pirate was dead and rotting. Marcos would be wise not to kick a sleeping dog.

He must have brought his boat up the Thames from the east where there are no bridges. Taking that route a masted yacht like the Triton can navigate its way right up the river and moor just a stone's throw from beautiful Tower Bridge. She is one of my favourite bridges, a colourful fairy tale, spanning the Thames like a stick of Brighton rock.

I jump the sorry excuse for a security fence and enter the Centre Basin. It's easy to identify the correct boat. I take a little time to watch the activity aboard the matt black, 55 foot yacht, moored up against Pontoon C, just as Marcos had said she would be. I hang back, stay close to the buildings that surround the pontoons and keep to the shadows. In my mind's eye I can see the boat slipping into its mooring ... just a touch of bow thrust and reverse throttle, churning up the murky water and stopping, then smoothly easing into position to nestle against the dock. He's been here a little while. Days, perhaps weeks. A human would call it imagination, or creative visualisation, but for my kind these mind pictures are just another of our survival tools. We have retained the ability to pick up on subtle changes to the environment and energy patterns. Vampire senses gather up all the remnants of an event and then our brain plays it back like a home movie running just behind our eyes.

Most predators have some form of the gift. Humans had it before they dulled their senses with domesticity. Humans call the last vestiges of the sixth sense intuition, clairvoyance and a whole number of other mumbo jumbo names – I call it sensitivity. Disruption of atomic particles remain after any action, and my kind are still sensitive enough to tune into these distortions much as an observant human trapper can follow spoor. Traces of disruption to the ether dissipate, usually after just a day or so, sometimes a week.

Vampires pick up patterns of minor disruption to the status quo, vestiges of activity at the subatomic level and sometimes these can last longer than days or weeks. If something very powerful and inharmonious to the balance of energy has occurred such as extreme violence, a murder or some massive destructive force has been unleashed, the traces can linger much longer. But without doubt, the most lasting wound to the ether is cut by high human emotion. The monkeys, when exposed to traumatic external stimuli are capable, through the activity of uncontrolled ionic current flows within the neurons of their brain, to produce neural oscillations forceful enough to stamp a deep footprint in the fabric of time. This leaves a scar that can be clearly read … sometimes, for centuries.

The mind pictures continue to play behind my eyes. A healthy, agile, human female steered the boat expertly into the dock during daylight. She jumped onto the wooden pontoon and wound a Hawser expertly around one of the dock cleats. A middle-aged human male, presumably one of the marina office staff, had been waiting on the pontoon for Triton's arrival. The girl threw him a rope and he tied the second hawser, cracked a joke and tried to engage her in conversation. Questions: Was she alone? How was she managing the big yacht solo? She had been polite but cold and unforthcoming. Eventually, a little confused, the marina worker got the message and wandered away. I shook my head to clear some other unrelated images of carnage that clung to the vessel's sleek carbon fibre hull. I noticed movement on deck, took a deep breath and focused back on the now.

The woman I'd seen in my mind's eye was standing on the pontoon in front of me. She had stepped off the boat to look around. She's very alert … obviously been told to expect company tonight. Sadly for her, but luckily for me, humans have such poor night vision; even with all the electric lights blazing she can't see me in the shadows. Human eyes have evolved to detect movement. My species, their natural predator, has consequently evolved a preternatural stillness. Even if I wasn't cloaked in shadow, most human eyes wouldn't immediately register my presence.

The pontoons are surrounded on all four sides by restaurants, offices and luxurious, new apartments. Two sides are new builds, very tasteful, and on the other two sides are old warehouse buildings, some of which have been converted into luxury living spaces for yuppies and Russian gangsters.

The Docks feel a little too claustrophobic to suit a pirate. The fact that exit can only be achieved through a lock gate that is closed at this moment makes it a crazy situation. The boat exudes the beauty of a thing well made and looks as though she's swallowed time and money like a hole in the ocean, but Marcos is obviously prepared to temporarily relinquish her if things go bad. He'll be fine at a pinch. A footloose vampire can always find an escape option, the least of which being a quick dive into the diesel-streaked water to freedom. I just hope he knows I don't welcome house guests.

From where I stand against the wall of the docks, Tower Bridge is obscured by the Dickens Inn, but I can still see clearly across the esplanade to Ivory House. There is nothing suspicious.

From a hatch emerges a figure I know and he stands on the teak decking while casually scanning the surrounding area at a full 360 degrees. Only another of his kind would be aware that he has taken note of everything that moves or breathes within 50 yards of his boat.

Marcos and I first got to know each other in the 1500s when we crossed paths in Pacific Polynesia. Vampires go where the pickings are rich and easy and Tonga was in the throes of a bloody civil war. The Tongan Tu'i Tonga empire that had dominated Samoa, Tonga and Fiji from Nauru in the Northwest to Niue in the East had been shaken by a Samoan revolt, triggered by the sudden rise of the Malietoa dynasty. The Tongans fought back and there followed unsettled, bloody times that continued into the 16th century until the Tongan Tu'i Kanokupolou dynasty wrested power back and went on to rule for two hundred years in relative peace.

Marcos and I met in the turbulent period when the disappearance of Pacific warriors was unremarkable and even leaving their eviscerated bodies in the sand didn't raise a hair. I had travelled to Polynesia during one of my many attempts to shake off my bat shit, crazy cousin Ezserebet and had, I'm ashamed to admit, been indulging in a kamikaze-type feeding frenzy from which I hadn't expected to emerge with my life. I'd been marooned on the 'friendly' islands by the crew of a Dutch exploration ship who had taken it into their superstitious heads that the boxes of scientific earth samples in the ship's hold, one of which was my bed, were the cause of the run of bad luck and pestilence the ship had been suffering and needed to be jettisoned.

Marcos found me on the island of Eua and offered me a way out. At the time I was despairing and dissolute, grubbing about during darkness in the interior rainforest, and spending my days deep in the cave networks of Eua's raised reef.

The whole idea of sea travel has always been difficult for me ... a boat feels like a trap, a dead end, but for Marcos, a boat will always represent freedom.

He told me that he'd been born to a long line of pirate vampires – the Atl Clan, and believed he could trace his ancestry back to the creatures that inspired the Incan civilisation. His dark, smooth skin and the high, flat cheekbones suggested this could be possible. Memories of my time with the Atl seem ludicrously archaic now –maritime hijackings, kidnappings and ransom, extortion, black-marketeering and smuggling. Interminable ocean passages terminating when we would make land fall, at as yet unchartered exotic lands, ripe for pillage and butchery. There we would sojourn and indulge in hedonistic excess until, sated and bored, we would return to the black ships and freedom. In the days before technology illuminated every corner of the globe, the Atl were the jet set … their lifestyle seemed very rock'n'roll.

To Marcos, another vessel on the horizon represented, and still does, a travelling larder, full of fresh blood, perhaps gold and tradable goods – a vulnerable catch waiting to be caught. The Atl tribe lived and thrived by doing just that, for centuries. They always tried to eliminate witnesses, but of course, over the centuries there had been slip ups and the legend of phantom pirate ships had emerged and spread among seafaring humans.

Human mariners were deeply supersistious and held an unshakeable belief in the goulish tales of ruin. To sight the dreaded black flag bearing the Aztec Miquizli, promised certain, mysterious doom. The Aztec Miquizli – a human skull stripped of living flesh, is an archetypal image, a universal symbol of death encoded deep in the human collective consciousness. The skull on the Atl flag left no doubt as to the intentions of the crew sailing the black 'death ship'. The sudden, unequivocal challenge to mortal combat alone often served to create a disorienting panic in their victims.

During the darkest nights, with the waning of the moon, the black ship would materialise on the horizon, as though birthed from the inky ocean. The vampire ship would appear to rise out of the moonless waters within range of a musket shot and close fast on its target. The cry would ring out: "God save our souls, it's Old Roger, God help us all." In the idiom of the day, Old Roger was the name of the Devil and the sailors feared it was Satan himself coming for them out of the fog. I couldn't fault them for making that mistake because my time spent sailing with Marcos had certainly convinced me that should the Devil exist, he could not be more inventive and wicked in the art of torment and torture than the Atl.

The vampire pirate race have always made their intentions clear, something I find to be both cruel and perverse. It is a point of monstrous honour among them that the whole ritual of seizing, pillaging and destroying a ship from start to grisly end should be the ultimate denouement of life, spirit and hope. The process has to unravel slowly and horribly ... purposefully, like a relentless nightmare, the kind from which you can neither escape nor wake, and which seems to last for years

Of course, the cleaver monkeys took up the idea of maritime thievery with gusto. There were many human pirate ships preying on their own species by the 1600s.

To borrow from the terror and dread the Atl Miquizli flag excited, human buccaneers were inspired to adopt the Jolly Roger for themselves, with the addition of two crossed humeri. The whole world soon came to recognise the symbol of skull and cross bones on black as the pirate ensign. The monkeys had stolen the Atl emblem and with it their identity. Nevertheless, among the human pirates persisted a belief in the existence of the ungodly originals, and they would have a tattoo of a violin needled into their skin, in the hope they would be sent to Fiddler's Green rather than Davy Jones' Locker should the Atl find them and take revenge on their wicked souls. The horrors that human pretenders have inflicted and continue to inflict to this day on their victims in the name of piracy, and they are many, will never equal those of the originals.

Marcos moves to the mast and lowers a small flag - a plain, black oblong - that looks like an Ad Reinhardt knock-off trendy corporate logo, but my eyes can make out the tiny, black on black, Miquizli in the top left corner. He stands for a while as if in casual reverie; from his vantage point he can check out the entire wharf. He is fully aware of my presence, and, satisfied at last that all is clear, he makes the smallest beckoning gesture with his hand and I emerge from the shadows.

On my approach I can see Marcos is well fed as always. He is conceited and understandably so. Over feeding softens the hard planes of his face and serves to take some edge off his high Andean cheekbones. He looks like an American, private school, trust-fund man/child, untempered by life's cruel furnace. Hard to gauge his years… could be early thirties or pass for late teens. My little trip down memory lane is to remind myself of the true nature of the creature that lurks beneath the polish. His black curly hair, which hangs casually around his chiselled face is so shiny, it appears wet. Black, heavy brows frame piercing eyes of aqua green. Marcos' eyes appear to have been infused with the colour of the ocean and I can almost see the luminescent waters of the Philippines, studded with small lush islands of green.

When I first met Marocs, other than in paintings, I had never seen the sea in daylight; water is always black by moonlight. Long before colour photography, Marcos' eyes had shown me how the ocean can appear when illuminated by the sun. His eyes create a fascinating magic against his brown skin much as does phosphorescence on the dark sea. His skin is very smooth, pale cocoa, and he moves with the easy grace of a young surfer. He evokes a fantasy landscape of pristine, untouched beaches on idyllic secret islands, except that the images are no fantasy - they once existed. When we sailed together I visited those places and felt the sun's residual heat warm my bare feet as we walked across untouched, sandy shorelines. Those islands still exist, trammelled by tourists, waterways polluted and littered with plastic and trash.

Marcos wears traditional Atl jewellery, one twenty-four carat gold sleeper-style earring, which catches the yellow light of the Dock's lamps. He hasn't changed a bit and stands before me wearing a fitted, black Henley-style T-shirt over 'Seven for all Mankind' jeans, 'Sebago' boat shoes and a gold, submarina Rolex watch. The earring looks completely contemporary; everything that goes around comes around.

'How many on board?' I ask as I approach, but I already know the answer.

'Just the two of us,' he replies with a nod to the woman who is checking the mooring lines.

'That's a lot of boat for just two.' I am in no mood for more surprises tonight.

Marcos smiles. 'I helm nights, she helms days ... easy peasy. Haven't you heard of autopilot, Eddy? Wake up and smell the coffee.'

I can still understand why I had initially liked Marcos. It's his easy grace, but I've subsequently learned it pays to keep your guard up when dealing with buccaneers – once a pirate, always a pirate. The Atl have a moral, or more accurately, an ethical code which I could never completely decipher. It appears to be simple: strongest takes all and weakest deals with it. I know there is more to it than that; I'm missing something and my inability to fully understand explains my incapacity to predict Atl behaviour, and that makes me nervous.

I take the opportunity to have a proper look at his travel companion, who is an exceptionally lovely monkey. Her hair, clearly once light brown, is sun bleached with red and gold. Her skin seems to radiate solar heat, and her features are Caucasian, but there is something else in the mix that has given her skin the ability to turn the colour of caramel. Her full lips should hold a man's attention but they can't compete with the magnetism of her eyes – the iris is almost orange, the colour of burnished copper. Everything about her makes me think of burnt sugar. I wonder if that is how she would taste.

She acknowledges my scrutiny with a nod of greeting, jumps back aboard and disappears below deck.

'What's your pet's name?' I ask, turning back to Marcos. He looks at me quizzically before replying:

'Emergency Rations.'

There is a pause before he lets out what can only be described as an 'ahoy me hearties' laugh. I shake my head. It's funny, but only because I know for Marcos it's true.

'Her name is Thalassa. She's a fully certified Yachtmaster, qualified diesel mechanic and a fine athlete. She is a creature of the islands and the sea, Eddy. What do you think?' He gives me a self-satisfied grin.

'I think you're one lucky son of a bitch Marcos, you always were. You must make a very handsome couple. I've come to think of you as the organ grinder of the sea - incomplete without a monkey. It must have taken some time to find such an accomplished familiar. How would you feel if one of your own were to eat her?'

Marcos takes an almost imperceptible step backwards, not a retreat, only an adjustment of balance. He's completely grounded yet flexible. I see a flash of knife blade in his right hand. The fashion for jeans that hang almost off your hips certainly allows room for concealed weapons.

'Not me,' I hasten to add, 'not me, although I'm flattered you feel the need of a knife to deal with that possibility. I always thought you believed you could take me ... no problem. No, I'm not one to cross lines without a good reason, but speaking of reasons, I am wondering what brings you to London after all this time?' Our eyes lock. This part is never easy with vampires – we tend to become very English at moments like this. We're terribly uncomfortable with hellos and goodbyes, that are always so full of hidden agendas and danger.

Unlike the English, the root of a vampire's discomfiture is not derived from inadvertently revealing our true feelings, possible impoliteness, rudeness or, God forbid, passion. Our unease is that of a lone hunter, our nature demanding virgin territory. Hellos and goodbyes between vampires always teeter on the edge of deep and murky emotions surrounding the transgressive urge to vampicide.

'I take this to be your way of greeting and welcoming me to London. Hello to you too, Eddy. You look well, if a little bedevilled and beset. How have you been doing, old friend? Is it not good to see the familiar face of a comrade after so long? It feels good to me Eddy. I have missed you, my old shipmate, but I am surprised you want to greet me with an insult after so long an absence.'

Marcos shoots me an ingratiating smile but his eyes have hardened.

'OK, that said, I can see you're all business tonight so let's get right to it. I'm here because about six weeks ago,

I received the first of a number of emails. I can't trace the sender and have no idea who they're from, other than they were generated here in London. London has become the 'go to' city for over seventy per cent of the world's mongrel vampire population; that holds no fealty or allegiance to any of the three Great Houses. Did you know that, Eddy? You have set up home in a veritable snake pit.'

I shrug. 'Be it ever so humble …'

After a pause Marcos continues, 'The origin of the communications could be anyone. The motivation of the sender, unclear. The messages were cryptic at first: "I have information you may find valuable" … blah blah. I was more interested in finding the bilge rat that had got hold of my email address and seemed to know what I am, but then the information became more specific – dates, times, places. In the end, I felt I had to follow up, and here I am.'

Marcos and I continue with the macho eye lock. He is trying to read me and I am wondering what he can see because I'm not picking up anything from him – subterfuge, truth, nerves … nothing. He is completely stonewalling me. That's a new talent he's developed, and I hope I'm returning the favour. Maybe he thinks I've been sending the emails. I am one of the few vampires that know how to contact him. The problem with interpersonal relationships between us vamps is we are just so twisty. We're complicated … we have baggage. A few hundred years of experience does that to you.

'And these emails you've received, Marcos, they contain information, times, places for what?' Marcos heads toward the hatch and beckons me to follow. I look around the Docks and can feel no other presence. No point in getting cold feet now. I am here for information.

Below decks, the saloon is surprisingly luxurious in a polished hardwood, shiny brass sort of way. The boat has obviously undergone an expensive refit and the exterior has had a modern minimalist facelift, but below decks, care has been taken to preserve its original atmosphere. The galley sits to one end of the main cabin and has been modernised and upgraded; I can detect the hum of gadgetry. I assume by the cutting edge, wind-driven generators and solar panels I noticed above decks that somewhere in this vessel is an impressive freezer full of human blood. Marcos sits at the chart table and fires up his computer. He stands and waves for me to take his seat in front of the screen. The emails pop up. No sender ID. Messages at first cryptic and teasing. I agree with Marcos … Sprat to catch a Mackerel nonsense … to be ignored. Then they change. The first of these reads: 'EB in London'.

I glance up at Marcos. He shrugs. 'Yep, that one caught my attention too.'

I continue to read, short, succinct, increasingly specific. 'EB outside HD's house CG'. Holy macaroni, that one unnerved me. What the hell is going on? Someone or something has witnessed Ezserebet Bathory, ancient vampiress, as she stood, silent as the grave, in Cadogan Gardens and watched the house of equally ancient vampire Herronimus De Vere. This has to be resolved, I have to claw back some sense of control and confidence because as it stands, I want to cut my losses and run. I'm further out of my depth than I realised and I'm going to take a leap of faith with Marcos, I have no choice.

'Ezserebet is in London. I believe she has eaten my pet and recently abducted me and attempted to subject me to what I assume was planned to be a prolonged, sado-erotic, torture session. Gratefully that was cut short.

Nevertheless, she is here in London, not yet satisfied and mad as a butcher's dog.'

Marcos visibly blanches under the wind-burnt skin. He still has a slight tan from the daylight burnings he sustained during his last escape from EB. He looks through a porthole and gives the wharf another sweep with his pirate eyes. 'Arrr!'

'Mmmm, my thoughts exactly. Might this be the time to try for a permanent resolution to that problem?'

We head back up on deck together, both of us suddenly unwilling to be in such a confined space.

Looking down into the black waters of the Thames, Marcos shakes his head. 'I've thought of you many times, Eddy. The years slip away and before you know it, fifty, a hundred have passed, but I have often considered dropping in on you. Maybe we'd grab a bite together … reminisce. Now this.' He makes a sweeping gesture toward the cabin and the computer. 'I came to London because you stubbornly and wantonly ignored my emails. You put me in a position where I either held my hands up and said, it's not my problem, or I physically came to your home turf to give you the heads up, Eddy. I'd heard rumours you were already halfway to full hibernation … shuffling around London like a zombie in your filthy old army coat … an easy target. I was concerned for you, old friend. Now I'm involved in a 'thing' between you and Ezserebet. Tonight, you want me to help you kill her, but tomorrow night I'll discover you're still schtupping her.'

I shake my head and start to protest but Marcos holds up his hand.

'I know how it is with the two of you, Eddy. I know you are obsessed. Why do you think we can no longer truly be friends? Your loyalty and motivation where she is concerned will always be divided. You're compromised. I find myself wanting to protect you, but it seems the games have already begun. If she really wanted you dead and if you really wanted her dead, it seems you've both already had the opportunity. I can't believe I've allowed myself, through some misplaced sense of duty, to be pulled into this bullshit again. Sink me! Eddy, I could kill you myself!'

Leaning back, he shouts towards the hatch, 'Thala! Smartly now, get ready we're departing.'

Thalassa's head emerges from the master berth. She looks sleepy and confused. Marcos barks again, 'We're weighing anchor, now!'

Her hands start rubbing her coppery hair. 'The lock is only open at 12.15 and 15.45 hours Marcos. We can't leave. I told you when we entered the Docks, every night we choose to stay we are here until noon the next day whether we like it or not.' She looks exasperated and distressed, torn between obedience and the impossibility of obeying Marcos' direct order.

I catch her eye and command her in my vampire voice. It isn't easy; there is some resistance. I sense she must be a handful. 'No, no, go back to bed. Marcos is joking.' She looks at me doubtfully. 'Go on, back to your bed my dear. Be calm. Sleep.' Reluctantly, she begins to retreat.

'Don't you fucking dare commandeer my human, Eddy, you arrogant picaroon. What the hell are you thinking? I'm a sitting duck here. Ezserebet isn't in the grip of a sexual obsession with me, as you seem to believe she is with you!'

Marcos' eyes roll upward and then flicker to the left and right very quickly. It's as though fury has resulted in apoplexy and he's actually exhibiting a momentary bout of Nystagmus. I've heard the expression 'apoplectic with rage' but I've never seen such a strange reaction, but then he is a savage at heart.

'Calm yourself, Marcos, you're going to blow a gasket. Your 'mincers' are dancing.'

'I'm just a loose end she has yet to tie off, unlike you, Eddy. If Betty ever decides to torture me to death, she'll follow through.'

I look around and decide for a gatecrasher, he's protesting way too much, and much too late. He wasn't invited to this party, not by me anyway.

'This is a bit of a bottleneck to squeeze your ship into if you are really in the mood to run. This venue makes it hard to escape from Betty or anything else. You don't look like you're in the mood to scarper, Marcos. You look like you've been nursing the need for vengeance in your breast far too long. The poison's beginning to seep into your system. It will cause you damage, old friend. You want and need action. Did you hear they arrested a Lithuanian pirate here just last year?'

Marcos looks at me as if I've gone mad. I'm being a little disingenuous ... The boy needs distracting.

'I'm not joking, it happened just over there in E Dock. He was commandeering some millionaire's £550,000 luxury vessel but wasn't aware of that piece of information the beautiful Thalassa keeps trying to explain to you. The lock gate only opens twice a day and he'd missed his window. He got ten months for the theft of the bottle of wine he was snorking while he tried to get the motor going. I should think you'd get a bit of a longer sentence than that if the humans got a chance to search the freezers on this ship.' I laugh, and sit down on the deck.

I just want to divert and talk him down a bit. I've laid out the situation too quickly, blurted information. The events of the last few days have left me dazed and confused, so I can't blame him for reacting defensively. It's one thing wanting a confrontation with Betty in theory and it's quite another to know she's on the warpath and up for a 'left and right'.

'Marcos, listen. I know your history with Ezserebet. I know you can convince yourself when you're out at sea, sailing in some vast ocean, that you need never see her again. That it's over for you. In your bones you know that isn't true. She will be aware of you out there, somewhere, existing. She took it into her head once to systematically annihilate your entire clan. Do you think that kind of obsessive madness just stops?

'Take it from me, it doesn't. She leaves loose ends just to give herself something to grab hold of when the depression hits and she can't find the will to live. You're just a project she's shelved. She's put you aside for a rainy day, and that day could be any day. Listen, she scares me too, believe me I'm not going to baffle you with bullshit, but you were young the last time you crossed swords with Betty. Now you're older, wiser and stronger and the thing is, I could really use your help.'

He turned to me. Beyond anxious, his fangs have begun to distend. 'Are you saying I'm a coward, Eddy, that I want to leave because I'm afraid? You don't think every night of my existence I feel the weight of unsatisfied honour? My ancestors have stopped whispering demands for vengeance. They now scream at me during my day's rest …horrors from the great beyond. I came here didn't I? I responded to those anonymous emails that featured you, while you were happy to ignore mine. All this could be a trap, set for me. If I start something Eddy, I want to be sure you'll help me finish it and see it through, to the end. I know you of old and if you were with Betty recently and you really had wanted her dead, I don't see how she could have gotten away. Are you going to let me down when it comes to the point, Eddy? Because if you have any remaining scruples where Betty's concerned, I need to know. Now!'

I am feeling a little more comfortable with Marcos. Perhaps there is a credible explanation for his timely arrival in London. I am also feeling a little sympathy for his situation. It's true, for centuries I have had a blind spot where Ezserebet is concerned. I waited for him to reach out to me after his family tragedy but I never heard from him. Suddenly now, that doesn't seem so surprising. From his perspective I am not to be trusted where Betty is concerned. For many years that was true, but that part of my life is now over – too much water has passed under the bridge. The tiresome repetition of history repeating itself has worn on my affections. I've been on an endless loop of broken promises and broken bones.

From my earliest years, Ezserebet has circled around and above me like an albatross over a ship, me below, looking up at her with both awe and dread. My appetite for her unpredictability has long soured my stomach. I have come to fear her congenital Batthyanyi madness as I've watched it blossom into full psychosis. She will be the death of me eventually. It really has boiled down to me or her.

Time for me to speak up.

'I haven't been myself of late. I'll admit I could have handled everything better – your attempts at communication, my encounter with Betty and my general living situation. I will do better, but for now we, or I, if you choose to leave, have to deal with the situation as it stands. I have very little understanding of what goes on in Betty's malfunctioning head. How or why she decides who she will play with is a mystery, but she never leaves a stone unturned, Marcos. She never leaves well alone. She knows you still live and more than that, you thrive and gain some pleasure from existence.

'The same goes for me. She's getting worse, she can't stand to think that others don't wrestle with the same demons that torment and make her life a living hell. She will eventually get around to finishing what she started with your clan. She'll come for you one day, Marcos. In the same way, she'll eventually tire of playing games with me and end it. You know, and so do I ...'

Marcos shakes his head. 'If that "one day" is today, Thala's bound to end up as collateral damage. If we engage with Ezserebet head on, there will be nothing I can do to keep her safe ... she's just a human ... I can't watch her 24/7. I can't protect a human from a creature like Ezserebet. I'm enjoying life at the moment, Eddy. I know you don't understand or agree with my appetites. Perhaps I disgust you a little, but do you have any idea how long it takes to find a Lassie-Lucy like Thala? A damned long time! You know us vamps can't be around our own kind too long – it always turns ugly ... but it's a long life, Eddy and I've been lonely. I can't help but think, long after Thala's aged and died, hopefully of natural causes, I will still have an eternity to finish my business with Ezserebet Bathory!'

'I get it, I really do. Your human looks lovely. I don't want to go into it now, but I am in no position to judge your lifestyle. I'd rather this foulness hadn't started again with Betty. I have a life too ... I have something to lose. I promise you that I have skin in this game and that I will not hesitate, if I get the chance, to kill Betty. Let's face it, you're here, and you couldn't resist the chance to be one step ahead of her for once. The only real dilemmas you face are the same ones I do: One, can you trust me? Two, who sent those emails and why have they done so?'

I know Marcos will need a few moments to get his head around the situation. I stroll across the deck to the prow and start scanning the Docks. I've had to jump through the same mental hoops in the last twenty-four hours. One moment life is sweet and ordered, the next everything hangs in the balance. The truth is I don't think Marcos is afraid. The Atl were one of the Warrior Hawke tribes of the Vampire Nation. In peace, just as with the psychopathic percentage of the human population, they were an inconvenient nuisance, they were always difficult to control and never easy company. What the heck do you do with them? But when there was a battle to be fought, when the Vampire Nation was in need of some 'fuck off' scary backup, the Atl were close to the top of the 'to call' list. Marcos' skill set is the reason I'd come to the Docks tonight, and not just deleted the messages from Triton. Marcos can be a ditherer; he doesn't have the greatest judgement, but he is also one of the bravest, toughest characters I have ever met ... utterly ruthless. If his heart is in it, together I know we could finish this. The stakes are high – Angel's life depends on it.

Marcos wanders over to me. He's made peace with himself; his teeth have retracted - we are going to be civilised again.

'Eddy, you've seen her recently, Ezserebet, is she still...' He trails off.

The sudden nearness of his voice surprises me. Marcos had moved up behind me, close enough for me to feel his breath on my neck, before I'd noticed. I am still getting used to being around vampires again. After all these years of feeling untouchable, physically and mentally superior, it's taking some getting used to. He is looking into the blue, diesel patterns cobwebbing the surface of the black water. Reflections of sulphur yellow harbour lights and chopped masts dance on the ripples.

'She was always … volatile, but you say she's getting worse. Is she completely … how do you say …?'

Marcos is struggling for words; English is not his most fluent language. I raise my eyebrows and keep my voice dead pan.

'Two points brother, just so you're not disarmed on your first encounter with her after so long. One, Ezserebet is still the most beautiful vampire you or I will ever know, and two, oh yes, she's bat shit crazy, utterly and spectacularly barking.'

After a moment or two of silent contemplation, for the first time since Marcos beckoned me to board his boat, the tension eases between us and we start to laugh.

Thalassa appears in the hatchway. She is rubbing her eyes and looks very huntable in her PJs. I can't help but imagine her all sweaty with eyes bulging. The top buttons on her pyjama top have come open and for the first time I notice the multiple bite wounds, some fresh, some old and healing, around her throat and travelling down her chest. My thoughts diverge and follow two independent avenues of speculation. I just know she smells delicious when she is terrified, and I begin to feel excited at the thought of roughing her up a bit. Perhaps she enjoys it, perhaps she doesn't … I don't care.

Thoughts come unbidden. I'm hungry again, I don't want to play fight, I am completely alive again and I want to break something. The awareness I am not yet the complete master of my appetites fills me with self-loathing, I'm too old for this malarkey. The monster holds dominion. It will be a few weeks until the 'better me' is in full command, but that part of me is still aware, and thinks the wounds on Thalassa's body look savage and uncontrolled. There is never any need to leave wounds that will scar on a beloved pet. A strange way to treat a valuable servant. I also notice the bites have been inflicted by two different sets of teeth. Evidently I am not the only vampire with whom Marcos has made contact in London.

'There's been another email.' She ducks back down quickly and Marcos and I follow her below decks to the cabin.

Sender:

Topic:

Message: EB badly injured, gone to ground to wait for sleep of day, taken to earth in disused Post Office Railway, Whitechapel.

Interesting place to take refuge ... I would never have considered it a safe house of choice. The Post Office Railway system lays abandoned and I use it for a stop gap if I get in trouble near the Paddington Metropolitan line. At one point the old Post Office rail network runs close enough to Paddington Station to hear the voices of humans on the platform. A couple of hundred metres down there's a shaft that allows utility pipes and cables to run through from the PM line to the P.O. track. Whilst the aperture may not afford comfortable access for a human, at a pinch, my kind can squeeze through that shaft.

The Old Post Office lines were used to ferry post between sorting offices throughout the City on driverless mini trains. Originally there were eight stations in use and the track can take me under the Thames, west from Camden Town to Bermondsey in the south east, south from Pimlico to Islington in the north or east from Stepney to Marylebone in the west. The old P.O. lines should be crawling with vamps, but they're not. I consider it a refuge of last resort and have my reasons for not being entirely comfortable with the place. The old P.O. line just isn't the stretch of track to head for when looking for escape from the monkeys. It's still very clean and sterile. Whitewashed walls make me think of a medical research facility and these days the possibility of ending up somewhere like it if I'm not careful is a little too near the bone to ignore.

There's an annoying research team from the University of Cambridge that hangs about down there too. The team are supposed to be testing original cast iron lining sections for wear and tear due to earth erosion. That's bullshit, they're up to something. They've installed digital cameras, fibre optic sensors, laser scanners and real-time reporting instruments. Dangerous soil movements, my arse ... those young scientists are looking for an entirely different kind of movement. The type of instruments I've seen down in the Old Post Office tunnels are more suited to detecting and recording animal life.

These researchers spend their days and some nights checking their devices and gathering evidence that something moves around down in those dark tunnels... something interesting. PhD types make me nervous, especially when they secure generous government funding. I can't believe Betty can be unaware of the technological gadgetry embedded in that tunnel and the human traffic monitoring it.

The old P.O. line does have advantages as I've said, not least the comforting feature that parts of the tunnel system are no more than 2ft wide by 2ft high, making them tight and uncomfortable for a human to access. It's mainly those scaled down sections of tunnel we vampires have embraced for our own use. But I still avoid the place - too many corners and cul de sacs - the sort of speleology that can quickly turn the hunter into the hunted. Hyenas corral and bring down lions. Pleistocene wild dogs corralled and trapped great woolly mammoths, and in the right circumstances, humans could corral and capture a vampire.

Betty isn't stupid and she's never reckless with her own life. The plus side to such a strange bolt hole would be that using the decommissioned postal lines she could go almost anywhere she wanted in central London very quickly. Also, to turn a negative into a positive, the fact that those lines were only recently decommissioned and still feel and smell strongly of human activity means they aren't on the radar of most vampires. Betty would be right to assume it is one of the last places I'd think to search for her.

'Well it's now or never, Eddy. Are we going?'

Marcos looks excited. His anxiety has disappeared and I notice the whites of his eyes are already turning red. Subconjunctival hemorrhage is a sign of heightened response in my species. It is also a sign of aggression.

I feel my own body automatically react to a perceived threat, and the blood vessels in my own eyes start to rupture, causing my damaged eye to sting. The eye is still painful but it's almost entirely healed. I can see out of it again and have perfect, binocular vision. Amazing how quickly the blood lust will rise in the Atl. I look at Marcos and his skin is stretching back across his bones and the veneer of soft handsomeness is shrivelling. 'A devil, a born devil, on whose nature, nurture can never stick'. What's bred in the bone, I guess.

'Of course we're bloody going!' I keep my voice steady but my mind is racing, this is all happening very quickly and I feel like a lab rat in a maze. There appear to be options but somehow there is really only one direction to move.

'Are you ready for a fight, Marcos, because wounded or not, Betty is no pushover. There can't be any half measures – no hesitation. Are you OK with breaking one of our most sacred taboos? Because if you don't intend to kill her, you're better off waiting here.'

'You've got a damn nerve talking to me like that. I don't know exactly why or how the distance between us grew after the massacre of my clan but I'll own some culpability for that. I know I am a different vampire than I was before. I'm not so trusting. During my escape from the ship, I was caught in the sun more times than I can remember… it changed me … I went into myself. Knowing how things always were with you and Betty, I'll admit I decided you were no longer on my Christmas card list … but I knew there was something holding you back from reaching out as well.

'At first I thought it was awkwardness, what could you say to someone who has lost everything? It's not our way to be a shoulder to cry on and I wouldn't have wanted any of that, but you must know I took your holding back as a sign that you had chosen a side. If it came to a choice between Ezserebet and anyone else, for you Eddy, she would always be the one. I've been waiting for the day you realised that she's not saveable. I want her removed from the face of the earth and have for many years. Revenge is shamefully overdue. I am humiliated and dishonoured by her existence, but you may be one of the only vampires alive that fully understands what I'm up against.'

We look at each other for some moments, and I eventually step forward and take him into my arms. I have Angel waiting for me at home and if I can put aside my suspicion and doubts around Marcos' reappearance in my life, I could also regain a friend. Good things could come from this dark diorama that Ezserebet has constructed, in which she believes she can move us around like puppets. Perhaps we can surprise her with an unforeseen twist in the story. It is on the tip of my tongue to tell him about Tia, but I just can't bring myself to reveal all my secrets; I have so few of them left. I will tell him about my strange, new companion later and perhaps he will tell me about the vampire he's been allowing to feed on the lovely Thalassa.

'Well then, let's go.' I release him from my embrace and Marcos heads back down into the cabin only to re-emerge with some impressive fire power. He's been waiting for this moment. He is ready and, at long last … so am I.

CHAPTER FIFTEEN

Tia

Back in the house at Cadogan Gardens, Tia continued to lay on the leather sofa, basking in the heat from the fire. The vampyr had left and now she could sense he was otherwise occupied. He had, at last, really gone, body and mind, and she could unclench and luxuriate in the sounds and smells of the old house. It is a beautiful and fitting lair for a creature such as Edward DeVere. She had intended to hate him as much as she did the female vampyr that had entered and despoiled her territory, but it is proving difficult. For such an 'old one', Edward appears rather lacking in guile, but she knows this cannot be the whole story. Even when armed with all the physical resilience his kind possess, a creature doesn't achieve his degree of longevity by being a fool.

Arrogant son of a bitch vampyr that Edward is, he has a bumbling affect that is disarming, and, reluctantly, she must admit that she doesn't really mind Eddy DeVere too much. Jumping up to perch on the high back of the velvet sofa she allows her eyes to take in the tasteful drawing room. Beneath the stacks of books and empty wine bottles, ashtrays and pot plants brimming with cigar butts and cannabis roaches, she can discern a logical order, a place for everything and everything in its place - so smug in his domain. She snorts at the image of Eddy moving through this fortress cloaked in humdrum urbanity. A deadly spider in his enticing web. So sure of his place in 'his London'. But he doesn't know everything. Certainly, her existence had come as a surprise to him.

One day she would recommend he look into the history of Parliament Hill Fields, the mounds of grass still marking the sites of neolithic barrows. Those gentle grassy mounds began as stone burial crypts around 2400 BC, and it was there that early human Londoners placed the remains of their treasured dead, including their warrioress Queen Bodicea. They would use massive boulders to seal those barrows, that could be rolled away when they wanted to play 'Where's Wally?' with Grandpa's bones, what contemporary humans would describe as pagan ceremonies.

The Victorians believed they'd found evidence to prove that these pagan ceremonies included cannibalism. Actually, what they found in those time capsules of forensic evidence were signs of visits paid by Tia's ancestors, the homoraptors, to repositories of the human dead. Those ancient cold stone and earth chambers had served as walk-in larders to her forebears. Before humanity decided they were the only race of sentient beings that walked the earth, when they still had some respect for the rest of creation and tried to be accommodating, they had acknowledged Tia's ancestors and paid tribute. Visits from her forebears to the tombs of human warriors were welcomed and celebrated. Treasure recovered from bogs, battlefields or bandits by the race of homoraptor were duly deposited in the barrows.

Deep in caves beneath the fields of Amesbury, Tia has seen the homoraptor carvings that depict a time when her species and the humans enjoyed a mutualistic relationship. Four heavily muscled homoraptor perch on the horizontal lintels that once spanned the thirty vertical Sarsen stones of the temple at Stonehenge. Sitting atop the lintels, each homoraptor faces one of the cardinal points – North, East, South and West, it is mid winter and the carved rays of the sun set in the south-west.

Tia's species had once been considered guardians of, and a conduit to, the passage of human souls to other planes of existence. As the setting winter sun of the solstice turned the massive columns of Stonehenge into pillars of golden light, the Tribute ceremony would begin. The humans would lay out the departed, be they Warrior, King, Queen, Druidic priest or priestess, on the massive central sacrificial altar. As night fell the Tribute would be left in the protection of the four great homoraptor guardians until, with the rising of the sun the Druid Keepers of the Secrets would return to find the body stripped clean of flesh and the bones respectfully arranged in repose and adorned with stone battle axes, metal daggers and ornaments of gold and amber.

Inevitably as the humans need for control over everything living and inert grew, Tia's ancestors' visits to pick the bones of the dead began to prick their pride. Farming eased the fear of winter starvation and the deities of Life, Death and Rebirth gave way to more humanistic objects of worship. The monkeys began to perceive any force of Nature that came between them and their man God as disrespectful, and a new fashion of burning the departed began. As a result, her ancestors, the homoraptor Guardians of the Soul, became feared and were driven away.

All but expunged from history, their legend mutated until they became mythical, cartoon gargoyles and grotesques.

Eddy needs to understand that this is her London too. She belongs here every bit as much as he, perhaps more. Tia really didn't mind sharing, but this female, red-headed turbo-powered bitch of a vampyr is crossing the line. She has been cutting a slash and burn swathe through the East End and making life way too complicated. That particular vampyress has to go.

Before she'd felt compelled to intervene, Tia had watched some of the shenanigans between Ezserebet and Eddy back at the torture cavern and she harbours doubts around Eddy's commitment to the job at hand. Tia had come as a surprise to him but she has known of vampyrs all her life and she knows when it comes to *it,* they stick together. Regarding the matter of disposing of Ezserebet, Eddy is going to have the benefit of back-up whether he wants it or not. Tia needs to be on the spot when the action kicks off to make sure he doesn't get all sentimental at the last moment. She doesn't need to be here, hanging about in this creepy, old house. As beautiful as it is, it reeks of ghosts and other things she couldn't name.

In the depths of the house, Tia can hear the breathing, very slow, of the girl he calls Angel, and this is where things have become unexpectedly, and perhaps even mystically, complicated. She had not been at all ready for the moment when she had first laid eyes on the girl in the dungeon, covered in filth and almost dead. There was something about the mutilated girl that struck her as familiar. For the life of her, she couldn't pin it down but knew she had seen that face before.

A shiver runs through her. She wraps her arms around herself, and feels the comfort of her wings nestling in and pressing against her back. It was when Eddy passed the girl up through the man hole access in Milner Street and into her arms that it came to her. By that time, the girl had already begun whatever form of transmutation she is destined to undergo. There was no doubt that she had been transfigured in some way and it was then that Tia had remembered where she had seen that face before. She hoped she had concealed her excitement and shock from Eddy.

She had seen the girl's face in old, vegetable ink drawings in her people's sacred *Book of Mi*, Mi being the name of the first ancient tribe of homoraptors. The book records the legend of the Defender or Avenger. No mention of the being's gender – male or female, is specified but there was a general assumption that the Avenger, although a beautiful, almost asexual being, would be a human male. The Mi were wrong. The Avenger is female and whether she is still human is now arguable. Tia had held her in her arms, looked into that unusual face and been gripped by an absolute certainty. There was no mistaking that countenance – humble, gentle and fierce, perhaps best captured by Guido Reni in his painting of the Archangel Michael. Reni's painting, completed in 1636, now hangs in the church of Santa Maria della Concezione in Rome. He captured the strong profile of either a striking, warrior woman or a beautiful sensitive male. The girl from the dungeon is Reni's Michael personified.

In her youth, Tia had been fascinated by the stories of the Avenger and the fact that both her species and that of the humans shared the same legend, and had the same vision of the physical embodiment of that creature. She had sought out other depictions of Michael in human art. The earliest Tia found dated from 324, and depicted Michael slaying a serpent. That painting now adorns the

Michaelion in the ancient Near East, close to the site where Constantine defeated Licinius at around the same time as the painting's creation.

But she had discovered that the Michaelion had been built on the site of an older temple. Perhaps there existed even earlier representations of the Defender of Light. She is no esoteric, but she believes this 'being', or an incarnation of this 'being' – Michael the Archangel– lies unconscious and vulnerable in the basement of this very house.

To humans, Tia may be a monster but she is warm-blooded, as are all the other monsters she has ever encountered. Vampyrs are cold-blooded creatures, reptilian in ancestry. As far as Tia knows, only the vampyr, they that mimic their human prey so perfectly and the humans find so irresistibly attractive, are so utterly foreign. The slayer of dragons and serpents as depicted in art for millennia, the perfect visual metaphor for the vanquisher of the vampyr race, is here, nestled deep in the bowels of the lair of one of the oldest and most aristocratic of that breed.

To the Mi, Tia's own race of homoraptors, the being Michael – the destroyer, deliverer, avenger, defender or purger, depending on your interpretation of the ancient texts, is depicted as a warrior Angel, wielding a sword and usually clad in armour. Unbelievably, this 'being', now stashed in the crypt below, is destined to cleanse the world of the under-dwellers and creatures that revel in darkness.

This is the sticking point for Tia, many of her own kind chose to believe that this couldn't possibly include themselves. They believe that the race of homoraptor is to be freed from fear and hiding, to take their rightful place beside the humans. Through this cleansing, her race are destined to be delivered from darkness every bit as much as humanity. She has never been sure on that point. Yes, it is true, unlike the vampyr, she can emerge into sunlight and be active in the daylight hours, but she hates it. Diurnal activity is unnatural for her; it leaves her feeling vulnerable as it does every other Mi she has ever known. The simple truth is, she does revel in the night and dark places. They are her natural home, including tunnels, caves, crypts and dungeons.

She is teetering on the edge of a metaphysical cliff, facing what the humans would call a moment of destiny. The moment has come to her unexpectedly and it is certainly unwelcome. This could all be an unfortunate coincidence for the one below, an encounter with Tia nothing more than a freak convergence of chance, but there again, as it stands, on this night, in this house, there is a chance she has been left alone with a creature that her kind consider a supernatural being entrusted with a divine purpose. That purpose is a cleansing and a deliverance, but the question is: Of what, and for whom?

Tia stands up and, keeping her step light, she all but glides to the concealed wall panel. She presses it as Eddy had shown her. The door silently opens on its precision mechanism and an interior light illuminates the racks of deadly toys. From the wall of weaponry, she reaches up and lifts down the massive gatling gun, holding it in her arms for size. It is heavy, and fitted with a belt of about fifty garlic soaked, wooden slugs. She circles the room, Rambo style, making firing noises from between her lips, before placing it back. She smiles and takes another look at the arsenal and whispers to herself, 'Easy girl, we're not making a western here.' She reaches up and selects a rotating crossbow loaded with eight, sharp wooden stakes, and a pistol loaded with the same number of garlic ampoules, set in a barrel that can shoot them out at the velocity of a bullet.

She feels the weight of each in her hands and steadies her breath. She can't detect any other life force in this house, but then she wouldn't if a creature like Eddy didn't want her to. She must not fall prey to assumption.

Moving stealthy as a cat, Tia approaches the door that leads down to the lower floors. She has gathered from Eddy there are three sub-terra levels of ever decreasing size and increasing depth. The girl is on the lowest level. She puts her foot on the top stair and it gives and creaks under her weight. Damn, the whole house is probably rigged and booby-trapped with these little alarms, some of which she perhaps will not hear, but for all she knows could be as loud as a klaxon to a vampyr. She stands still for some moments. The breathing of the girl down in the basement continues, undisturbed.

There are strange juxtapositions of cutting-edge technology and Hammer Horror hokum dotted through this old house. Eddy, for all his apparent disconnect from the modern world, must still know how and where to procure and engage highly skilled tradesmen to work on his house. How did he guarantee their discretion? The interesting thing is there has been no lift access to the lower or upper floors installed – very smart thinking for one with superhuman powers. Moving through this enormous house is nothing to an immortal but for a human, it would pose a real disadvantage in a chase or a search.

She continues down through the first two sub-terra floors. Nothing remarkable - a swimming pool, sauna, small cinema - to be expected from the super rich. Except there aren't many humans that would care to take a dip in the pool. It looks like he's filled it with mud. Moving closer to the pool, she takes a sniff and doubles back quickly – weeds and algae, anaerobic bacteria with a whiff of ammonia, methane and hydrogen sulphide.

These vampyrs are beyond her understanding. Eddy has filled the pool with a pathogenic soup from which most humans would emerge with either cholera, scabies, typhoid, shigella, salmonella, botulism or at the very least, some suppurating boils and sores. The pool room is covered in the most luxurious, scintillating mosaics of hand-painted porcelain, glass and semi-precious stones. Tia wonders just how rich Eddy is. He certainly plays it down on the clothes front. He isn't flashy like some vampyrs, but the house tells a very different story.

She opens the door and pauses at the top of the flight of stairs that lead down to the lowest level. A cold draught of air pours over her like a death exhalation. Her body stiffens and she becomes aware of a slight nausea. *Just more vampyr bullshit.* She takes a step back. Every fibre of her being screams retreat, but she masters herself, takes a deep breath and moves forward and down.

The heavy door at the base of the stairs is unlocked. That should be a plus, but somehow it doesn't strike Tia that way. Everything about this house whispers 'come in' but every animal instinct tells you to run. She pushes it, and with effortless silence, the door swings wide to welcome her in. The utter darkness of the space beyond comes as a surprise. Her eyes take some time to adjust, and despite her nocturnal vision she is suddenly enveloped and caressed by gloom.

Only one description befits the room into which she has walked – a burial chamber. It may be shown on a set of floor plans as the basement storage room, but no breathing creature could mistake the atmosphere – it oozes death. At the back of the chamber, she can see what she's come for. The sarcophagus looks very heavy, but that is all right, she'll manage. She approaches the stone coffin and again pauses to listen. Angel's rhythmic breathing continues. Not a sign of speeding or pause.

She remains motionless a while longer, probing the shadows with all her senses. The silence throbs with malice, coalescing into a living presence that presses close to her, greedily drinking her warmth, sucking her into a miasma of despair. Her large ears twitch and turn toward a noise, muffled by the heavy thickness of the atmosphere and the hum of an old, beat-up chest freezer. Was that a rustle? Or had it been a sigh? She pauses again. Silence rushes back in, reclaiming the space like liquid filling a vacuum. It could have been her imagination. This place plays mind tricks, but she would swear the atmosphere of dread has changed to one of waiting. Her lip curls and she stifles a nervous yawn. The place is really giving her the collywobbles now and that takes some doing. *Just get on with it.*

Tia stands in front of the sarcophagus to assess the dimensions of the tomb. It looks damn heavy. She slowly circles and decides the best point to apply force is directly at the head of the thing. Placing the weapons on the ground at her feet, she presses her shoulder against the lid and gives a push. There is the slightest movement of the incredibly dense slab. *How had he managed to get this thing down here?* She takes a deep breath and pushes again. Standing up and stretching herself she studies the lid. It is a couple of inches offset now. The smell of the girl rises up through the chink. Not quite the usual living human stench, but unpleasant, nevertheless.

The breathing from within the stone coffin continues. Steady, rhythmic and slow. She pushes again and this time hits the sweet spot and the lid slides a bit further down. Now she has two feet of clearance and she can peer into the cask. Edward sure meant business when he'd chosen this crypt; even for a vampyr it would take some effort to open, and it made a lot of noise too. Perhaps he thought it would give him just the time needed to get down here and protect his human from harm. That was his plan obviously, but of course he would need to be here for that to work, and he isn't.

This girl is valuable to him. He wants her alive when he should really want her dead, and as yet, Tia can't understand why. He should have left her to die in the dungeon and kissed the feet of that crazy redhead for doing the job. Instead he's made her invulnerable with the dubious gift of vampyr blood. She had noticed the two paintings in the rooms above. They definitely depict versions of the girl in the crypt but had clearly been painted centuries apart and even to Tia's world view, that seems weird.

Has Eddy known and preyed on this girls' whole damn family going back hundreds of years, generation after generation? These vampyrs were always playing games, amusing themselves at another's expense. Perhaps it helped to distract them from their remorseless existence, helped them pass the years without going insane. Or perhaps this girl had always been Michael, the supernatural warrior Angel. In which case, she had existed before and the vampyr had defeated her many times over the course of history and all the tales of the victorious Avenger are mistaken. Whatever the story between the girl and Eddy, she would be glad to be out of it.

The girl's head is visible now, and she is definitely in the process of change. Eddy has dabbled in some mysterious alchemic voodoo right here with this little human. Angel damn near glows. It makes Tia shiver. She needs to pull herself together and just get on with it. One more shove and the lid swings down and to the side and the girl's upper half is completely exposed. Still in her filthy rags from the dungeon, covered in a patina of grease and street grime, nonetheless it is undeniable now – the other worldliness. Of course, that could be put down to the fact she had recently been bitten and fed by a vampyr, but still…

Bending over the open casket Tia took the chance to lean in close and take a good look at the stump on the end of the girl's arm. There is now a fingerless, pink growth extending from the wrist. Interesting. Leaning in further she can taste the girl's breath – sharp, aniseed, with a background of some herb. Was it Dill? Tia exhaled and studied the girl's inert body. There are still dried blood stains all around her lips and streaking down her chin. Nasty business, having your tongue cut out.

Satisfied, Tia crouches down and takes the weapon back into her hands. She stands again in quiet alertness. She could damn well swear she'd heard it again. There it is … a rustle … a sigh … a long, almost erotic exhalation of unbearable yearning. 'Cheese and rice' as Eddy would say, she is alone down here with who knows what. Holding the pistol at arm's length in a trembling grip she presses it to the girl's temple. Decision time. She whispers 'Bang!' and quickly reaching deeper into the casket, places the revolver next to the girl's good hand. She wont risk actually allowing her own flesh to make contact with the girl's. Vampyrs are known for their lightning reactions to threat and whatever this girl had once been, she is no more. She is now polluted with the distilled essence of those vile reptilian creatures. Nevertheless, Tia presses the weapon close enough that the cold metal just touches the hybrid's fingers.

Let the Destroyer rise for all she cares and either free her from the tyranny of the belly crawlers, or if it turns out her own kind are also among the unclean, send the whole lot of them to Hell. Either way, Eddy will just have to be collateral damage. She can live with that; he's brought it on himself, after all. Whether this whole thing is just some weird coincidence, hocus pocus or the wrath of God, she doesn't know and doesn't care. She is no philosopher – let the cards fall where they may. She is already way out of her depth. Right now she is more interested in things she does understand and perhaps can influence, like the extermination of the most immediate threat to her existence – the vampyress Ezserebet.

'There child, whatever manner of creature you now are, you must take your chances like the rest of us, I'll leave it in the hands of Izcuintli. May he guide you to wherever, or whatever you are meant to be. Angel or demon, I will take no further part in this dark magic. I have my own deliverance to take care of.' Pushing the lid back over the girl, Tia stands and wills her eyes to more effectively penetrate the heavy, pitch blackness of the vault. It isn't going to happen.

Suddenly dizzy and overcome with nausea, she leans against the sarcophagus. She is surprised to find she takes comfort from the sound of the heartbeat coming from within that stone casket and the proximity of another being that breathes and is alive, because, sure as hell, they are not alone down here. An alien presence shares this space with them and wants something.

'Whatever you are, stay back from me. I have no business with you.'

She isn't sure if she whispered the words to herself or if she had just thought them, but this time there is no doubt she hears, and more reliably, can sense movement at her left side, and it is close. She backs slowly toward the stairs. Her breathing is now ragged, all the oxygen having been sucked from her lungs, and the prospect of passing out becomes a terrifying possibility. The sensation of light-headedness intensifies and she stumbles, reaching out to steady herself.

Her left hand brushes against something solid and cold. Her fingers find some purchase and then she becomes aware that the coldness she has clutched for support, engulfs her hand. She feels long fingers gently, caressingly curl around her own. Tia freezes as the soft grip of the cold fingers tightens about her hand until it feels as though it is being crushed beneath hard ice and the bones scream. With a violent jerk, she pulls free and makes a frantic leap for the doorway, throwing herself through the opening onto the stairs and using her legs to kick the door of the deep basement shut behind her. She bolts up the stairs, past the opulent but putrid swimming pool, upward through the cinema and up the last flight of stairs to reach the ground floor, slamming every door shut behind her as she goes.

On reaching the ground floor hall, she stops and takes a deep breath to regain her balance and focus. Raising the crossbow to eye level, she slowly exhales and spins on her heels, turning a steady 360 degrees of the hall. 'Jeepers clucking creepers', she will be glad to get out of this house.

Slipping into Eddy's study, Tia opens the laptop to find the email. She hopes she can make it to St Katherine's before Eddy leaves. She has allowed herself to be drawn into this intrigue for one reason, to get rid of the female vampyr. That vampyress has earned herself a death sentence. Insanity she can forgive; psychopathic tendencies, again she can forgive; being an eater of human meat, preferably carrion, she is in no position to judge. But indulging in reckless self-destructive carelessness that could ultimately lead to the discovery and destruction of her entire species – she wont tolerate it. No way José.

The crossbow she ties across her back with a belt she finds in Eddy's upstairs dressing room. She takes the liberty of dressing herself in a pair of his trousers and a roll neck sweater. Boots on, old coat and beanie, she chooses one of Eddy's scarves and drapes that around her head, veiling everything but her eyes. Covering her head so completely used to bring stares but since the influx of Muslim immigrants to London, no one turns a hair.

She is ready. Patting herself down; she checks she has everything she will need including her black-lensed specs. With one last glance around the house, she allows her eyes to fall on the door to the lower floors, and pictures Angel's dirty, blood-smeared, seraphic face. She approaches and presses her ear to the solid hard wood. Silence … a pensive stillness has returned. Her lips close to the frame, she calls out, 'Good Luck.' A cold breeze rushes from under the basement door, broiling over her, seeping down the neck of her sweater, under the sleeves and creeping up beneath the trouser legs of the gaberdine pants, puckering the flesh across her entire body and probing her 'lady garden' with an icy finger.

Tia backs away, and, rushing across the grand entry hall, she bumps against the heavy front door before letting out a groan of horror. She opens the door and lets herself out onto the marble front step, slamming it firmly closed and taking a deep breath of cold London air. Her legs shake just a little as she sets off, her arms wrap around herself in a protective reflex.She whispers to herself, 'Good luck little human and good fucking riddance.'

CHAPTER SIXTEEN

The Old Post Office Line

Marcos and I drop down onto the tracks at Piccadilly Tube station and slip into the tunnels. Moving quickly, we make our way deep into the network. We squeeze ourselves through a utility shaft and follow the tracks until we are drawing close to the disused Post Office Rail Line. Marcos is giving off signals like a pressure cooker ready to blow. The closer we move to the Old Post Office station, the more tense he becomes.

I can't remember him being such a nervous Nelly type, but being left adrift at sea in an open top lifeboat for weeks with just a black sail to fend off the relentless sun has left more than physical scars. I imagine him burnt to char during the day, waking with the rising moon to searing agony and the stench of his own cooked flesh. Just enough night hours pass to recover the strength to survive, only to endure the ordeal again … and again. A memory that would not quickly fade - the sort of experience that could unhinge the strongest vampire, perhaps even result in a vampire version of post-traumatic stress. Just what I need.

At last we emerge through the network of tunnels and onto the right section of track. We come to a curve at one of the narrowest parts of the run and stop to listen. Where is she? A wounded vamp is the most dangerous kind. The thought of a wounded Betty has every fibre of my being on high alert.

Marcos seems to have calmed down a bit, now that we have reached ground zero. I can tell he's never visited this section of the Tube before, yet he is looking around as if searching for something, something he should recognise. He heads off in a westerly direction, suddenly purposeful. It's unlike Marcos to make a snap decision. I call after him – no need to keep quiet now. We both know there is no hope of surprise. If this is indeed the place Betty has taken to ground, she will have known of our approach long before we reached this section of track.

'Where do you think you're going?'

He turns. His eyes are very bright. 'I think this way.' He points in the direction he's moving.

'No shit Sherlock, and why is that?' He has no answer, none he is prepared to share with me. He shrugs and keeps moving. Great, after nursemaiding him all the way, now he decides to take charge. Well, my 'little voice' has other ideas.

I turn to look at him but he's already gone. I call after him, 'You carry on, brother, I'll head east. We'll soon hear if there's any trouble. Keep that garlic ready.' He must have taken off along the rail lines like a bullet.

I guess that's one way to handle the situation. I decide to take it a little slower. I want time to let my ears adjust to the unique echo in this section of tunnel. All the tunnels are slightly different; the curvature, depth, building materials all create an acoustic fingerprint. They each have their own quirks and the trick is to allow for the particular distortions and extraneous noises each tunnel carries.

Right now, I am editing out the scuffle and pitter-patter of tiny rat feet, and there are plenty of them. At any time, there's around eight million rats under London, maybe many more. Most humans never see one, a bit like all the other distasteful creatures, me included, that live right under their noses. There is a hum through the utility shafts – electricity, gas, water, noises from other tube lines – people and trains. Underneath it all there is a throbbing anticipation like a pulse. I can sense other vampires, plural. My inner voice has been whispering to me as Marcos and I approached these tunnels, but the kamikaze in me just wasn't in the mood for more procrastination. I am not much for games, but when I have to deal with 'game players', I find it best to just let them have their fun. Then stamp on them hard.

By now I have moved some way down the track toward the terminus when it suddenly hits me – the voice of self-preservation stops whispering and screams inside my head. 'Oh, Eartha Kitt!' With stone cold certainty, I know this whole damn thing has been a set-up from the word go. I've walked into a trap. I turn toward the closest escape route which branches off a little way behind me in the direction I've just travelled. About thirty feet ahead, I see that the way is now blocked by the shadowy bulk of three vamps. I spin back around to head off in the opposite direction and slam, cartoon stupid into Betty. I've never met another vamp that can move as fast and silent. She doesn't look injured – more importantly she doesn't smell injured. She glows with vitality as always.

She opens her mouth to say something amusing and droll. That's what I assume by the way her lip curls up at the corners. But before she can speak, I stab one of the garlic ampoules I've brought from my own supply into her neck.

In my 'lost years' spent creeping about the gaff, I haven't been entirely idle. Sometimes I fill 0.41 fluid ounce glass phials with my own potentized home brew, garlic extract and fit them with fine steel self-pumping syringe needles – I call these little beauties 'sticks'. I had grabbed a pocketful before I left Cadogan Square, as I always do. Better safe than sorry and all that. I am as surprised at myself as Bets' startled eyes assure me she is – at my lack of hesitation and the speed with which my hand darted up and struck. "Celerity is never more admired Than by the negligent."

This time I hadn't paused to consider. I'd taken advantage of her over confidence, her one vulnerability being an unshakeable belief I will always be in two minds where she is concerned. That I will always waver because I am always interested in what she has to say, and she's right. Even while she drops to her knees, one hand cupping the boil forming on her neck around the point of entry, I do wonder what her one liner would have been.

'Your wit's too hot, it speeds too fast, 'twill tire, my lady,' I whisper in her ear as I take her weight and let her gently drop to the ground, but I'm sure it would have been very funny, after all she'd had time to think about and savour this moment and choose the perfect put down.

I feel the vamps move behind me. The static electricity of their physicality hits me just before actual contact and that gives me a fraction of a second. All I need to feint a move, duck down and back up, then strike with two more of the 'sticks', while they are slightly off balance and still recovering from the anticipated contact that didn't happen. They both buckle at the knees and drop. The one I caught in the shoulder goes down surprisingly quickly and hard, but the older one I injected in the cheek, is writhing and keening and generally making a meal of it.

I spin round. There had been three – where is it? Betty lays still, her eyes open and staring. Apart from the pulsating boil on her neck, she looks surprisingly healthy. I nudge her with my boot and then reach down and carefully touch her neck. I'm not pretending that she doesn't still scare the crap out of me. No pulse … wait … no pulse, just wait, and there it is. Damn, but it's hard to kill this woman. Maybe there is something to her weird obsession with young nubile blood. I take another 'stick' out.

'Sorry Bets, it's you or me. We always knew it would boil down to this.'

I lean in for one last kiss. My lips touch hers, velvet soft. She stinks of garlic but I continue to press my lips to hers. She will always be my first love. 'Goodbye Blood Countess Elisabethae Batthyanyi, Princess to the House of Bathory.' I am suddenly and unexpectedly choked with sadness. We share so many memories. Why had it come to this? Where and when did she mutate into the hellion of nightmares I've come to know of late. There again, if I am honest, I can't remember a time she wasn't this way. I can tell myself she degenerated over the years but the truth is more stark. With the confidence of age, she simply stopped hiding and with maturity, I stopped making excuses and hoping I could fix her. I always knew there was something wild and depraved at the heart of Betty even when we were children.

I watched as she struggled with an inner Titan, hell bent on mayhem. It was exciting just being around the kinetic energy created from the battle she fought with herself. I lived in the eye of a terrifying electrical storm driven by the constant internal friction. At some point, Betty had conceded to destiny, submitted to the Batthyanyi curse, let go of any self-control, and embraced her licentious love of chaos, debauchery and blood lust. She was … and is … my

Goddess Kali Maa, my Lilith, and I will miss her. God help me but *I will* miss her.

The second 'stick' is kicked out of my hand just as it makes contact with her skin, leaving nothing more than an innocuous scratch across her wrist.

'Get away from her you filthy human fucker! Keep your perverted hands away. Get up and keep your hands where I can see them. Come on, stand up! Keep them away from your pockets you vamp-killing arsehole!'

Through the teary eyes of my sentimentality I focus. I've never seen this vamp in my life, nor either of the two dead on the ground now that I come to think of it. 'I don't know where you got that idea, but I can assure you ...' I stand up and move toward him. '... I've never fucked a human.'

I lunge for him, but he ducks back. He is a big boy, massive, taller than me and heavily set. I name him Cujo and decide that should be his WWF moniker if he ever takes up the sport he was clearly born for. Although big, he's still quick on his feet and his teeth are fully extended. So... it appears Betty has an admirer. He takes another step back. I know he is only backing up to lure me toward him and put more distance between myself and her defenseless body. Self-sacrificing loyalty... very commendable. Coming down the track from the east, I can see and hear more vamps. It appears Betty has been slumming it and become the dominant female to a nest of scallies. I wonder how many more disciples she's gathered down here.

'Ezserebet told us all about you and your human fetish. You make me sick.' He lashes out with an uncontrolled, impassioned swipe, managing to cut me across the cheek with his extended nails. It's always the face ... I'll have to start wearing a mask. Perhaps some sort of helmet? We circle each other. Although he is bigger than me he is also a lot younger and that's to my advantage.

From behind him I suddenly see Marcos emerging from the tunnel. The vamp facing me doesn't react to my approaching reinforcement. Marcos reaches us, sidesteps Cujo and pushes straight past me, completely disinterested in my situation with 'Man Mountain'.

Falling to his knees next to Ezserebet, Marcos presses his fingers to her neck. He throws his head back and lets out an echoing howl of anguish and relief before shouting, 'Oh thank God she's alive.'

That makes me look, makes me stare, makes me feel like a numpty idiot. Marcos lifts her up and puts her straight into the arms of Cujo.

'Take her out of here, back to the boat. Hurry. Thalassa will know what to do.'

I've finished processing Marcos' actions and got my head back in the game just as the cavalry arrives – six of them. I'm surrounded and they push in close but are all clearly young, not quite confident enough to touch me yet. I should have seen it coming of course, but Marcos and Betty's shared history involving genocide of the Atl had made this scenario too far-fetched for consideration. The love lives of vampires beggars belief.

Marcos moves forward toward me and I can't help but state the obvious. 'You sorry, back-stabbing, son of a bitch, Marcos. She killed your entire friggin clan!' He winces, then looks me straight in the eye.

'She did it for me, so I could be free. You always act like some kind of tragic prince, sensitive and misunderstood, a milk maid! Your mother and father bred you, then dropped you into this world like a rotten, hot potato, with a bag of gold - an entitled orphan. Poor little rich Voivode vampire had to sink or swim, but like a scurvy dog you always do swim, don't you? Well, I never felt bad for you, Eddy.

'You don't know what it means to have your fate mapped out, stretching before you like an endless sea passage with no hope of making land. Ezserebet is my saviour. I had never conceived of deliverance until she came into my life and showed me it was possible, and offered it to me. If you want the truth, I was dead and ready to feed the fish, until Betty came and she has transformed me.

'No one controls her, although my clan of blaggards certainly tried, and look where that got them. We are together, now and always. She doesn't love you, she doesn't want you. This whole delusion that she's hounding you across the centuries is your own construct. It is you that can't leave her be. She's told me all about the stalking and the gut-aching pleading. The obsessive, possessive, manipulation you've put her through, always ending in violence when she feels suffocated and rejects you.'

At this point I stifle a giggle. Marcos notices but he shakes it off. He's on a roll.

'She has finally had enough. In truth she wants you dead, Eddy. Part of me hoped it wouldn't have to end like this, that you could shake off this fixation and move on. I feel sorry for you, you've become a pathetic shadow of the vamp you once were, but Betty comes first with me, and that's just the way it is.'

Marcos spreads his hands, an apologetic gesture, but his eyes tell another story. He is no reluctant cat's paw. He wants to kill me. Some part of him knows he's never going to take my place in Bets' heart … there just isn't much room in that stone hard little walnut. He's itching for a fight to the death and Betty was hoping to watch. How she loves her blood sports. No one can play on an insecure lover's jealousy like

Bets, and I'm beginning to get the feeling Marcos' life has been purgatory ever since that black widow crawled under his skin and laid eggs. But that isn't going to stop me letting him know what a fool he's been.

'So, let me get this straight. Betty kills your entire family, more – your entire clan, to free you. To deliver you from the tyranny of destiny. But there seems to be a problem with this picture, pea brain. You're still controlled, Your new master – Elisabethae Batthyanyi, is the most despotic, absolutist on the planet. You imbecile! I always knew you were weak minded Marcos, persuadable, and I made allowances. You just aren't the sharpest tool in the box, but this, this is a whole new level of stupid. She is playing with you!'

Well, I tried. I knocked and I can see there is someone at home behind Marcos' glazed eyes, but he just isn't answering the door. Too confused. Marcos is a lost cause. He just doesn't have the tools to handle a creature like Ezserebet.

'Shut your mouth you scabby harbour rat. You can't stand the thought that you aren't the one she wants, but that's just the way it is. Ezserebet and I have something unique, something powerful. I don't know what you did to piss her off, but whatever it was Eddy, it was the last straw. I wish it didn't have to go this way, I really do, but here we are. It is time to prepare for your doom.'

No matter what he says, his eyes are shining with hatred. Marcos wants me dead, and backed up by a gang of itinerant dog-ends, he's found the confidence to give it a go. I thought I could control it but I just can't. I lose it … not the wisest move when confronted with a possessive boyfriend. I do the one thing a jealous vampire, intent on first unmanning and then shredding his rival to death, cannot abide. I start to laugh, loud and hard. All this mayhem and for what? Just another attention-seeking stunt.

Marcos swings a jab and hits me hard on the jaw. It hurts a bit and I can taste my own blood. My laughter stops. All of a sudden, nothing about the situation strikes me as humorous. I take a deep breath, close my eyes and let Eddy go, allow him to evaporate. The carefully constructed English gentleman, ironic and self-deprecating, bumbling through life's relentless shit storm with a joke and a shrug, disappears.

I wish my disguise were the authentic me. I often fool myself that it is, but it isn't. The real me is coming back though. He has been waiting for my control to slip ever since Betty nearly drained me dry back at the dungeon. I am not my camouflage even though I so enjoy my shell of humanity. I rarely let it fall entirely away, but alas, beneath, I am something other. My body has been transforming since my encounter with Tia at the church. Then Betty damn near killed me and my cell turnover shot through the roof and is still climbing.

I am now desperately hungry. A powerful engine has roared into life and demands fuel. Exasperated with my pussy footing, the merciless, ravenous dragon is rising up beneath my disguise and is tearing away my human mask. My teeth have distended and my nails are elongated. I can feel my lizard skin stretching taut over my body and face and, with a surprising rush of sheer ecstasy and relief, all pretence vanishes and I am revealed. The expressions on the faces of the vamps that surround me confirm it. They become still and pale. Haven't they ever seen a real vampire before? The thought starts me laughing again, without much joy – an hysterical, rasping laugh that is interspersed with guttural battle screams of frustrated blood lust. The effect is electric.

They all take a step back, in unison, like a row of line-dancing ghouls. Except Marcos who, white as a ghost, steps forward. I know this is the creature in him wanting to assert himself as Alpha in front of his nest. The dominant female would, after all, only be interested in the dominant male. There is a biological imperative at work within him, but he doesn't look confident any more.

His shabby crew can be relied upon to hang back until the 'one on one' is over. A vampire pirate of the legendary Atl Clan versus a high-ranking Voivode of the Order of the Dragon and heir to the House of Basarab, locking fangs for the affections of the infamous Blood Countess. Priceless! This sort of theatre doesn't come along every day. Like the World Cup, this is the sort of entertainment that only comes around every four years, except with vamps being so lacking in passion, it is more like every four hundred. I am confident this will remain a spectator sport for the moment.

Marcos strikes out. Not quick enough - a fearful half-defensive move that just makes me angry. I snatch the hand in mid-air, twist the wrist until it snaps and stretch my mouth open wide, wider than any human could imagine possible; wide enough to take in the entire girth of his forearm and clamp down until the bone breaks. And with a shake and a tug, the lower arm and hand drop to the ground. Marcos' eyes widen and he instinctively reaches out with his remaining hand to push me away. Mistake. It's easier to snatch the arm this time. He is even slower - shock will do that. One of my hands reaches out and cups his elbow and the other snatches his biceps. I twist but this time at the shoulder joint. With a slurping pop, I rip the arm off at the shoulder socket. He screams and I'm ashamed to say it starts me laughing again. We're just having some 'armless fun.

235

My mouth widens and flips the top of my head back. Marcos whimpers a little. That pathetic little noise pushes me completely over the edge. I've had enough of witnessing his terror. This time I snap down on his head and take half his face. What sort of a vamp loses his head over a woman? Hardy ha ha. Before me is weakness and my kind don't like it. We're programmed to root it out of the gene pool. Don't come into the kitchen if you can't take the heat. Ezserebet likes to stoke up a particularly hot kitchen – she likes it smokin'.

With a gurgle, Marcos drops to the ground, sans half his head and I plunge my hand through his ribs, rip out his black, pulsating heart and hold it aloft for his buddies to have a good look. I throw my head back and roar. It feels *so* good - it's been way too long since I really let my hair down.

My true ancestor, Crocodylidae, is reasserting and I, its ultimate successor, am expressing some of its more effective characteristics. I can slow my metabolism at will if I wish and embark on a century-long persistence hunt, but I can also move very fast over short distances. My species is dangerous because of our speed but not just in the chase; more importantly in our ability to strike before our prey can react and retreat.

The element of surprise allows me to snatch up and hold onto my prey using my sharp teeth that have evolved for tearing and mercilessly gripping flesh. Those lethal teeth are set in a jaw furnished with powerful muscles that can snap shut with a force of 5000 pounds per square inch. To put it in context, a Rottweiler can produce an impressive 335 pounds per square inch and a Hyena 800–1000 lbs.

I stretch backward in a joyous yoga move and hear the pop as I crack every joint in my body and stand glorying in my power – in my freedom. I've been at it so long I had ceased to notice how much effort it took to hold my monster down. No wonder I get tired. People have described me as laid-back or laconic, but in truth, I'm just bloody exhausted from fighting the urge to rip their silly human heads off.

The noise and the smell of blood has at last woken up the disparate band of disenfranchised that make up Betty's nest. They move forward and I can't help but smile as I notice they are all keeping one eye to the side, making sure they don't inch ahead of the pack. There are six that I can see, and they spread out and surround me, but I can hear more. There are at least four others deeper in the tunnels. Perhaps they are the rear guard; I assume two to the east, two to the west. I can hear them as peripheral noise. 'Something' has started them scrabbling like rats. I would recognise the heavy footsteps of the one I named Cujo and he is not among the vampires in the tunnels. He has disappeared, I assume per Marcos' orders with the unconscious Betty to the boat and escape.

So here we stand – three males, three females and me, although one of the females may be male, but I'm not prepared to bet my house on it either way. The vamp of indeterminate sex wears black leather, jacket, boots and gloves. Not fat – a solid curveless body embedded with multiple piercings. I am initially weighing up the females because generally they are the most vicious.

The second of the females is smaller but I sense nastier. She is super slim, snake-hipped with a shirt too short, exposing belly button and hip bones above tight jeans. Those jeans would have to be a size 0. A long-legged child's size. She is skinny to the point of androgyny, a 'she' who could again as easily be a 'he'. Her head is slightly too big for her body. Blonde spiky hair, very underfed, but still hanging on to the appearance of youth. Dark circles under her eyes and a look of jaded overindulgence. A surfeit of experience in those sapphire peepers confuses the rebellious teenager disguise. Someone has been burning the candle at both ends and it is starting to show. She stands defiant, unnaturally still and planted while she makes relentless eye contact with me. Aggressive, spoiling for a fight, she is damn near starving and the gnawing need for blood has turned into a reckless, directionless rage. I can sympathise.

The last female sports a 'do' that looks like it came straight out of the Court of King Louis the Beloved and perhaps it did for all I know. A pompadour that involves a generous curly mullet of layered hair that covers her head then rises from her forehead and is back combed, two to three inches high from her scalp. Tresses and curls pour down her back from under the mullet. The hair is a rich, dark auburn and it is either the most luxurious head of hair I've seen for some years or a wig. I'll take a bet on the latter. If it proves to be the former, it could explain her twig-like frame in that all her meagre nutrition is being sucked up by the parasitic super abundance on her pate.

Typical of Betty to keep her 'hangers on' hungry. She's obviously made an executive decision that she will be the only female in her nest allowed to carry enough weight to have breasts. Betty is such a greedy baby. It's never enough to be loved, she has to have all the love in the world and she is such a miser with her own affections. Hundreds of years of the same old tricks and still she hasn't noticed that fear and dependency always lead to hate. She clings to the twisted belief that if she lavishes enough torture and debasement on her groupies, they can't help but worship her. I have a feeling the shine has already worn off for a few of the misspent 'youths' that surround me.

One of the male vamps wears skinny jeans and a Super Dry hoodie. Curly hair peeks out from under the hood. He could have been the inspiration for Michelangelo's Angel of Arca di San Domenico in the Basilica at Bologna, Italy. His skin is so pale it makes me think of Michelangelo's words: "I saw the angel in the marble and carved until I set him free." Perhaps this was the very face that inspired such poetry, but I doubt it; he still has the impatient, confused energy of the very young. He too is hungry, all the fat has been pared off the perfect triangle of his upper body. Under the hoodie I'm sure is the Brad Pitt Fight Club six pack. His cherubic face is now distorted by two savage fangs and his pale skin is starting to take on that reptilian green-blue pallor.

One thing is clear, some of these vamps are heartbreakingly young and still tragically impressionable. They are the vulnerable cast-offs, turned out to let Nature take its course: survival of the fittest. They've been left to find their own way, guided either by accident or fiendish design. Some vamps are born to mothers with all the maternal instincts of an amoeba. I know how it feels to find yourself alone, unprotected, confused, in desperate need of a mentor, or just a helping hand to point you in the right direction. These stragglers have had the misfortune to encounter the Countess Bathory during the most needy period of their long lives. Securing their fealty would have been like taking candy from a baby. Betty can be such a heartless bitch.

Although it is difficult to articulate thoughts while I am in my current state, it is even more difficult to enunciate and form words through my true reptilian mouth, for I am fully myself for the first time in years and far from human. I manage to speak:

'I don't want … to kill you.'

Their eyes dart around the circle, seeking to read reactions to my statement on the faces of their cohorts. I know they want to take the 'out' I've thrown them and just slowly back off to be swallowed up by the darkness and obscurity from which Betty plucked them, but they are held back by peer pressure. I can also tell that the exchange between Marcos and myself has sent a frisson of confusion through the whole nest. Betty may have gathered a rag bag of stragglers and renegade misfits to press to her cold bosom, but these kids who have nothing to lose, aren't completely feral – they are aware of vamp etiquette. The execution of a lone vamp engaged in a vendetta with their Queen will earn them 'uber' cool maverick status on the street. I know they see this whole adventure as a rebellious flipping the bird to the vampire establishment that scorns them. The cool romance of becoming an outlaw, a 'beast' I believe is the modern slang, appeals, but the massacre of an entire clan is quite another kettle of fish. Perhaps until a few moments ago, they were unaware that their new Queen was the perpetrator of the Atl blood bath. So the question remains, who will be strong enough to not give a damn what a bunch of loser vamps think and get smart? Who will be the first to say, "I'm out", chalk it up to experience and just walk away to fight another day?

We enjoy a moment of indecision, a little communion of sizing each other up. They obviously feel buoyed by numbers, whilst I just feel resigned to inevitable carnage. Meanwhile I can hear screams, grunts, crashing and scraping echoing through the tunnels. I sense the band of merry vamps surrounding me, are finding it just as hard as I, not to be distracted by the noises of combat filtering down from the western track.

The 'man/woman' steps forward. She feels she has something to prove, I assume, and lunges at me with bared teeth. I grapevine to the right and snap a chunk out of her side. I spit out a mouthful of meat and bone still covered with a layer of leather jacket and the gobbet lands at her feet. I think there may be an entire zip still attached, pocket and all. It feels like something's chipped my tooth. She yelps and wobbles with a surprised 'what just happened' look on her face and drops to her knees. Her five cohorts move in unison on me. I handed these losers a 'Get Out of Jail Free card' and they're throwing it back in my face. I detest a lack of grace in response to generosity. I lose all reason and cogent thought and become one with my long suppressed fury.

I am now a vampire berserker lost in the red fog, and at last submit to the demands of my inner dragon and relinquish all self-control. I lose myself in an orgy of violence and savagery. Crunching, slurping, ripping, I am beside myself with ecstasy. The civilised *me* it has taken hundreds of years to construct, exits the creature and floats free. Disembodied, I hover above, looking down on my vampire-self and watch the horror unfold. Dispassionate but fascinated. Below me, my body moves in a seamless tao of death – a Tai Chi of annihilation. From my vantage point, the decimation seems too easy. This contest is a mismatch and I feel a little sorry for the young vamps that are losing their chance at immortality in this ignoble, petty little battle, but I don't pity them too much. They should have known better.

Eventually, the frenzy of brutality subsides. The last of the vamps falls silent and still and the sounds of butchery abruptly end. My consciousness returns to my corporeal self and reasserts itself behind my eyes and I rise up amid the gore. The last vamp standing, awash in blood and guts. I am replete. In my hand the auburn tresses of the pompadour 'do'. A 'syrup of fig!' I knew it.

The air is full of red mist and I laugh and roar only to stagger backwards straight into the arms of the two rearguard vamps who had been, until recently, loitering out of harm's way 30 metres or so down the east tunnel.

The chuckle brothers have obviously made the bold decision to disobey Betty's orders as I suspect these two were meant to hang back and regroup if things went pear-shaped. I feel a blade slice across and through the back of my leg, deep enough that I hear the grate of steel across bone. It drops me momentarily. I reach back, grab the blade and yank it forward hard, bringing one of the vamps with it into the path of my snapping jaws. 'Didn't let go fast enough, asshole.' At least that's what I try to say, but it just comes out as a gurgling snarl.

The second vamp has reconsidered his strategy and put some distance between us. He raises a modified harpoon gun and hits me with a wooden stake. I start to twist away from the stake's trajectory the moment my eye catches a glint of steel but the shaft passes close enough to graze my ribs, taking skin and a slither of bone with it. The graze hurts, Yew wood - good choice. Ancient pagans and superstitious monks believed it had the power to drive away demons. I'm so allergic to the damn stuff I won't even handle arrows made from Yew without gloves. The wound stings and sizzles. It's going to fester for days, but it's not life-threatening.

The vamp is still fumbling with a re-load. The carpet of vamp bodies around us has made him a bit shaky. I reach for the harpoon gun and pull it toward me. 'Here, let me help you with that.' This vamp isn't so slow and releases his grip on the weapon the moment my hands touch it. Hearing my poor excuse for a voice seems to be the signal he's been waiting for and he takes off at great speed, away from me, back down the track from whence he came. He's out of sight and if a human had been present, the vamp would simply have seemed to disappear. Covering my hands with a piece of leather jacket, I load a Yew stake into the harpoon gun and take a blind shot. Nevertheless, it connects with something. I hear a grunt of pain. I'd hunt the clown down and finish him off but I'm past caring.

Dead or alive there is no way I'm chasing after the cretin, even if I could. From down the line, I hear another howl and a grunt. Silence follows. Covering my hands again with the piece of torn jacket, I recover the wooden arrow shaft 'Mr Leg It' had been attempting to load. I slide down to sit on the ground, the tunnel wall against my back and wait until I see movement from the direction of the sounds and raise the bow.

A pale face resolves atop a long, dirty old mac. Tia emerges, looking like some hideous flasher. What the hell is she doing here? She is dragging something behind her and holding an arrow shaft in her free hand.

Reaching level with me, she drops the edges of a tarpaulin and I stretch forward to look at what she's hauling – Mr. Leg It, another two vamps I don't recognise and … Cujo. No sign of Ezserebet though.

'Where did you get this one?' I ask, kicking big boy with the toe of my boot.

'Hello Eddy? If that is Eddy. Man, you look like hell, I can see why you vamps like your human suits so much. Don't trouble yourself to thank me for tidying up your loose ends Vampyr, I wouldn't understand you if you tried. But I assume by the way your freaky eyes are popping in this one's direction,' giving Cujo a poke with the arrow shaft, 'you're interested in the big fella. I took him out in the tunnels. He was carrying Betty, and looked pretty freaked out actually, and not by me, I would add. These two ...' she pointed to the mystery vamps. 'I took them out at the terminus, down there, where I came in, and this guy...,' pointing at 'Leg It', 'I ran into him on my way here, just up there on the tracks. I had the element of surprise .... it was spoilt a bit by this.' She held up the bloody Yew arrow shaft and used it to point to the ragged hole in her trouser leg. 'Luckily not too deep! Did anyone ever explain to you about not shooting unless you can see your target. Fortunately this vamp really wasn't focusing on me or anything coming from ahead, he was all about getting away from what was behind him. You, I presume. Thought I'd bring them all along with me. We should leave things tidy down here. No need to alert the humans to a vampyr invasion of Central London. I'd like to make life a little easier, not even more difficult.'

I struggle with my jaw, but manage to make myself comprehensible. 'Thanks, we tend to decompose very quickly, but you're right, we should drag all of these into a quieter tunnel. There's a service line access close.'

My camouflage is reasserting itself. My jaw has popped back into socket and my lips are reforming. I am pretty sure Tia can understand me. I think catching me 'in flagrante' has taken the wind out of her sails a little. She looks shaken, of course that could be because I just shot her in the leg with an arrow. She smells a little afraid, fearful but defiant – a good offence being preferable to an apologetic defence. She's putting up a confident 'front', but she knows I am not happy to see her.

I swallow hard, my throat is raw but I manage to croak out, 'Isn't there somewhere you should be?' It looks like Tia has decided to disoblige me in the very important matter of watching Angel. I am in no mood to be lenient with acts of disloyalty.

She crouches down and after a cursory sniff, starts dismembering bodies, making it easier to stack them in her tarpaulin. She takes the opportunity to snack while she works. She starts chewing feverishly on a femur and I get the impression this is a nervous reaction, a bit like a dog licking its lips and yawning. It is taking me a while to come down from the high of free-for-all massacre mode and I am finding it difficult to control my temper. I don't like to be defied and her frantic gnawing is playing havoc with my nerves. She picks up on my mood and stops abruptly, fixing me with those bright amber eyes.

'No, I think I'm right where I need to be. I'm at your disposal if you'll excuse the pun.' She brandishes a dismembered arm at me before throwing it onto the stack. She is very methodical, I'll give her that. I continue watching. Now that immediate danger has passed, my burst of explosive energy is ebbing.

'You just sit there and catch your breath, Vampyr. I can see you've been busy. You don't look yourself, that's for sure, and you're injured, but I have to admit by the look of things, you really aren't as hopeless at this vampyr stuff as I'd thought. I'll be back for a second load soon and then we'll get out of here.'

I watch as she clambers up the tunnel wall and squeezes through the conduit pipe feet first, dragging her grizzly cargo up after her. Like a nightmare version of Santa's elf.

I am surprised when she comes back for the second load, let alone when she returns a third time and helps me to my feet. She takes some of my weight as we limp back through the tunnels. We are both aware I am making a decision but I don't think she has any notion of how close a call this is. I have been considering the wisdom of cleaning house – a scorched earth approach. I have found in the past that when things get this complicated, it can be helpful to stop making value judgements and just kill everyone. I can always make new friends after all. The jury is still out for some reason, perhaps because I just can't stomach any more death tonight.

We haven't spoken a word. There is a huge elephant in the tunnels with us and a heavy, *I told you so* feeling radiating from my winged friend. I'm not sure I should even be thinking of her in those terms anymore. She has left my little Angel alone, but, if the chuckle brothers had received backup, if those two idiots had been four and Cujo had doubled back and not been stopped by Tia, I may be dead now. If she hadn't used some initiative and followed Marcos and I down to the heart of this waiting nest, I can't be sure I'd have made it out alive. The big problem is Betty – she is unaccounted for. Tia hasn't mentioned her again and her body wasn't in the tarps. Looks like mission failure. Without wishing to sound obtuse, I just have to ask:

'Where is Betty?' I know there is a threatening edge to my voice. The element of resigned exhaustion is softening my aspect, but I am barely in control – the dragon still abides.

'Wait a moment. I think I'm experiencing a déjà vu moment, Eddy. I'm just trying to lend a hand here, cos you seem to need it. You are the Johnny on the spot that gets all the one-on-one opportunities with Betty. I turn up after the fact and try to pick up the slack as best I can. It's your plan that's gone 'Pete Tong', but all you have to say is "Where's Betty, Tia?". Well… I haven't got a 'scooby'.

When I finished with the big fella, and that was not easy, she wasn't where he'd dropped her. I backtracked, searched all the way along the tunnels but then I bumped into two more vampyrs and by that time, I could hear bloody hell breaking loose up here with you. I decided to concentrate on the job at hand and hope you'd know something about where she might drag herself, she looked pretty 'out of it.'

It strikes me that it really wouldn't be that much trouble to just finish the evening in a tidy fashion. Kill Tia, dispose of her and forget her. But I've lost the impetus. I just hope Betty had been moved by other members of her nest to safety. My fear is that she escaped under her own steam. If she has been taken to a safe house by her followers, without Betty pulling their strings, I'd guarantee they won't have the 'teabags' or initiative to instigate any further action against me or mine.

Betty rules with an iron fist. She rarely bothers with the velvet glove, and I know from experience she relishes breaking cronies' independent will to action. She would hold total control over any group she moves with. It's just her nature. Control makes her feel safe. Whilst Betty remains alive but unable to command, all her minions will be far too afraid of the consequences of making a wrong move. The second option makes me quicken my pace.

Unbelievable though it may be for most vampires, if that resilient she-devil has managed to somehow drag herself out of this shit storm, she'll be spitting tacks and burning to soothe her injured pride. Bets' desire to humiliate me has turned into a gory fiasco. Her ego will be dented and demanding reassertion.

Tia gives me a 'leg-up' when we reach the conjunction of overhead pipe work and I pull myself through. My sliced leg is useless for the moment; the tendons are completely severed. I wonder if Marcos is actually dead. I'd entered a crazed blood lust and now I can't be sure I dealt with his vampire remains vigorously enough. There's a method to killing a vampire. You have to be thorough as we tend to regenerate. I need to know.

'Did you dump the dark-haired vamp? The one with the gold earring was Marcos. I'm assuming you already knew that?'

Tia grunted. I think it was a mirthless laugh as she continued to push from behind while I clawed my way forward. Finally, we slid out and onto the Piccadilly line.

'Well?'

Tia sighed. 'He's gone – dead, defunct, kaput. You really know how to pick your friends and lovers, Eddy. A soul could be excused for thinking you have a death wish… it makes being around you kind of dangerous.'

'Well Tia, if I was unsure of your sex when we first met, I apologise. The fact that you feel the first and most critical point you need to press home to me is that this is somehow entirely my fault confirms that you are all woman.'

My leg hurts, but it's a good hurt. The cells are multiplying and connecting. We continue along the track as before, my arm over Tia's shoulder and her arm around my back, supporting me. I am grateful for the help. I would manage to get where I'm going on my own but we are making good progress and I'm desperate to get back to Angel.

'I think I'm owed a thank you, Vampyr. I think rather than being testy with me you should be damn grateful.'

Her voice has taken on that gravelly timbre that I believe signifies anger or maybe fear, perhaps both. She has good reason for the latter.

'Believe me Tia, I am grateful for any assistance you may have given me. What that amounts to is mute as I was doing OK before you turned up and may have continued to, or not … we'll never know. For what it's worth, I thank you sincerely for your potential help. I would have thanked you more if Ezserebet had been in that tarp. The truth is that when this is all over, I had intentions to bestow the gift of both material and logistical aid to you and your dependants, or clan or whatever you call your compatriots. I'm assuming there are others like you, and they too were going to benefit from my considerable largesse, because I pay my debts and you did make a difference back at Ezserebet's dungeon.

'I really don't want to disturb our entente cordiale, but I should in fairness make something clear to you right now. You have betrayed me. You have left Angel alone and unprotected against my express wishes. If any harm has come to egyetlenem, to my dearest love, you will wish you'd never been born.'

Tia drops her arm from around my back and shrugs me off her shoulder. 'You are beyond belief, Vampyr. Why has arrogance been bred into your kind? What advantage is there in your being a race of arseholes? I didn't sign on to be a babysitter for the weird, science experiment down in your creepy basement. You are meddling with things best left alone and I'm out. The next time that crazy redhead takes a pop at you, you're on your own. Just keep her out of the Elephant & Castle or maybe you'll be the one wishing you'd never been born.'

She stands and glares at me for a moment and then takes off at a brisk jog and is quickly out of sight.

I call after her, 'Tia, I assume you left Angel to make sure I killed Betty. That is the only loose end that needs tying and you failed to tie it, Tia. You failed! If she's got back to Angel before me, you had better start running and you had better keep running.'

She is gone, out of sight but not out of earshot. She can hear me all right. Damn it! The Yew scratch is impairing my ability to heal and the leg is starting to hurt in a bad way. I keep going till I reach the next conjunction of lower sewer lines and head back toward home. I am sweating blood by the time I get there – literally. Pulling myself out of a sewer cover on Milner Street, I look like hell.

The night is nearly over. I can smell the approach of dawn, and the damn birds have already started their infernal twittering. I am cutting this fine. I really don't have the strength for any acrobatics and let myself into the house the traditional way, with a door key. I slam the door shut behind me and lurch for the basement. The pink glow of morning already spreads across the hall from the stair's stained glass window, and I can feel, as well as see, the steam start to rise off my back as the weak sunlight hits me.

The heavy basement door is hung on rising hinges and weighted to always slam shut. Once behind it, I lean my back against it and take a deep breath. I am feeling the drugged quality of my daytime sleep washing through me, pulling me down into the embrace of darkness. Nothing else matters as much. Everything has narrowed down to two simple imperatives: check that Angel is undisturbed and then find somewhere dark and safe and sleep.

CHAPTER SEVENTEEN

Ezserebet

The full moon shines down on Ezserebet Bathory, turning her red hair to glassy copper in London's chemically charged air. She moves quickly across the roof tops until she comes to that of 52 Cadogan Gardens. Here she stops and prizes open an attic skylight. Beneath the glass, toughened steel security bars are bolted to relatively new RSJ beams, expertly installed beneath the original tile. The bars have been attached to the roof in such a way that pulling them out from above is possible, although not easy, but removing them from within would be a tough job.

'Interesting ...what has Eddy been keeping in his attic that he doesn't want to escape?' She smiles. He is such a wicked man, so many secrets, so many irons in the fire and all the while he plays the part of the unwilling hostage to fate. He might fool others, perhaps even himself, but he's never fooled her. If only he were as simple and tiresome as he would have the world believe, she could have killed him and been done with it years ago, and at last, she would be truly free. Unfortunately, he didn't bore her, not a bit. Eddy drove her mad with his monkey books and art and music.

Frustrated her with his ridiculous scruples and maddened her with his ability to disengage from her with the flick of a switch.

Eddy also disgusted her. His penchant for a certain type of human was gross and he had the brass balls to call her perverse, but ... he never bored her. Gripping a steel bar in each hand, Ezserebet exerts steady pressure until she hears bolt nuts pop and the security bars come away. She's made some noise but there is nothing to be done about it.

She drops down into the loft space and is surprised by the juxtaposition of 'stuff' that has been left to gather dust and clutter the gaff; most of the junk is shrouded in thick, cottony spiderwebs. There is a lot of Eddy's old objet d'art, ancient medical paraphernalia and contraptions, and, of course, more of his Nancy boy books. Poetry… blah, blah, she smiles again despite herself. Her hand idly rolls her gold Caran D'Ache lighter, a present from Eddy and she considers the idea of burning the old house down. She has always found a certain satisfaction in arson, but she isn't in the grip of a compulsion, unlike Eddy's little human pet. She can take it or leave it. Still, the idea of seeing all this combust in a purifying explosion of super heated destruction is tempting.

Abruptly, all the dust and cobwebs disappear to make way for an area of cutting-edge medical equipment, white benches, computer screens, instrumentation, all manner of gadgetry. Dear Eddy began experimenting with mechanical drawing and storing of blood from still living human donors long before the humans thought of it, and here is the evidence that he is still twiddling about with science twaddle - and he has the nerve to call her crazy.

Ezserebet suddenly feels a little light-headed, wobbles on her feet and sits down amongst the taxidermy and old coats. This time she hasn't lost consciousness, which means she is growing stronger, but she needs to take a moment. 'Szar!' she murmurs out loud. She is frustrated with the debilitating symptoms of garlic poisoning, and she has yet to fully shake off its effects. On the bright side, she should be as dead as a door nail. The shot of potentised garlic that Eddy stuck her with was almost pure sulphur. It could probably cure human STDs and should have proved absolutely lethal to one of her species.

If Eddy had been paying attention, he would have noticed that she had been poisoning herself with doses of garlic for centuries, starting with microscopic, homeopathic potencies, and slowly but steadily increasing the dose. Occasionally, she has overdone it, just to see what would happen and in each case, it had taken her some months to recover, but she *had* recovered and, more importantly, discovered that the 'old chestnut' was true - what didn't kill her made her stronger.

Other vamps must have thought of doing it before but they didn't have the 'stones', and she could understand why. The symptoms of garlic poisoning, even in the most minute dosage, are horrific. The closest description of it she had ever heard came from a human she had seen on the Discovery channel describing his attack of acute seasickness. After a few hours, his shipmates had secured him with ropes to the guard rails of the boat because each time he vomited over the edge, in an attempt to make it stop, he would try to wilfully throw himself into the briny. Add to that the gruesome physical symptoms and it wasn't for the *gyenge szivü*. She tried to think of the English ... sissy ... yes, not for the sissy.

Having made so many enemies over the millennia, Ezserebet lived her life in a constant state of hyper-vigilance and she had felt the need to prepare for a random, yet inevitable, attack by some grudge-carrying pussy with a garlic syringe. It would be too ironic if she were to meet her end at the hands of an obsessed halfwit because he popped out of the wood-work when she least expected it. Now it took a decent dose of garlic to have any effect on her at all. That said, the stuff Eddy had been concocting and distilling up here in his quaint Frankenstein-esque State of the Art attic lab, was powerful enough to choke a vampiric horse.

She smiles again as she leans back and catches her breath. Yes, she should be as dead as a Dodo. The thought sobers her up. It stings a little that he could actually do it. Did he really want her dead? But here she is … alive. The poison had hit her hard though; her breath stinks and her tongue is coated with furry slime. She would take a bet that the toxicity of her flatus alone could kill a young vamp and the damn fainting spells continue. She rubs her thumb across the blistering scratch on her wrist. Would he have stuck her a second time?

She sits until she begins to feel better and is soon back in command of herself again. As long as she stops for a little when the hypoxia hits, it will pass and she will be fine. Standing up she tests her feet. She laughs out loud … she is fucking indestructible. She can almost hear Eddy agreeing with her. Despite everything, she still chooses to believe in him. The problem with Eddy is he never knows what he really wants. After all, what he really wants is her, and to that end she needs to get moving. Somewhere in this house he harbours the annoying little trollop with whom he has become obsessed. She needs to tidy up that loose end before he finishes making mincemeat of the rest of her devotees at the Post Office lines and returns like a knight errant to protect his damsel in distress.

She couldn't resist the temptation to play games with Eddy when she fortuitously stumbled across the little doppelgänger of his lost love, but now she is wishing she had just killed the human and left well alone. This time she has really stirred up the hornets' nest and been stung for her trouble. Now she wants the fun and games to be over, to kiss and make up and the natural status quo to be re-established.

Ezserebet descends the stairs, moving through the house, and letting the ambience wash over her as she goes. Very elegant yet modest. Understated in that 'I'm so rich I don't give a damn' kind of way. Every piece of art and stick of furniture could fetch a small fortune on today's market but has been chosen purely for its beauty and to suit the owner's taste. She likes it very much.

She is trying to stay cautious but it's proving difficult. She mustn't let her guard down too soon but it has become increasingly evident that, although almost unbelievable, the house is empty. Just her own and one other weak heartbeat, and that must belong to the doppelgänger. Her teeth distend at the thought. She has visited this house before and has already seen the oil paintings depicting Eddy's human muse, read his drippy balladry, felt his longing like an interminable toothache for the lost object of his desire. Now, thanks to her own stupidity, he has found his lost love and has installed her somewhere in this house.

From the sound of the slow, weak heartbeat, the girl is still close to death and has been left alone and untended. Just what the hell is that all about? Why would he rescue his human only to leave her in such a precarious position? To what end? She can feel the blood vessels rupturing in her eyes. They will look like two red marbles by now. Eddy's obsession should strike her as pathetically funny but it doesn't … it makes her blood boil.

She continues her descent, passing door after locked door. Rooms untouched for years, no doubt stuffed with treasure. Hermetically sealed time capsules to be opened and plundered on some future rainy day. How can he bear to be such a vampire cliché. Count Eddy, prowling through his Chelsea mansion like a sated lizard, a greedy dragon guarding his gold. Now, to cap it all off, sick with love, he has stolen his adored maiden and locked her up in his cave to be his bondswoman, except the creature below is no maiden and hasn't been since the dawn of puberty.

Eddy's paragon of virtue had lost all sense of self during her short, excruciating life. Betty had made sure of that. The creature below was never allowed a safe harbour in which to rest for long. She had bent the girl's guardians to her will and if they couldn't be bent, she broke them. By the time Ezserebet had finished guiding young Angel's development, the girl Betty had picked up off the streets of Soho six months ago, was an utterly broken 'thing'. Selling herself for the price of a hot meal and warm bed for the night. The idea of being put aside in favour of such a filthy little beast makes Betty shudder.

The house is so quiet and deserted. Careless ... too careless, it is making her nervous. It is all well and good pretending Eddy is a hapless romantic, but that isn't the whole story. Eddy is one of the few monsters she shares this big old world with that scares her – perhaps the only one that does. He under promises and over delivers in the monster department. That is why she loves him still. Perhaps that is why she knows, even if he doesn't, that he needs her. He was always so attracted to the light, gravitating toward it like a moth to the flame. She understands his need to feel the burn of experience. Ezserebet keeps her own larder stocked with the unfulfilled promise of youth, the tender and good, the mystery of naive blood. She loves them too, in her own way.

But Eddy's obsession with this damn girl is beyond the pale, and that is all it amounts to, just the age old longing for the thing we cannot have. The universal conundrum, shared by human and monster alike. The Portuguese are the only monkeys that thought to create a word for the universal exquisite melancholy: *saudade*. As Manuel de Melo put it, "A pleasure you suffer, an ailment you enjoy." Well, she had always thought she'd look good with an Afro 'do' and that wasn't happening either. Life is a bitch and then you die. He is just going to have to get over it. Note to self, she would celebrate tonight by having a Portuguese virgin for dinner - Celtic, Roman, Suebi, Buri and Visgoths… what a mix… yum yum.

Ezserebet moves on until she steps down from the grand staircase and her feet touch the wood of the ground floor. The door to Eddy's study stands open and the stillness is broken by the hum of electronics – computers, fax machines, and background noise from other devices … storage fridges perhaps. She has no interest in his gadgetry.

She moves through to the drawing room, the remains of a real fire still glowing in the hearth – a rarity in modern London. She noticed as she crossed the roofs that he had some kind of filtration system fitted to the old chimneys. Eco-friendly Eddy? More likely he just didn't want to draw attention from the new breed of 'thought police' among the human herd – EU nannying, government controls and invasive watchdogs. Big brother's big eye watches from every lamp post. Meanwhile, Eddy continues to do exactly as he pleases. She could kiss him.

Her eyes focus on the door to the lower floors. That's where she'll be. A shiver of nerves runs through her body.

Never wise to ignore the 'little voice', but she cannot detect any guards, booby traps or infrared trip wires, yet she is edgy. She has a tendency to paranoia. No one can have a family like hers and avoid that. But just because you're paranoid doesn't mean they're not out to get you. Could he possibly have left his special human, his precious Madonna, so completely defenceless?

Eddy is such a strange, contradictory scallywag. It would be typical of him to add a little frisson of risk to his night by exposing something he holds so dear to the mercy of chance. Such a deep roller. 'Oh Eddy, we are made for each other.' She smiles. It is now becoming clear some part of him wants … no, needs her to save him from himself. She won't let him down.

The stairs creak and groan. Completely orchestrated. No point in sneaking, she may as well be banging a drum. Such an antiquated intruder alarm … difficult to disarm though. She passes the first basement level, through the exquisite bathing pool grotto and on down to the second sub basement, continuing down the secret stairway to minus three, and into the true crypt of the house. What darkness is this? The complete lack of light washes over her with quenching bliss. This is the place she is meant to spend the daylight hours, wrapped in Eddy's arms. Two soldiers weary from a long campaign, but still dangerous, still up for the fight. With a little zhooshing, perhaps a bath tub, some manacles, and this crypt could really work for her.

Ezserebet stops abruptly mid stride. What was that? Sounded almost like a sigh of resignation … or pleasure. She stands silent, her heart beating a little faster, Some 'thing' else is down here. She can hear the steady if slow heartbeat of the girl. That hasn't changed, but there is an indefinable fullness to the silence. Suddenly confused she pauses. The girl's heartbeat is not as it should be - slow yes, but not struggling - it's muted, different, but not weak, and then there is this growing awareness of an 'otherness'.

Ezserebet shivers. She feels as much as hears the sound of a held breath, the presence of anticipation ... longing. Some 'thing' definitely shares this house with Eddy. 'Be careful Ezserebet,' she whispers, 'you are now dealing with an equal.' Cautiously, she steps down onto the flagstone floor. So bone chilling cold. Cold as the grave.

It is as though she has entered a ship's cargo hold. Good Lord, but Eddy knows how to hoard. An archaeologist's fever dream heaped and piled up around her. Unopened crates with way bill stickers from Cairo, Ethiopia, India, Tibet. He certainly seems to have eclectic tastes when it comes to plundering antiquities, or perhaps he has been hunting for something. Against a far wall stands a beat up, old chest freezer. Even frozen, she can smell the blood; it has the nasty whiff of the NHS. Storage in plastic adds a chemical flavour to blood that leaves a bitter taste on the back of her tongue. She never touches the stuff. 'Stale blood and human concubines! What the hell are you thinking, Eddy?' Her eyes move straight to *the* sarcophagus. It isn't difficult to identify. To her vampiric eyes, it appears to glow ... it contains the only source of warmth.

She approaches and circles it, cat-like and excited. 'Oh Eddy, how tasteful!' That makes her laugh as she is ready for something tasty. Recovering from garlic poisoning takes a lot of energy, and she is hungry and needing this as much as she wants it. 'Well, little human, this is what happens when you come between me and that which is mine.'

She only wishes she had the time and energy to start where she'd left off with their torture session back in her dungeon. It is inconceivable that Eddy has allowed this little scrap of mammalian flesh to become such a thorn in her side, to bait her with his obsession, and pretend he doesn't know how it will end.

The strangest part of the whole fiasco is that he had come looking, not for his treasured Angel, but for some serving wench called Jackie. He'd seemed genuinely upset at the thought of her having eaten his servant. That whole conversation had been nothing short of bizarre. She hadn't lain a hand on the creature but she'd played along. She had followed him to some stinking little hovel in the Elephant & Castle, assumed residence of said servant, found a greasy little polka dot hair band behind some bins, belonging she supposed to Jackie. It smelled like milk pudding, disgusting. And then she had been forced to all but dangle pieces of Angel under Eddy's nose to get him to take the bait.

If he had just answered his bloody emails like everyone else on the planet, Marcos could have dropped him a clue months ago that Ezserebet had found his muse. That she had pipped him to the post and found his Angel first. Hanging around London for hundreds of years, waiting for her rebirth had done Eddy no good at all.

She reaches out to touch the stone tomb and runs her hands over the cold surface. 'Hello!' She presses her ear to the stone and waits. Nothing of course … not even a little flutter from the light, monotonous heartbeat within. What a surprise that she is alive at all. The little female human is stronger than she appears.

'Hello kedvesem, it's just me again, little one. Remember, I picked you up up in Soho and took you home with me for some fun? You can call me Aunt Betsy. Now don't be afraid, nyugodt. I'm not going to hurt you this time. I'm just going to kill you … it will be quick. Just give me a moment to get this lid off.'

She gives the lid a few tentative nudges, but it is much heavier than it looks. She takes a deep breath and, pushing with all her strength, the stone slab slides with a rush across the top of the coffin and settles at a right angle across the stone trough opening, forming a crude cross.

'Szar!' She spins around at the feeling of cold breath on her neck. What in hell's name was that? Her heart is pumping now. It is thrilling to be afraid … only Eddy can pull that trick off. 'What have you got down here, Eddy?' The skin on her arms hardens and puckers. If she were human, the hairs would be standing on end. Her hands run over the edge of the cold stone and she allows them to take her weight. Her heart is pumping now and the garlic nausea is returning. The presence seems to grow stronger and become a little more insistent. 'Just bugger off whatever you are! I'm busy, menj a fenebe!'

A human would have been out of here by now, but if Eddy thinks some creepy vibes are going to distract her, he's mistaken. Turning her attention back to the sarcophagus, Ezserebet steels herself. She made a mistake but she will correct it. "To live, to err, to fall, to triumph …" No party tricks are going to stop her from finishing with this nonsense tonight.

In the darkness, the open mouth of the stone coffin unveils the girl's face like the moon appearing from behind dark clouds. She is Sleeping Beauty, waiting for a lover's kiss. Filthy, matted hair, grime-smeared face, still stinking of human sweat, fear and excrement – what man could resist? It is true, even when Betty had first spotted the girl, when she was just three years old, riding on the carousel by the Natural History Museum, that she had possessed a luminescence visible to vampire eyes. That radiant quality seems to have multiplied and is noticeably stronger.

Something is different. The girl's mouth is shut but the lips look less bruised and brutalised, and she could swear if she prized those rose-bud lips apart, she would find a tongue.

Ezserebet pushes the slab a little further down until she can see what should be a grisly, seared stump at the end of the girl's arm. Now, on the end of the wrist, there is a pink nugget of flesh, roughly hand-sized at the edge of which tender embryonic shoots have formed where fingers should be.

With a shiver of realisation she remembers the rest of the James Joyce quote: "... to recreate life out of life. A wild angel had appeared to him, the angel of mortal youth and beauty, an envoy from the fair courts of life, to throw open before him in an instant of ecstasy the gates of all the ways of error and glory. On and on and on and on!"

She takes a sharp in breath, shocked by the jolt of true horror. 'What have you done, Eddy? What in the name of all that's unholy have you done?' She takes a step back and it feels like she's backed into something, something dense and heavy and cold, but the presence evaporates on contact with her physicality.

She turns ... there is nothing there. She runs her fingers through her thick red hair. It is enough. No more play time. She must get this done ... destroy this abomination and get the hell out of this basement. It has been a long time since she felt remotely this vulnerable and the novelty has worn off.

She takes a step back to the side of the crypt. The girl lays still; no sign of any quickening, but she is definitely not the same. Her hand is regenerating, and under the filth her face glows. As yet, the girl still presents as very human and it does appear that she is protected by nothing more than a shivery sensation of 'the willies'. The girl is obviously in the grip of a profound healing stasis and apparently utterly insensate.

There is a noise from behind her. The door she left open is now closed and she hears a click as if a key has turned in the lock. She waits. Nothing ... no more noise. Leaning in close to the girl's neck, it is becoming hard to concentrate. How Eddy conjured up this reaction in her of eerie dread she has no idea but it is nothing more than a party trick to scare little monkeys, and what alchemy he has employed to heal his little mammalian strumpet is a mystery to be unravelled at some other time. Right this moment she will not be deterred. Nevertheless, she is so distracted by the awful sensation growing within her, that she is having difficulty making her teeth extend.

As she leans forward again to strike, a presence leans in behind her, spooning her, pressing itself to and about her with menace and a lustful impatience. She's getting angry now. 'Huzz a picsaba!' She needs to get on with it. The mixture of fear and rage does the trick. Ezserebet's teeth drop like a drawbridge and she strikes lightning fast at the girl's neck, plunging her teeth deep into the soft, still mortal flesh with murderous ferocity. She draws hard and syphons off a quart or more of blood in one suck and then pulls back, taking a good pound of meat in one swallow.

She steps back, watching with satisfaction as the blood pumps and gushes from the open wound. So gratifying to watch this creature, whom she can hardly believe is her rival, fade away. Since Eddy stabbed her with a garlic ampoule, the wound on her own neck has been tingling and stinging. As the girl's blood spreads throughout Ezserebet's system, that discomfort eases and stops. She notices that the edges of the wound on the girl's neck are already shrinking, pulling together and knitting. Exhaling she steps forward, leans in for a final, lethal inhalation of blood and flesh, then, feels a hard object press deep between her own ribs.

She pulls back to investigate but is not quick enough. A thud and another in quick succession followed by a feeling that she's been combination punched in her side. Was that the crack of two small explosions, and the smell of cordite? She has been shot. She looks down incredulous, and presses her fingers to the flower of blood blossoming on her shirt. The sting of two garlic-filled bullets entering between her ribs and spreading poison as they ricochet around her gut makes her eyes widen and bulge. Involuntarily, she lets out an unexpected, agonising scream. She drops hard to the ground, cracking her knees on the stone. As she falls, she notices a pistol in the girl's hand.

Ezserebet can now see, too late, that there is already a new alien presence alive and established in the little human. The girl Betty had lifted from the streets some months before had already been conditioned to victimhood and inured to pain. She'd hardly put up a fight when Betty picked her up. Accustomed to feeling helpless against fate's stone-hearted battering, the girl had instinctively submitted to a stronger will and accepted tragedy as her destiny.

The new presence is as yet very separate and distinct from the young street kid, but its interests are now bound to this scrap of humanity. This 'thing', sleeping in Eddy's basement is not the creature Betty has tormented over the years, and eventually abducted and tortured. That part of the girl is present but sleeping, eyes closed, still phlegmatic in unconsciousness, while the new 'other' lies quiet and still beneath her skin but is awake; watchful, patient, and ready to defend its frail host. The 'other' raised the pistol and shot her, quickly, efficiently and with merciless, expert timing before Ezserebet could react.

The human behaved to threat as would Crocodylidae. The girl has taken on characteristics of homoreptilia, making it impossible for Ezserebet to remain in denial and she accepts the horrific truth. She knows what Eddy has done. Would he really go so far … create an abomination so against the natural order, that it will anger the entire Vampire Council, and earn himself a place on the 'most wanted' list? Of course he would.

Ezserebet's consciousness is draining away and she is grateful for the coming mercy of oblivion. The garlic stings and burns like acid in her veins and makes her writhe in agony. Waves of hideous nausea are churning through her. Just as she prepares to allow herself to embrace the blessed surrender to nihility, she feels the grip of two, large, strong hands. The hands clamp around her pelvis, press hard and knead deeply before running down her thighs, tightening their hold around her ankles and pulling hard. She feels herself move just a bit, and then a little further, until she is being dragged across the cold stone floor, slowly but steadily.

What is down here with her? What is happening and where is it taking her? She tries to see but her eyes won't focus. She can't move. The garlic has paralysed her muscles, leaving her defenceless as a baby. Inside the prison of her unresponsive body, she rages and screams but her temper tantrum only serves to make her heart pump faster, circulating the poison more efficiently and magnifying the symptoms.

Blackness rises behind her eyelids. She feels sure she will soon pass out and she almost weeps with relief and hope. Whatever has hold of her abruptly releases its grip but she can still hear activity … scuffling and scraping. Damn it all but she is rallying. She can identify the sound of a flagstone grinding against the stone floor. Then the gliding, molesting pressure returns to her torso, running lasciviously across her breasts, concentrating briefly on her nipples and then continuing down her body, pausing over her mons pubis, an intense painful sensation of impatient probing.

At last, mercifully the hands move on across her thighs, suddenly, painfully concentrating their tangible presence and viciously clutching her ankles once more; a powerful yank and she is being dragged again. She feels her knees bend as they pass over the lip of an opening in the floor. Her mind races and she realises it must be the well. She experiences the sensation of being hauled onward like a sack of coal until she feels her back bend as the floor gives way beneath her hips and with a gasp, the falling begins.

Her body drops into nothingness and utter darkness; the feeling of plummeting downward becomes interminably prolonged. As much as it feels that way, it would be most unlikely that Eddy's well is actually a chasm that penetrates down to the centre of the Earth. Ezserebet tries to brace for the inevitable impact of a crash landing, but her muscles won't respond. Her fear turns to confusion as the interminable plunge continues until she longs for the certainty of hitting bottom. She begins to hope the whole episode is just part of an intense garlic-induced hallucination. That the ferocious grip of a greedy leech surrounding not just her feet and ankles now, but her whole body, is just the horrific symptom of toxic delirium.

The powerful hands squeeze her head tightly. They seem to have grown larger - large enough to hold her entire being in their greedy clutch while the kneading and probing continues. From far away, as though a mile above her, she can hear the distant sound of scraping as the large flagstone is dragged back into position to cover the well shaft opening. The weightless falling continues, deeper and deeper and the presence grows and becomes more physically concrete with every passing moment.

Gradually, some motor control starts to return to Ezserebet's body. She can feel her lips move and at first, it takes all her will to produce a whisper. She persists until she can drag enough air into her lungs to scream: 'Eddy, Eddy! Hell's Gates, Eddy. Get me out! Get me out!' Her words echo into the unknown and bounce back to her, unheard.

CHAPTER EIGHTEEN

Eddy

Even before I enter the house I can hear the sobbing … not loud but exhausted. It seems she may have been awake for some time … cold, alone and in the dark. Not good. It's almost sun up – a strange time for an awakening.

I cautiously descend into the heart of my home, my inner sanctum. My heart beats a little faster. I can hear Angel's ragged breathing. I pause at the final door, reach for the handle and see the 'knobbly Knee' is in the keyhole. It's been turned, locking the door from the outside. I turn the key, remove it and hold it in my palm. How very curious. What will I find below? An image of 'something' distorted, raging, hideous and perhaps ravenous, flashes behind my eyeballs. Well, learning to live with a female human, having been a man alone for so long, was never going to be easy. The poor girl is bound to come with a certain amount of baggage. I'll just have to learn to make allowances. We all have our little ways and we all need a period of adjustment when we first cohabit.

Stretching my head around the door, I see my Angel. She is pressed against the far wall, crouched down, squatting, rocking on her heels. She looks very small in the darkness, but her eyes are open wide and I know she can see me as clearly as I her.

'Oh Mother of Mercy, no, no, no ...'

Her voice sounds raw. She must have been screaming for help, but eventually, exhausted, she has given up, her throat shredded and sore. I let out a sigh of relief, although I am concerned for her mental state. At least she looks as I remember her. Physically, she's going to be OK.

I enter the basement and shut the door behind me. On the inner face I notice there are scratches across the wood and around the handle and lock. Angel has tried to leave but this door is made of solid hardened steel with just a wood veneer, for appearances' sake. I never lock this door from the outside. No sign of Ezserebet, but I can smell her. The crypt looks overturned like a small tornado has passed through. For the moment I assume that is down to Angel.

'Where am I?' Her question is a hoarse whisper.

'You're safe, you'll be fine now, but you still need to rest. It's nearly morning, the sun's rising fast. Don't you feel tired?'

Just looking at her it is evident she doesn't feel tired. She has her tongue back - she's speaking after all, with a slight drawl and a lisp, but she's making herself understood. I draw a little closer, noticing she has both hands. One looks cleaner than the other; it is pale pink and pristine as if it has been scrubbed hard. There is a patch of clean, pink, new skin on her throat too, which looks like a fresh healing site. She has sustained an injury while under my protection and I feel a stab of anger and shame. Nevertheless, I exhale with an inner 'phew'. Things are really starting to look up. Apart from the regeneration of missing parts, she looks perfectly normal. No aberrant manifestations of accelerated cell turnover. No obvious mutations. That's when the other shoe drops. The old hand, until now hidden behind her thigh, moves into clear sight.

My eyes settle on the source of immediate danger. The hand she didn't lose in the dungeon holds one of my custom-built pistols, loaded with my own weaponised concentrated garlic bullets. How did she get that? I sharpen up and pull myself together. I don't want to be hoisted by my own petard at this point. There have been developments of which I am unaware. I have walked into the theatre at the last act of a play and I am struggling to piece together the plot line.

I stretch my tongue out and lick the air and notice from the corner of my eye that Angel recoils with distaste at the sight. I'll deal with her delicate sensibilities later; right now I can taste Betty. My eyes slowly scour the room. Down by the side of the open sarcophagus I espy foaming black saliva. I lean down and quickly recoil from the nauseatingly strong odour of garlic.

So it appears my Angel has shot Betty. Well, good for her. I bet that came as a surprise. I follow the trail of vomit and gently fizzing bile; sputum and emesis that runs across the stone floor and ends at the well.

I move forward and out of the corner of my eye I see Angel raise the pistol. 'Easy now, I mean you no harm, I'm just going to have a little look around.' She lowers the weapon; the way her hand is shaking I doubt she could hit me any way. The stone well cap has been moved, and there are signs of fresh scuffs and scrapes on the flagstones to one side of it. Hewn from Galena rock, I'd chosen and fitted the cap stone myself. The slab is damn heavy even for me, and as well as being packed with lead sulfide, it also has a high silver content giving it the added benefit of being too unpleasant for some creatures to handle.

As I am not entirely sure what the 'uninvited visitor', residing in my well, is, I had decided to go for belt and braces on the capping stone. Whatever manner of entity lives at the bottom of my well it appears that silver doesn't bother it one bit. I made sure the slab was a tight fit too. Hewing the stone had been hard work, but it was worth the effort. I wanted the cap stone to be all but impossible to move, for either human or monster. Unfortunately, my eyes are not deceiving me … the well has definitely been breached and then reclosed from the inside by the look of it. I double check, to be sure there are no signs that tools have been employed to prise it open from above. Holy macaroni, this is an interesting development. I take a deep breath. I'm not sure how many more punches I can roll with tonight.

Angel is still in the corner, rocking, mumbling prayers. I wish she would stop that. Her singsong liturgy is creating a buzzing in my head. I'm trying to think, hells teeth and damn it, she's breaking my concentration! Why would my uninvited and most definitely unwelcome house guest, resident in my ancient well for the past hundred years, choose to make an appearance tonight of all nights? Given that it had, why was Angel overlooked? She's still here and apparently untouched, physically at least. Mentally, I'm not so sure.

I don't think the same can be said for Betty, who I think may have become intimately acquainted with my 'guest', given the trail of vampire bile and puke. The temperature has dropped a few more degrees and there seems to be a new intensity to the chill rising from the pit. This place is now far too cold for Hell and I surprise myself by shivering.

I press my ear to the slab covering the well shaft. 'Ezserebet, do you hear me? Betty, are you down there?'

Nothing, no reply. Not that I expected one in truth. I am aware of the same old stillness, the familiar sensation of patient waiting - the loud silence. I've had many of these one-sided conversations with my 'guest' over the years. I'm used to filling in the gaps. I've never heard a word echo up from the well, but 'it' speaks to me nevertheless.

My amygdala, which takes up a good fifty per cent of my skull space, hears it speak, and it says, 'I'm here, come on Eddy, come down and satisfy your curiosity. I've been waiting ... you know you want to ... it's just a matter of time.'

Well, I'm not going down that bottomless pit any time soon, and certainly not at break of dawn. I shout at the lifeless stone: 'Damn you both, you'll wait a long time for me, mother fucker. Keep her and may she bring you all the joy she's brought me!'

The sunlight striking the earth above is taking on mass. I stagger back as it presses down on me with the gravity of Jupiter. I need sleep ... my mind is racing. Angel looks traumatised; my sudden shouting at the well hasn't helped. There she sits, rocking, avec new hand and tongue, chanting those infernal prayers. I have to hold my temper, aware that she needs me now. She needs comfort and placation, but I'm so tired that I can't think straight. Why can't she just sleep till evening like any new vampire should? It sure doesn't look like that's going to happen. She is wide awake and showing no symptoms of day paralysis whatsoever.

Then there is Ezserebet, damn her, always complicating things. I want her dead – I want to be free of her interference and 'tom tit', but damn it all I don't want her down there with 'it'. I shudder at the thought. What the hell is 'it' anyway and why tonight of all nights has it stirred? Above all, why has 'it' actually left its hole and manifested? Something tangible dragged Bets down the well as she wouldn't have gone of her own free will, that's for sure. I hadn't thought until now that 'it' was capable of inflicting any physical influence, based on the fact it hasn't done so before. I have sometimes sensed the intensity of malevolence emanating from the well, directed at me, but I've assumed that if 'it' could do some physical harm, 'it' would have tried by now. My eyes involuntarily move back to Angel. She glows ... she is radiant, a dynamo of vitality ... she is actually giving off heat. Could it be her? Have I inadvertently provided a power source that the entity inhabiting my well can plug into?

Betty must have been completely immobilised by the shot from Angel's gun – perhaps even killed. Any other vampire would be dead, and rightly so, but Betty must have been doing something to counteract garlic poisoning or how else could she have survived the shot she took in the tunnels? I am clutching at straws, but I can't help but hope that another shot or two of the potentised garlic serum in one night must have finished her off. Surely it's time that I got a break.

Betty may well be dead, in which case I'm not interested in what 'it' wants or what 'it' does with her corporeal remains. 'It' can turn her into a coat stand for all I care. I'm trying hard to embrace this scenario and get a good day's sleep, but it's no good, I know Betty is still alive; I can feel it in my bones. A vamp of Betty's age biting the dust would normally involve some form of small, wet explosion but there just isn't enough blood, gore and acrid body juices to support death. I want her gone, I absolutely do, but I can't live with the possibility of her starving, entombed with 'it'. She needs me. What a bloody nuisance.

But for now, it is no longer a choice – I have to sleep. My head is pounding; it feels like someone is pushing a needle through my right eye, and my teeth feel loose. Angel's throaty whisper drifts up to me and rises to a scream: 'I'm afraid of the dark. There are monsters down here!' She has turned away and is pleading to the wall rather than to me. She really doesn't seem to want to look at me. She swallows another exhausted sob.

I move closer and crouch down next to her, almost touching, but there is something about her stiff, hunched shoulders that keeps me cautious. She still has the pistol. 'Listen, I'm here now. You're not alone. We'll work through the darkness together. We can talk this evening. There's so much to say and you must feel tired. Aren't you sleepy, my darling? You should be – the sun is up. Can't you feel it?' I sure as hell can. I feel as though I've swallowed an overdose of valium and jumped into a hot bath.

'No, I'm awake, I couldn't sleep here. Please, please just let me go.'

Her eyes move toward me. She still doesn't seem to want to actually look at me. Her gaze slides across me like a fried egg off Teflon. She is keeping her eyes just a little above my head or to the side, and I wonder how I appear to her. I didn't check myself in the hall mirror … stupid. I run my hands over my face and realise I am sated on vampire blood and in the throes of a primordial buzz. There's a good reason vampicide is strictly forbidden; there's nothing like vamp blood – it's the only reason I'm still functioning at this time in the morning.

The vampire in me is still very exposed. The Yew wood scratch has no doubt left me hollow-eyed and my mask of humanity hasn't quite reformed. Angel looks terrified, traumatised – on the point of a psychological fracture. I can only imagine the torture to which Ezserebet subjected her. Why should she wake up and consider me anything other than part of that? And damn it, I'm not looking my best. I hope she can't remember too much of all that took place in the caverns. She was almost dead by the time I found her, and should have no recollection of me.

'Are you hungry?' Her eyes sweep the floor and I realise I've touched a nerve. She doesn't want to admit it but I can tell she is famished; it takes a lot of energy to regenerate a hand.

'Yes.' It is just a whisper. The admission has cost her as it must seem strange and wrong to feel sick with fear and yet at the same time, ravenously hungry for something you do not dare to name.

'OK, I can do something about that.' I'll have to use what I've got. I don't have much time and it's all that comes to mind – I need to pull this whole cock-up together, and quickly. 'Listen, take some deep breaths … try to calm down. Come and lay with me.'

I move to the far side of the basement and slide aside a heavy stone tile that is set into the foot of the wall. The tile is only small, two feet by two feet. I don't need or want it any larger as it isn't meant to draw attention. I get on my belly and slither a little way into my hole where the dark, damp, cold awaits. Delicious – it feels so good.

'Listen, in a few hours I'll explain everything.' I can hardly form the words and my eyes are drooping as I speak but hers, I notice, are suddenly wide with terror, literally bulging. She's looking at the hole into which I have started to crawl. I stretch out my arm and beckon her to join me. She isn't coming to me. I am her blood Lord and she should obey. Hell's teeth, why isn't she responding to my commands?

I slither back out, across the stone floor knowing I don't have time to indulge her fragile hypersensitivity. I bite into my wrist and puncture the skin, and hit the ulnar artery deep. My blood is thicker than a human's. It doesn't spurt out like a geyser of sticky water; it oozes like rich oil. She watches my wrist with utter horror, as though a deadly snake is rearing up to strike and she seems to freeze as I press it to her lips.

'Drink, just drink – we'll talk tonight,' I mumble.

She pulls away from me with more force than I'd have thought possible of her. She spits the blood out from her mouth, gags and wretches, puking up dark black, red bile. She starts wiping inside her mouth and her lips with the filthy sleeve of her dress. Most unexpected.

'Please let me go!'

She's found her feet and is circling me a little unsteadily, but there is something about the way she moves that is giving me pause. She shouldn't be so alert, so active mentally or physically. This whole encounter should be impossible.

I have to sleep and she is moving toward the door of the lower basement. She wants out but can't know that escape into the daylight flooding the upper floors will mean agonising death. I don't want to imprison her down here with me. I don't think I'm capable any way. She still holds on to the pistol, waving it uncertainly in my direction. I have to protect her from herself and the terrible possibility of a baptism of fire, but how?

She bolts for the door. She has undergone 'the change' all right. She is fast and I can't out-manoeuvre her in my current state; the torpor is dragging me down into that place where I cannot move and now I am ceasing to care.

She is climbing the stairs, four at a time. It is still first blush of dawn to human eyes, but there is enough light to guide her to the ground floor and there is already enough light filtering through the doors she has left open in her wake to make my skin tingle. She should be screaming by now.

'Angel, stop! Please stop.' I follow as far as I dare to the foot of the last flight of steps, but she is already at the top, on the ground floor. The first tentative shaft of dawn sun bursts through the London smog belt, filling the hall behind her with UV, burning my eyes, blistering my face, singeing my hair as effectively as a blow torch blast.

The light refracted through her hair forms a golden aura, surrounding her head with a luminous rainbow colour disc. She isn't suffering – she is bathed in daylight as though dipped in liquid gold and she is fine. I retreat a little way back into the shadows where she can't see me, but I can still see her. Shaking and still sobbing a little, she continues to stare down, some part of her aware that I cannot follow. The pistol still hangs from her hand. The light is dazzling … steam and smoke rise from my searing flesh.

'What are you?'

I can hear the horror in her voice as she speaks. I retreat a little further. My small inner voice whispers, 'You are in danger, Eddy – real danger.'

'Darling?' I call, coating my voice in soothing glamour, like liquid honey. Even to my ears I sound drugged. A pregnant pause is the only reply but I can hear her holding her breath so I continue:

'If you are hungry for human food, I think you might find a cottage pie in the freezer.' I can't believe I've heard myself say those words - like a fussing nursemaid. But I am exhausted and Jackie's 'cook one today, freeze one for next week', popped into my head. Well, she'd said she was hungry and I must play my cards very, very carefully. Her response is another ragged sob, this time with a hint of confusion.

What am I supposed to do now? Angel is in my house, wide awake, in daylight. I am going to sleep soon whether I like it or not. I can collapse here and burn all day or retreat to my chamber. I move further backwards towards the stairs and my crypt. She raises her arm, and for a moment, wishful thinking makes it appear she holds out her hand for me to take, beckoning me to join her. Whoosh! Something skims across my upper arm, just breaking the skin and it stings like hell. She has shot me! Three inches to the left and the garlic bullet would have gone straight through my weary heart. She's very nearly caught me with a direct hit and I had thought she couldn't see me back here, deep in the shadows. 'Fuzzy duck!' Would I never learn? Tia was right – I must have a death wish.

Throughout my relentless existence I've now found my Angel three times. Twice, she's nearly been the end of me. Maybe the third time will be the charm. I can do nothing to defend myself now … nothing but sleep. Who knows what I'll wake to, or if I'll wake up at all. Perhaps the police or the scientists or the 'Ethan Hunts' from town planning, will be hanging over me with a stake to plunge through my lizard heart. She is above ground now and I can hear her running through my house, covering all the floors very fast, faster than humanly possible – super human. What is she now? I can't think straight. The day sleep courses through me, sedating me with its powerful opiate. A burning sensation travels up my veins from the wound on my arm toward my heart. I can hardly breathe, and can only find the energy to whimper rather than scream.

I am on my belly now, clawing, dragging, writhing into my darkest hole, and I pull the heavy stone tile back into place against the wall. I have no confidence that she won't dislodge it – she will if she wants to. There are no lights down here. She said she is afraid of the dark, but soon she will realise there is no dark for her. A big part of humanities' fear of the dark is simply the helplessness of being unable to see the approach of a predator. Angel will see now, no matter how impenetrable the gloom. How long will it take her to realise? The darkness can no longer hide mysterious terrors; no monsters will be concealed in shadow. All will be revealed to her splendiferous new eyes.

I am falling into a nightmarish half consciousness, not my usual peaceful rest. I can hear her tapping on computer keys, lifting the phone receiver, lowering it, lifting it … the ring tone … emergency services – Angel's answering silence.

Incapable now of action, vulnerable, all but insensate, there is nothing more I can do but sleep and hope that she will find some food and somewhere topside to rest. Maybe she will avail herself of the plumbing and take a long bath. I was hoping to bathe her myself and then perfume and adorn her – my darling, egyetlenem. I don't think that dream will happen any time soon.

But who knows, maybe with some time to consider, as the sun goes down, she will become calm. Stranger things have happened. We will be able to talk the situation through, objectively, peacefully, and get to know one another. I will appear thoroughly human by tonight, myself again and pleasing to her eye. She will see me as if for the first time – young, handsome and charming.

I look forward to a longed-for reintroduction and a third chance to get it right. If she can find it in her heart to embrace some equanimity over the next few hours and not do anything impetuous or rash, she will find that life can be so much more than she has ever experienced or hoped possible. What fun we will have.

I move toward optimism, my default position – my answer to 'rock and a hard place' situations. I take my mind to a happy place … Angel and I talking, sharing a joke, enjoying each other. I can be charismatic when I need to be. The two of us are alone, sitting in my comfortable drawing room before a large roaring fire. I will make her feel protected and safe. I will make her laugh and know she is adored. I will make her love me. I smile in my sleep and can still see us together and the fire roaring in the hearth. Always the fire, roaring. What's with the roaring fire? The shrewd omnipresent voice of survival cuts through my catatonic little death: 'Because you can smell it, dummy. Smoke!' I try to move but I am in the rigid grip of paralytic stillness.

So this is it. I'm going out with a sizzle not a bang, to end my eon-spanning odyssey as a strip of crispy bacon, and know it was completely self-inflicted. The acrid smell of burning furniture drifts down to the basement levels.

Was that the sound of a key in the door? No one has a key to my door except me, and of course… what the hell is going on? I struggle against the day sleep, but I can't move, trapped like a living statue in my own hard skin and pinned under the gravity of light.

'Cooee. Helloooo. I'm back!'

I can feel myself convulse in my sleep with apoplectic rage. There is a nervous, apologetic edge to a very familiar voice. Footsteps across the hall, a pause at the basement door, the sound of it being opened, just a crack. The minute but unmistakable traces of a distinct – milk puddingy pheromonal signature waft down on the air currents.

'I'm back … long story. Tell you all about it later, Mr Edward. Hope you wasn't inconvenienced… or… a bit worried. I've had a right old time of it. You'll laugh. All's well that ends well tho - eh? Ummm. Later then.'

The basement door shuts. The familiar voice whispers to itself, 'Please, please, please for 'Robbie Williams' sake, don't be annoyed.'

Don't be annoyed! *Annoyed* doesn't touch it. If I make it through this day sleep and should awake to darkness, the first thing I will do is pull a certain person's, fuzzy-haired head clean off.

A sharp intake of breath and the unmistakable cadence of Jackie's voice:

'Hello, who are you? Oh no. No, don't be frightened, petal. I'm Jackie. Oh, don't be frightened, flower. I work 'ere. See – a key. Honestly, I'm s'posed to be here. You OK darlin? You're looking a bit worse for wear, sweetheart. What's 'appened to ya? What's that smell?'

More hurried steps …

'Shit snacking crackers – we'se on fire!'

Sound of running feet, followed by whooshing sounds.

Could that be the sounds of the kitchen fire extinguisher being deployed for a purpose more fitting than being brought down with force to crack walnuts on my Italian granite kitchen surfaces? Is my cretinous, and as it turns out, 'prodigal' housekeeper, capable of such fast thinking action? I hope she is, but that is all I can do as the last traces of awareness leave me and I am pulled into the deep, dreamless void.

Not much can reach me now but I am aware that a beloved presence exits my house.

My Angel is gone … again.

She has run back into the grubby, diseased, arms of old London and that heartless whoremonger quickly envelops and gobbles her up with one burpless gulp. I am powerless to stop her. Helpless and all but paralysed, pinned beneath the weight of the Sun's life-giving radiation like a butterfly under an entomologist's glass.

I surrender to my weakness and mumble a last:

'Whatever ...'

With an heroic struggle, I muster my last tiny vestige of strength to slowly, deliberately, cross my fingers.

To be continued ...

GLOSSARY

Cockney Rhyming Slang

Barney – (Barney Rubble) – trouble
Cheese and rice – Jesus Christ
Chicken pluckers – fuckers
Clucking -fucking
Eartha Kitt – shit
Ethan Hunt - Cunt
Friar Tuck – fuck
Fuzzy duck - fuck
Hank Marvin – starving
Jackanory – story
Jam tart - heart
Knobbly knee – key
Lady Muck - fuck
Left and right – fight
Mince pie – eye
Mincers - eyes
Mop and bucket – fuck it
Loaf of bread - head
Nelly – (Nellie Dean) – Queen, or effeminate man
Pete Tong - wrong

Pork pie – porkie - lie
Rubber duck – fuck
Scooby do - clue
Syrup of figs - wig
Turkish Delight – shit (shite)

London Slang

Money : pounds (readies)

Nicker or quid – 1
Tenner – 10
Score - 20
Pony – 25
Bullseye – 50
Monkey - 500
Grand – 1000

Bint – unpleasant woman
Bollocks - nonsense
Bullseye – fifty pounds
Clocked – seen, saw
Cock up – fiasco
Collywobbles - nerves
Crap - faeces
Dicking around – wasting time
Fluke – oddity
Friggin - fucking
Gaff – place of residence
Gobsmacked – shocked
Leg it – run, escape

Malarkey - nonsense
Ninny – nincompoop – silly, idiotic person
Nonce – child molester
Numpty – fool, unwise person
Old chestnut – cliché
Pear shaped – difficult or wrong
Peepers - eyes
Robbie Williams – exclamation (as though a deity)
Scallywag - rascal
Scarper – run, escape
Shag – have sex
Schtupping – having sex
Snorking - drinking
Stones – testicles
Teabags – testicles
The willies - creeps
Twunter – mix of: twat – woman's private parts, munter – unattractive person and wanker – masturbator (male)
Zhoosh – improve, jazz up

HUNGARIAN

Jo utat kivanok – I wish you a good trip
Bolond menyet – crazy weasel
Szivem – my heart
Csillagom – my star
Dragam – my darling
Balzsamot – balm, ointment
Fenek – bum, buttocks
Bikaszem – bullseye

Szep a szemed – you have beautiful eyes
Szar – shit
Egyetlenem – my only one
Gyenge szivu – faint hearted, cowardly
Kedvesem – my dear
Nyugodt – calm
Menj a fenebe – go to hell
Huzz a picsaba – get the fuck

43529776R10174

Made in the USA
Charleston, SC
30 June 2015